The Woman Who Loved Too Well

The Woman Who Loved Too Well

A Novel by

David Orsini

Quaternity™

Other Books by David Orsini

Bitterness / Seven Stories

The Subtleties of Seduction

The Ghost Lovers

CONTENTS

Chapter One

Marc and Jean-Claude

Marc glared at his squadron leader. Though he had always liked him before, he positively loathed him at this moment.

"Do you know what you are saying?"

His staccato inflections turned the question into an accusation.

"Jean-Claude is alive, and we are not going to do anything to save him."

The major eyed him directly. He was a tall, vigorous man whose ruddy complexion gave him the appearance of excellent health. He did not permit himself to glare back or to give any other sign of his displeasure. There was in him as usual an understated self-command and a hardened demeanor. No more than five years older than he, Yvan Pelletier had been through it all. His three closest friends, who had been among the squadron's best pilots, had recently died in air battles over Berlin, Stuttgart, and Dresden. Only a week earlier, his girlfriend—a feisty nurse assigned to a London hospital—had been killed during Nazi strafing raids.

Marc understood all these things. He was also aware that Pelletier refused to pity himself and that he refused to pity others.

When he answered him, Pelletier spoke matter-of-fact words that set before him once again the dilemma facing them.

"There is nothing we can do to save Jean-Claude. A commando raid against the Germans who captured him might have worked, if they hadn't moved him to a new prison. We don't know where the Germans have brought him. Believe me. We have done all that we can. There is no way to free Jean-Claude."

His dispassionate words did not keep Simone from urging him to see their problem differently.

"Yvan, this is not like you. You have never before refused to help a pilot in your squadron. There has to be something more that we can do."

On this January afternoon in 1942, they were sitting in a booth within a shadowy corner of the pub that stood a half-mile away from Marc's and Pelletier's air base in Lincolnshire. On any other day, Major Pelletier would have perceived Marc and Simone as one of the many romantic couples in the room. Marc Roussillon was tall and dark-haired, and his big-boned physique and manly grace suggested that he was a well-trained athlete.

Marc's brown eyes met him directly and drew him into their steely regard. Pelletier well understood that an encounter with this twenty-two-year-old pilot involved quickened awareness and subtle calculations. If he were to ask him to describe his scanning impression of the place where they were meeting, Marc would have offered an accurate location of entrances and exits, of the eight persons seated nearest those exits, and of the man and woman who were dining at the booth next to theirs.

If their meeting were less fraught with tension, Pelletier would have—even in this dark period of his life—allowed himself to admire more than an instant the poise and decorum of Simone, Marc's wife. She also was twenty-two. She was, besides being very young, one of the two or three loveliest women he had ever seen. Her blond beauty and delicate bones lent an ethereal expression to her manner. But her warm spirit and her confident inflections told him that she was very much a woman of this world.

They had shared a torte filled with zucchini, eggplant, and tomatoes, as well as a few rounds of Glenmorangie scotch, pungent even with its caramel and vanilla textures. Called by Marc away from her father's home in Sweden, Simone had made a special effort to join him here in England for this meeting with his squadron leader. Because Pelletier had always shown a soft spot for her, Marc hoped that her presence would draw Pelletier into a new plan for saving Jean-Claude.

In the distance, smoky vapors rose and coiled about the crowded bar and about the wider spaces of the pub. The tangy fragrances of food—beef stew, cider apple chicken, trout braised in Riesling wine, and lemon sponge cakes—floated languorously into the vaporous atmosphere. French and British pilots in blue Air Force trousers and brown leather jackets were drinking whiskey, rum, and ale at the bar. Some of them were sitting at tables or in booths while eating lunch and making contact with old friends or new acquaintances. They were talking about the latest rugby matches or about hunting trips they had taken in South Africa or about the skiing they had enjoyed in the Swiss Alps before the war. Most of these men were partnered with pretty girls in colorful dresses who lived in the town and who liked the company of combat pilots. Caught within the cacophony of voices, Vera Lynn, Frank Sinatra, Betty Grable, and Edith Piaf were singing romantic ballads on jukebox recordings.

Marc and Simone perceived all of this reality of people and fragrances and sounds. But they were aware of it as merely an oblique reference point that reminded them where they were and why they had come here. The reality that was far more pressing belonged to themselves as they continued to negotiate with Pelletier about the fate of Jean-Claude.

When he heard Simone's words that urged him toward a workable escape plan for Jean-Claude, Pelletier reflected upon them for a moment. Then, while his cold brown eyes observed her with the courtly respect that he subtly anchored to his otherwise stoical manner, he told her once again the harsh truth of things.

"I know how much Jean-Claude means to you and to Marc. But, as valuable as he has proven himself to be, he is only one man among all the men and women who are fighting the Nazis. He is as important as you and I are, but no more than that. What has happened to him may happen to us. We knew that from the time we entered this thing. Our squadron won't help win this war if we send our pilots and commandos into a rescue attempt that is bound to fail."

Marc refused to accept these words.

"We've got to help him, Yvan," he said. "We can't let Jean-Claude die."

Pelletier answered him quickly. This time his voice carried a trace of bitterness. His curt intonations suggested that these would be his final words about the matter.

"Forget about Jean-Claude. When it's our turn to die, no pilots in our squadron will be thinking about us. They'll be thinking about staying alive and stealing whatever pleasures they can from a world that loves nobody."

Just as swiftly as he had spoken, he swallowed the remaining drops of his scotch, threw his napkin next to the lunch that he had barely eaten, and rose—tall, brown-haired and formidable—to his full height. Then, bowing to Simone and brusquely patting Marc on his shoulder, he hurried away.

Silence overtook Marc and Simone now, an austere presence that lingered as if watching them. Not even the raucous and hearty sounds around them dispelled this stillness that held them in its bond.

It was a few minutes before Simone chose words that meant to encourage Marc.

"We did our best," she said. "Maybe, if he knew Jean-Claude as well as we know him, Yvan might have been willing to make a new rescue plan."

Marc answered her with new determination.

"I'm not giving up. We've got to help Jean-Claude."

"How?" Simone asked. "How can you make the impossible happen?"

"I'll find a way. I'll think of something."

To arrive at the truth of Simone and him, Marc felt, a person needed first of all to know about their relationship with Jean-Claude Jourdan.

He and Jean-Claude became friends six years earlier at

Le Rosey, a private school in Switzerland. There, on a manorial estate in Rolle and—during the winter—in the alpine ski resort of Gstaad, they excelled in rigorous academic programs as well as in a wide array of extracurricular activities. They boxed, fenced, played soccer and swam as members of the same teams. Tall, dark-haired and vigorous, they might have passed as each other's fraternal twin. When they were at their homes in France or when they visited their homes in Argentina or England, they played polo. In the summer following their junior year, they studied architecture in a program for gifted students at the École des Beaux-Arts in Paris. Even at sixteen, both of them knew they wanted to design and build modern cities and comfortable homes for the needy as well as for the wealthy and the middle class. In their senior year at Le Rosey, they spent a week in the laboratory of a renowned bacteriologist. Under his guidance, they experimented with white mice to fathom the nature of a cancerous tumor.

During their winter and summer recess from school, they kayaked in Finland, trekked across the High Atlas Mountains in Morocco, and snorkeled in the Galápagos Islands.

One time, after breaking his leg in a ski accident on the rugged slopes of Gstaad, Marc struggled through a long and painful recovery. Even with the assistance of excellent physio-therapists, he found his convalescence a bitter experience. At first, he proved to be a difficult patient. Deprived of the agility which had always defined him, he spent too many hours brooding about his predicament. His sudden inability to participate in the world as a self-reliant individual made him feel inadequate and even destitute. Because his parents were absent from his life much of the time, busy with their careers in classical music, he had learned to cultivate a strong-minded independence. Thoughts of his mother's warm regard of him cheered him in those hours when, sometimes weary of the rules and the competition at his school, he looked to his life at home for solace. But his memory of his father's coolness toward him left him uneasy. The memory made him sad. He loved him no less. But his emerging belief that his father might not love him intensified his need to rely on his own powers to make his way in the world.

Now, because the ski accident had taken his freedom from him, his suppressed need of his father rose up to goad his anger and his uncertainty. It was Jean-Claude who brought him back to the familiar self that he trusted. For two months, while he was bound to a wheelchair and then to crutches, Jean-Claude guided him smoothly through the long halls of their school and into the spacious classrooms. On every one of those days, he joined him in his physiotherapy. There, with the surgeon's assistant, he accompanied him in the careful exercises which accelerated his recovery. He viewed Jean-Claude's presence as a validation not only of his loyalty, but also of their unbreakable bond to each other.

During these hard weeks, he would from time to time speak to Jean-Claude about his father, who was the renowned violinist Henri Roussillon. To remark upon the tense undercurrents of his relationship with the father that he loved so much was an altogether new experience for him. Had he been in the best health, he would have refrained from any words that might cast a pall upon the image of his father. But his awareness that Jean-Claude enjoyed a successful relationship with his father persuaded him to open himself to this best of his many friends. That Jean-Claude was an only child might have explained Monsieur Jourdan's wise blend of sensible rules, consistent discipline, and genuine love. Above all, there was love, which Monsieur Jourdan conveyed through his open-hearted praise of Jean-Claude and through his generous gifts.

Yet, even though he himself was not an only child, Henri had—for the first ten years of his boyhood—never failed to express his love for him openly. The love he offered him had been equal to his paternal love of his daughter Nicole. But then, and for no reason that he could fathom, his father grew distant and even cold. If he continued to involve himself in his son's life—in all the hills and valleys he journeyed through and in all the milestones and disappointments—their relationship had become nonetheless a simulated camaraderie. At that time, he did not know that, because of his father's infidelity, his father and his mother had grown estranged from each other. At sixteen years old, however, he still needed his father's encouragement.

"I love my father," he told Jean-Claude on a rain-swept Sunday afternoon when, injured and brooding, he felt helpless and imprisoned in his convalescent bed. "But I no longer feel close to him. Even when he is there beside me, I feel he has turned away from me, and I don't know why."

That time Jean-Claude fell silent, uncertain perhaps how to advise his friend about so personal a matter. But Marc's seeking his counsel nudged him forward to words which were far wiser than he imagined.

"Your father still loves you," he said. "He's involved in so many of your activities. He attends your swim meets and your soccer games, he sails and horse-rides and hunts with you, he teaches you the violin and the piano, and he takes the time to converse with you in several languages so that you can feel comfortable with all of them."

To his friend's words, Marc listened very carefully.

"Everything you say is true," he told him after a moment's reflection. "But something is missing. There should be something expressed openly. There should be affection offered unconditionally."

Jean-Claude, more confident now and just as serious, counseled his friend further.

"You mustn't dwell in these thoughts so much," he said. "They'll rob you of your realistic view of things. You're seeing mystery and indifference and coldness when you have no cause. Your father is probably one of the many fathers who do not care to express their love in any emotional or sentimental way."

He wanted to believe his friend's words. Ordinarily, the assurance and the intelligence behind those words might have convinced him that this uneasy subject of his father and himself required no further words. But the thought of Monsieur Jourdan's warm-hearted fellowship with Jean-Claude compelled him to say more.

"Your father is not embarrassed to let others know that you are very important to his happiness."

"Sometimes, I think he overdoes it," Jean-Claude said. "Believe me, there are days when I wish I had a father like yours. In his own way, whether he is joining you in one of your activities or corresponding with you from some far-away city on his concert tours, your father shows his affection. It exists as an unspoken pact between the two of you."

He allowed himself the hint of a smile. That day, when he had felt so miserable, Jean-Claude's comradely words pleased him, even if they did not entirely convince him.

Noticing his newfound ease, Jean-Claude drew him into a light-hearted thought.

"Hey, buddy, let's trade fathers."

The surprise of the words roused him to genuine laughter. Jean-Claude laughed, too. Their laughter was as hearty as it was invigorating. For the rest of that week and for all the other hours when he recalled this dialogue between them, he realized all over again and even more profoundly that Jean-Claude was the essential presence in his life. He was a brother. He was a mentor. He was the one person on whom he could count.

That their friendship pleased Jean-Claude's parents seemed like a further validation of believing they were brothers in spirit, if not by blood. Their having been born on the same day, though in different countries, persuaded even the Jourdans to regard their figurative brotherhood as a twinship. Their privileged backgrounds, their interest in architecture, and their aptitude for languages and science, as well as soccer, kayaking, and polo, made their friendship seem inevitable.

One time, while he was a guest of the Jourdans at their *estancia* in Buenos Aires (which was located about fifty miles from the Roussillons' ranch there), Jean-Claude gave him a prized Criollo. He had noticed how smoothly Marc rode him in a polo tournament in which, as teammates of young and hardy gauchos, they proved their mettle. All during his visit to the Jourdans, Marc had spent time riding and caring for the Criollo. More than once, when he was in the stables feeding him or cleaning his stall or brushing his coat, he had commented on the sturdy and compact body of the horse. He had praised its strong, short limbs; the ampleness of its bones below the knees; and its exceptionally sound feet. Even before coming to Buenos Aires, he knew the history of the Criollos. Descended from Andalusian and Barb horses, they had adapted to the harsh environment of the pampas. There, the extremes of climate—intensely dry, hot summers and severe winters—proved intolerable to all but the most vigorous specimens. Even the coats they had developed were a form of self-preservation. Dun-colored with dark points and often with a dorsal stripe, the coats protected them from their enemies by rendering them inconspicuous against the dry pasturelands they inhabited.

"This Criollo knows how to survive," Marc said. "He knows what to do when he is in a tough situation."

Perhaps it was the capacity of the horse to endure hardship and danger that stirred his love of the animal. Possibly it was his easy compatibility with the horse's movements or his awareness of how openly the Criollo returned his affection that inspired his respect and his devotion. Whatever it was, it drew to itself Jean-Claude's attention and persuaded him to give the horse to him.

"You share an affinity with him," Jean-Claude told him. "You belong together."

That day, as a youth of sixteen, he beamed with a rare happiness that he had not known since his early boyhood. Quickly, he embraced Jean-Claude as the brother he believed he would have for a lifetime.

Simone grew very fond of Jean-Claude, too, not as though he might become her lover, but as though she might become his sister. She had given her heart completely to Marc, but she perceived nonetheless that Jean-Claude was a very attractive young man. Tall, dark-haired, and rugged, he wore his handsomeness with a casual understatement that made every-thing he did appear extemporaneous and natural. More than a few times, Jean-Claude and his latest girlfriend joined Simone and him on romantic excursions. They canoed on the Seine, enjoyed a boating holiday in Brittany, and vacationed on the French Riviera, in the Azores and in Tahiti.

By the time Simone, Jean-Claude, and he had completed their studies at Le Rosey and their first two years at the École des Beaux-Arts (and in Simone's case at the Sorbonne, as well), war was already flaring its violence across Europe. When the Nazis invaded France, the three of them offered their services to the Resistance—Simone in league with her father in Sweden and he and Jean-Claude as pilots in the Free French Air Force who were flying with the British. In these first months of the war, they made danger their friend and overcame their enemies.

Then something happened that changed everything for the three of them.

In September of 1941, Jean-Claude's Avro Lancaster was shot down during a successful British and French commando raid against the Nazis who had overtaken Norway. For a time, the Free French Air Force thought they had lost Jean-Claude Jourdan.

His comrades saw his plane shot down in Oslo and believed that he had died. But the Germans had dragged his wounded body from the plane before it exploded. He had broken both legs, had dislocated his shoulder, and had sustained a concussion. Traumatized by the shock of the crash and by his injuries, he would have died if the Germans had left him unattended. But they considered him an important source of information. They were also aware that his skill as a pilot had made him a hero in his country. More than a hero, he had become a symbol of French fighting power. Now he was their prisoner, and they were going to break him. They would turn him into an image-writ-large of the militant French who were being defeated by the Nazis.

Calling upon the services of their best surgeons, the Germans repaired his body and brought him back to vigorous health. Then, they brought him into one of their military prisons in Oslo and began to torture him. They wanted him to divulge information about the military plans of the Allies and about the identity of the French, Swedes, and Danes working for various Resistance movements.

During their first interrogations, they hung him from his wrists with heavy weights tied to his legs. Even his firm shoulders and his strong biceps could not subdue the agonizing pain that made him imagine that his arms were being pulled from their sockets. Yet he told his enemies nothing.

Within that same week, the Nazis bound his naked body with chains. Then, as though they were making a tourniquet, they pressed the chains deep into his flesh. Not the jagged cuts or the purple welts that rose from his skin or the red blood spurting out of him could break his resolve.

Nor did the Nazis break his spirit when, after stripping him naked and hanging him from his feet, they beat his body with barbed wire sticks. That time, he passed out of consciousness. When he awoke, he was in his cell, cold and shivering and alone in the clammy pool his own blood had made.

For weeks sometimes, because he had fallen ill with dysentery or pneumonia or random infections and because they feared he might die before he had given them the information they needed, his captors left him alone. An aged physician, a well-trained nurse, and nutritious meals would rouse him to good health once more. Then, the Nazis would proceed to a new cycle of interrogation and of torture.

They forced him to run in circles while he was carrying heavy logs. On those days three big-boned guards would kick him while he was running and disarrange his careful balance. The logs would fall away from him and the guards would go on kicking him. Then, because he had not cried out an appeal to them or screamed in pain, they would wait for him to gather the logs once more and heave them onto his shoulders. Only then would they leave the room to which they had brought him from his cell early that frigid morning. A young recruit, stationed at the threshold of the door, would stand watch over him and laugh if a log fell away from him and caused him to lose not only his balance, but also the pile of logs he had struggled to keep in place.

On other days, the Nazis burned his arms and his legs with lighted cigarettes, with the fire of wooden matches, and with hot candle wax. Again, they hung his nakedness from heavy wooden beams that spanned the width of the ceiling. This time they hung him from his ankles and beat his penis and his testicles with a heavy rope. The pain ripping through his groin threw him out of consciousness.

In spite of all these ways of torture, Jean-Claude was determined not to die. Tight-lipped and grimacing even in those hours when the Nazis left him alone in his cell, he knew he would stay alive as long as he withheld the information they were seeking. Only because the Nazis were determined to break him had they allowed him to go on living. He knew that they would go on alternating their savage use of him with periods of medical care and recovery. But there would come a day when they would realize that he would never betray his country or the countries of any of the Allies. On that day they would kill him.

At this time, about four months after the Germans captured him, the British discovered that Jean-Claude was alive. One of their double agents in Oslo (a Norwegian nurse) had been called to assist the German physician on an evening when he was caring for the injured French pilot who was being tortured in the building which the Nazis used as a military prison. Within hours after tending Jean-Claude, she transmitted a coded message to the British officer who was commanding the new Allied headquarters at South Vågsøy, about three hundred fifty miles from Oslo.

When he learned what had happened to his friend, Marc urged his squadron leader, Yvan Pelletier, to organize a raid into Oslo, so that their teams of pilots and commandos could rescue Jean-Claude. The British and the French were, in fact, willing to organize the raid. But no sooner did they learn of Jean-Claude's being alive, than the Nazis hurried him away to a location which remained unknown to the Allies.

For days, Marc brooded about the capture of his friend and soul mate. A murderous rage was rising within him—a rage so fierce that he began to believe that he would run mad. Aware of his muted fury, Pelletier quickly assigned him to dangerous sorties. A pilot that angry will, he believed, make an unbeatable killer even in the most formidable battles.

Flying with the hunter squadron Alsace and alongside the City of Glasgow squadron, he logged sixty or seventy new hours in direct combat while at the controls of Spitfires and Hawker Tempests. The dogfights and fighter sweeps and strafing raids over German ports and cities fed his wrath without appeasing it. That Jean-Claude was going to die at the hands of the Nazis was a bitter fact. That he could not help him continued to torment Marc. He felt that he was abandoning this best of all friends who had always rallied to his side during the most complicated episodes and in the darkest periods of his life.

Then, about a month after he learned that Jean-Claude

was still alive, there came to him a plan so dangerous that it might have given him pause, had his need to save Jean-Claude not become an obsession. He would be drawing Simone, the wife whom he passionately loved, into the danger. He saw no other way. He saw, in fact, that Simone was absolutely essential to the success of his plan. The plan needed her because it involved a man over whom she had tremendous influence. That this man was in love with her made him indispensable. His name was Gerhard Hauptmann.

He believed in his wife's courage and in her wiliness as much as he believed that she could save Jean-Claude. So, without yet telling her of his plan, he arranged a discreet meeting with her in Switzerland.

This was the year when Simone was staying with her father (Knut Bergman) in Sweden. Because he was an eminent mathematician and a nuclear chemist, the Nazis were trying to draw him into their atom bomb project. They were unaware that she and her father were decoding the Nazis' military correspondence that was being transmitted from their High Command in Germany. She was also serving the Allies as a courier and as a double agent in missions that brought her into Berlin, Munich, and Strasbourg. Every day, she risked her life because of her hatred of Nazi tyranny and because of the memory of her mother, who had been a lovely egalitarian

French woman.

In these same months, she was allowing Gerhard Hauptmann to court her. He was one of the officers whom the Germans had sent to persuade Professor Bergman to join their atom bomb team. By intimating that she loved him, Simone meant to disarm him. She did not want him to ask her father too many questions about his current activities or to press him too insistently about bringing his scientific knowledge to the Nazis' bomb project. He knew nothing of her marriage. Nor was he aware of her underground activities.

To him, she presented herself as upright and virginal. That she refused to adorn her face with cosmetics impressed him, as did the modest way she wore her blond hair, which was combed to form a coil at the nape of her neck. The subdued colors of her dresses and tailored suits, which were black, gray, and navy; her straight-backed carriage that expressed a delicate femininity even as it resisted overt sensual rhythms; and her understated inflections—all these things enhanced her decorum and in his eyes made her both different and extraordinary. The thought that she remained untouched by a man roused Gerhard's respect for her and roused, as well, his carnal interest. His willingness to defer to her celibacy both surprised and pleased him. In his mind, her virginity was proof of her patrician background. His willingness to leave her untouched until they were married was, he felt, a courtly gesture offered in the conviction that eventually he would enjoy days and nights of unstinting pleasure with a woman worthy of being his wife.

So, upon his careful inquiry of her, did Simone explain to Marc whenever he asked her to summarize the encounters with Gerhard that had taken place in the home of her father.

When he met her in Geneva, Marc told Simone that it was through Gerhard that she could save Jean-Claude. She would need to negotiate with Gerhard. She would have to convince him that Jean-Claude had been her childhood friend. Lying, she could tell him that Jean-Claude was, in fact, a distant cousin. Drawing upon the demure persona she had established with him, she must remind Gerhard that Jean-Claude carried the blood of Germans as well as of French and Swedes. Even in this violent period of European upheaval, his father had remained a prominent Swiss banker. In his mother's line there had been distinguished barons and brave generals.

"You can save this man," she must tell Gerhard. "You can help him escape. Without bringing any blame on yourself, you are the one who can do it."

On that evening in Geneva, within the modulated luxury and careful privacies of his parents' chalet, he had outlined the plan she would have to carry through with absolute conviction.

For three days, they'd had the chalet all to themselves,

because Henri and Marianne were in London, busy with wartime activities. There had been time to socialize with loyal friends and trusted newcomers. There had been time to be together. For those three swift days, they had taken joy once more from each other's company. They had skied and danced. They had attended a concert of chamber music—Chopin, Brahms, and Ravel. They had dined well and had drunk champagne. They had made love with the fervor and the intensity of their earliest times together.

"Chance gave us these three days," Marc told Simone, "and we have used them well."

"We have, indeed," she said. "These days have been very good to us."

He had not yet drawn her into his plan to rescue Jean-Claude. But she sensed the melancholy that shadowed his show of happiness. Intuitive, she imagined that he had something important to tell her.

When, in the last evening of their brief reunion, he did explain his plan to her, she listened carefully, as though he were mapping a combat strategy for the pilots in his bomber squadron or summarizing the sort of maneuver of which her training in the Resistance had given her knowledge.

"I'll do all that you want me to do," she said. "But I think that you are magnifying the influence I have over

Gerhard."

They were sitting on a comfortable fur rug before the warm glow of the fire-place, drinking brandy and feeling almost contented because, despite the ongoing war and the uncertainty of their own fates, they had experienced a few days of extemporaneous pleasure.

"He's in love with you, isn't he?" he asked her rhetorically. "He wants to marry you. I think that you have plenty of influence over him."

"Don't forget who he is," she answered him. "No matter how romantic he tries to be, Gerhard has the heart of a Nazi."

"You must make him believe that your future with him depends on his granting your wish. More than anything else, you want him to save your 'cousin' Jean-Claude."

She drew closer to her husband. With a light, feminine touch she clasped his rugged hand. Then, just as lightly, she touched his lips with a kiss.

"I'll do my best," she promised him.

For a moment, as she glanced upon him warmly, there flashed across his seeing the image that was Simone when she was a fourteen-year old school-girl braving out an uncertain moment with a bright smile and an assertive remark meant to subvert her vulnerability. Whenever she was feeling the pressure of having to win a crucial swim meet or of skiing down an unforgiving slope or of enduring the betrayal of a friend or of a day's early promise, she stood up to her fate with that charming smile of hers and with words as quick-witted as they were casual. The memory of her as she was then moved him with a gravity that surprised him. In that springtime season, she had been newly radiant because of their love and still innocent of the hard war years that were to come. The imagery that his memory scanned was, he thought, like a face concealed beneath a face on a canvas that the artist had painted over when he revised its meaning.

The imagery stirred his affection and persuaded him to embrace Simone with intensities that were both sensual and protective. He felt her body straining to subdue the apprehension that beneath her cool exterior his words had quickened. Now he knew where she stood in this difficult assignment he was placing on her shoulders. Not even her love of him or her empathy for Jean-Claude's peril could quite dispel her uncertainty about the outcome of their plan to rescue their friend. Her muted unease ignited his concern for her. He had been taking for granted her much-tested courage and her capacity to bring upon herself unforgiving risks.

"You don't need to do any of this, you know," he pushed himself to say. "There's so much danger in it."

She saw the effort he was making. He was straining to

believe what he was telling her. For that, she was grateful, because she understood how difficult it was these days for her husband to be soft or sentimental.

"Don't worry about me," she said, her voice carrying along its edges a matter-of-fact hardness. "I'll do the things that need to be done. Besides, we couldn't live with ourselves if we didn't try to save Jean-Claude."

Chapter Two

Simone and Gerhard

When, shortly afterward, Gerhard visited her in Sweden, Simone played out the whole intricate scenario that Marc had devised so that she could save Jean-Claude. She did not tell her father about Marc's plan. She did not want him to worry about her or try to dissuade her from playing this far-too-dangerous game with Gerhard.

"Don't become too involved with this German," her father had warned her at the start of Gerhard's visits. "Remember that he is a Nazi and that by inviting his special attention you are playing with fire."

"I know how to handle him," she said. "I'll keep him at bay and still make him believe that you and I are his friends."

Gerhard did not see her alone. Always, when he had visited, she had received him in the company of her father. Now, especially, in the days and evenings when she began to carry out Marc's plan to save Jean-Claude, she was careful to maintain the elegant propriety he had come to expect of her. He had grown used to seeing the other upright persons who were in the house with her father and with her. The housekeeper and that good woman's husband, who served as the gardener and the general caretaker of her father's property, were there. So were the cook and her husband, who managed the stables as well as their wine cellar. Middle-aged and meticulous in carrying out their various duties, they had impressed him as a sensible and hard-working staff. In any one of his visits, the gardener or the keeper of the stables might bring an important message to Professor Bergman, or the cook might carry in a silver tray of tea and cakes. On other afternoons, the housekeeper might serve Gerhard wine or scotch or bourbon.

When he visited in the evening as one of several guests, the housekeeper, the cook, and her husband would orchestrate the smooth turnings of an elaborate dinner.

"I love visiting your home," Gerhard once said at the end of an evening when, after the other guests had taken their leave of the dinner party, he stayed behind to share more wine and new anecdotes with them. "Being here with the both of you, I feel that I have returned to the years when there was no war and when I believed that happiness was within my reach."

Simone noticed the sensitivity of the remark and his yearning for a time that the war had stolen from him. But it was her father who responded openly to Gerhard's words.

"Maybe there will be such a time again," he said. "Maybe we'll all believe in happiness."

If Gerhard was the only visitor, Simone and her father would receive him in their parlor, fully engaged in conversation about the harpsichord concertos of Bach, for instance, or about the poetry of Rilke, the novels of Knut Hamsun, and the latest German aircraft. Then, after a while, Professor Bergman would withdraw from the company, leaving his daughter to complete the evening with decorous poise and well-trained modesty. But never did Gerhard feel absolutely alone with her. The father who had retired to his room and the staff who were asleep in their quarters remained an oblique presence. At any moment, they might appear unexpectedly. This careful propriety pleased him. It reinforced his belief in Simone's purity and in her decorum.

He did not intend to fall in love with her. But he had done so. He believed in her. She was upright and genteel. She was demure and honest. The beauty that attended her required no adornment. In his eyes, she appeared without artifice. He desired her in a way that he had not desired any other woman. There was in his feelings toward her a vaguely sentimental interpretation of all that he thought she represented.

The purity of her womanhood roused him, even as it held him to a Spartan discipline. He had never before met a woman whom he could rightly regard as untouched. Meeting her for the first time, he accepted Simone as the fulfillment of the ideal he had discovered only in his dreams. That she was a here-and-now reality brought him as much surprise as pleasure. She was the woman he wanted to marry, so long as she remained virginal.

To safeguard the ideal, he willed himself to an unfamiliar celibacy. At least with her he remained celibate. The stray women with whom he slept during the months that he courted Simone did not taint his dream of her. He did not dream of the women to whom he casually made love. When he did dream, he dreamed of Simone. He loved her passionately then, in all those nights when imaginary sexual intercourse became a pleasure more intense and more enjoyable than any he had known with other women. He loved her passionately now in his anguished dreams of her.

She was living in Uppsala with her father, the eminent mathematician Knut Bergman. After her schooling in Switzerland and after two years at L'École des Beaux Arts and at the Sorbonne, she had deferred her studies because of the war. That part of her biography was true. Nearly everything else she told him turned out to be a lie. From the day they first met, she pretended to favor Hitler's plan for Europe. With a shy reticence that touched him, she said that she had no skills that she could offer to the Nazi cause.

"The bookish and secluded life which I have always maintained has not prepared me for the harsh world," she said.

She spoke to him quietly, as if she were sharing with him information that was confidential yet essential if he wanted to understand who she was.

"But, even without an advanced scholarly training, I have taken my place in a university environment. I find that I can be of some use as an assistant to my father in his mathematical studies and as his secretary at the university where he teaches."

All these things she told him incrementally, after—as a frequent visitor to her father's home—he drew her into the careful rhythms of polite conversation. Never, though, did he impose upon these early dialogues with her either romantic innuendo or an intimate glance or gesture. He told himself that he must not move too quickly. To do so would be an affront to her upright character. There would be other days when he would court her properly, the way a well-born gentleman courts a young lady who has breeding and beauty and who belongs to his class.

Besides, he had come to Uppsala to see her father. His superior officer had sent him on this quiet mission which the chiefs of staff of the Army High Command regarded as very important, because it involved Professor Bergman's joining the Germans' team of scientists who were hard at work building an atomic bomb. It made no difference to Adolf Hitler or to the primary officers on his staff that Sweden had remained adamantly neutral in the wars which were tearing the old world apart. Regardless of his country's political scenario, Professor Bergman must participate in this planning stage that would yield a new and mighty world order led by the Germans.

"It is not Bergman's proficiency in mathematics which has drawn Hitler's attention. His excellence in that field is, of course, commendable. Rather, it is his genius as a nuclear chemist which makes his presence on Germany's atomic bomb project essential."

So his commanding officer told him, as he explained the importance of his drawing Knut Bergman into the Germans' plan.

A few weeks before Gerhard's first visit to Knut Bergman in November of 1941, a team of high-ranking officers had failed to persuade the professor to take an active part in the creation of the extraordinary world envisioned by the Nazis. During that week, Simone and her father told the Germans that Knut Bergman had a proper reason for remaining in Sweden. He had a serious heart ailment that prevented him from accepting any formidable assignments.

"My father needs to rest," Simone told the one-star general and the three colonels who, on a three-day visit to the area, had been urging Professor Bergman to join the Nazis' atom bomb team. "I'm following all of his doctor's instructions, so that I can give him the right care. I don't want to lose him."

With a courtesy equal to that of his daughter's, Professor Bergman eased the disappointment of his German visitors.

"In the near future," he said, "after my body has adapted to the new medication which my cardiologist has prescribed, I might be able to accommodate a more demanding schedule. Be assured that I am most sympathetic to the idea of a new world view."

None of the military visitors noticed that not once had Professor Bergman linked Hitler to that prospect. Nor did Gerhard discover until Simone's betrayal of him that her father was in perfect health.

These German officers went away with mixed feelings. Though they were not bringing Knut Bergman to Hitler, they were carrying a conciliatory letter from him, which held out the promise that he might one day soon be able to join an atom bomb team. Not even Hitler protested the broad and unspecific language of the message. There was nothing in the letter which indicated that Professor Bergman was going to league himself with the Germans.

Preferring to regard the letter as a hopeful sign, the Army High Command now sent Gerhard to secure the professor's commitment to the bomb project.

"You will be the one who brings Bergman to Berlin," the one-star general told him.

His words sounded clipped and imperious. On this afternoon, his shock of red hair, broken nose, and scar-faced features, as well as his tall and hardened frame, gave him an especially formidable appearance.

"Knut Bergman and your father are friends."

For a moment, though he stood at attention and held himself within stoical disciplines, Gerhard was caught surprised. The general was expecting the impossible. Without hesitating beyond that moment and while maintaining a self-assured demeanor, he told him so.

"The two men have not seen each other for many years, sir. From all that you have told me about Professor Bergman, I cannot say that his having been my father's friend so long ago will make any difference at all. The professor will come to Berlin only if he wants to come. I doubt that I can influence him in that direction."

The general gave him an order.

"You must," he asserted. "We are counting on you. Don't let us down."

The interview was over. Recognizing the moment, Gerhard saluted his general and quickly left the room. The general's arbitrary manner did not dispel his doubts about this unexpected mission that would bring him into Sweden.

His father had known Knut Bergman many years earlier, when they were beginning their careers in London—Anton Hauptmann as a young military officer attached to the German Embassy there and Knut Bergman as an enterprising mathematician and research scientist teaching at Oxford. They and their wives had socialized amicably, pleased that they shared so many beliefs and interests, even as they remained tolerant of one another's dissimilar politics.

Now, in November, more than a year after Germany had invaded Denmark and Norway, Gerhard came to the spacious home of Professor Bergman to persuade him to join the bomb team in Berlin.

He admired the Aryan look of the professor. Even in his sixties, Knut Bergman made a tall, imposing figure. The cragged features suggested a life lived with rugged intensities. The mane of white hair that looked vaguely unkempt and the cold blue eyes that steadily penetrated the imagery before them belonged to an unpretentious and no-nonsense individual. The big-boned shoulders and the unusually large hands indicated the physical resilience and manual dexterity that Time had worn down without negating all of their powers.

"You are exactly as I imagined," Gerhard told him. "I've heard so much about you, that I feel I know you well."

"Ah, but you must look more closely," Professor Bergman advised him. "I may surprise you."

"I want to be surprised," Gerhard said. "I would like you to say that Berlin is in your future."

"Please do not want it too much," the professor said. "Surprises should not be coaxed."

Momentarily light of heart, the professor meant to disarm him. In his own way, he was telling him not to push too hard the request his commanding officers were requiring him to reiterate. A patient detachment (he was implying) can make even a young, hard-grained military man appear philosophical. It might teach him to accept whatever the Fates care to allow.

Thus far, the Fates had nearly always been kind to Gerhard. His father had been a high-ranking officer during the First World War and afterwards an influential ambassador. Through Anton Hauptmann, he had inherited a hardy genetic identity. Through him, he had acquired characteristics which were as militant as they were leaderly.

He was (he'd been told) an extraordinary physical specimen. His blond hair, blue eyes, and chiseled features impressed an observer at once. With his muscular bearing and his well-grounded self-possession, he easily commanded attention and commanded as well whatever room he entered. He was quietly aware of the powerful effect that his presence had upon others. In the company of the men who belonged to his regiment, he made a pragmatic use of his husky voice, level gaze, and unusual height. Standing at six foot, four inches, he employed with tough-minded confidence his massive frame and his militant expertise. The men who served alongside him feared him as much as they respected him. Some of them loved him, with the unspoken love men bestow upon the man they have accepted as their mentor. In the company of his superior officers, he used his presence differently. He had a canny ability to subdue the effects of his physicality whenever he was in the same room with them. Because of his relationship with his demanding father, he understood that even his strongest advocates would resent being displaced by the charisma of a subordinate.

From early boyhood, he was taught to demand a great deal from himself. At the private military schools he attended as a youth and later as an officer candidate in the Junkerschule and in the Waffen-SS, he showed himself to be supremely athletic. He was an excellent swimmer and skier, a fine horseman and fencer, a first-rate marksman, and a seasoned hunter. He also excelled as a pilot, a mountain climber, and an auto racer.

He spoke several languages with ease and with natural, understated inflections. Knowing German, French, Italian, and English, as well as several of the Scandinavian tongues, enhanced his profile as a young officer who would move with assurance through many parts of the world. His wide travel began in his early years when his father's military and diplomatic assignments brought the Hauptmanns to South America, North Africa, and China, as well as to England, Italy, France, and Belgium. Only when he was eleven years old and a well-publicized scandal threatened to tarnish the Hauptmann name did he withdraw from the world—and then only temporarily.

That scandal involved his parents. His mother had grown weary of her husband's arbitrary disposition and the insistent militarism he brought from the battlefield into their home. In Belgium, she fell in love with a man ten years her junior. He taught at the University of Liège and was also an established poet. He had lost his wife in the second year of their marriage, when she gave birth to a stillborn child. For three years he had lived as a lonely widower. Then, one summer afternoon while boating on a sun-tinted lake, he met the woman who he was to learn on that day was Mrs. Hauptmann, the unhappy wife of an eminent German general who often served his country as a diplomat. That the poet needed her as much as she was in need of him made their being together seem inevitable. Together, they came to perceive, they could build a life that was as fulfilling as it was exciting. At the end of a year of soul-reviving trysts, she summoned the resolve to leave the ill-conceived marriage which her class-conscious relatives had arranged for her twelve years earlier. She willed herself to leave her son behind, too, because she understood that his primary allegiance had always been to his father. Elated, she hurried away with her lover and settled in Italy.

His father found them living in glamorous comfort within a villa on the Italian Riviera. Quickly, he shot them again and again, until their bodies were riddled by the bullets from his Luger. Without pity or remorse, he watched their blood flow across the marble floor of the atrium where he had confronted them. Setting his emptied pistol on a table nearby, he calmly told a servant to call in the police. Not even at the trial that followed would he show remorse or the troubled brow that hinted of an interior anguish. For two days, while tabloid newspapers made a tawdry affair out of the unorthodox union between Anna Hauptmann and Friedrich Buchholz, the all-male jury listened carefully to his father's story. It took them less than an hour to deliver a verdict of "not guilty." They forgave him his murders. But they could not forgive his mother for betraying her husband's trust and for violating the sanctity of marriage.

Perhaps it was the dishonor that his mother had brought upon herself which influenced Gerhard to distrust women. A vigorous and confident lover, he had known many women. Though he had a mild contempt for their sensual displays and for his urgent desire, he enjoyed sleeping with them. They were a man's necessary pleasure; they were the imagery exciting his spermatic power. In spite of his ambivalent feelings toward them, he never disparaged them—neither in the clubs, theaters, and spas that he frequented, nor in the private chambers that he shared with fellow officers.

But within himself he sometimes heard the voice that echoed his secret thoughts. "Every woman is a whore," that voice reminded him. "Only the tunes they sing are different."

He never thought of Simone in this way. Her beauty, intellect, and carefully modulated sensuality satisfied the romantic subtexts of his nature. His fragmented boyhood and his military training had taught him to suppress his yearning for an ideal partnership with a woman he could both love and respect. That Simone so completely fulfilled his image of an ideal woman not only made his heart leap. She also appeared to be in some profound and immense way his rescuer. Already, in these brief weeks of his knowing her, the promising implications of their relationship had revived his belief in the future. Once more, and for the first time since the war began, happiness seemed for him a realistic possibility. It was she in whom he believed. The innocent young woman whom she so artfully embodied in their carefully arranged meetings awakened his hope and his capacity for authentic love.

He also believed in her father. In spite of the savage influences that the war had wrought upon his character, Gerhard clearly perceived that Knut Bergman was a gifted scientist and a Renaissance man capable of rescuing humanity from its murderous impulses. What he did not yet perceive was that Professor Bergman was already making arrangements to join the Allied bomb team and that Simone was an agent for both the French and the Swedish underground resistance.

In February, a few weeks after her meeting with Marc in Switzerland, Simone initiated the plan that he had devised to save Jean-Claude.

On the evening which would become different from all the other evenings when Gerhard visited them, her father offered to their guest not only wine and cakes, but also a well-measured cordiality. Then he withdrew, because the evening had grown late and because he had to read his students' examination papers. He had no knowledge of her plan to rescue Jean-Claude. Marc had pledged her to secrecy, for fear that her father— who ordinarily consented to her risk-taking ventures— might dissuade her from a dangerous mission that he believed had no chance of succeeding.

It was in these moments, after the staff had completed their duties and retired to their rooms and after her father had once again played the role of an ingratiating host to a Nazi whom he disliked, that Simone broached the serious matter of Jean-Claude's rescue. Though she did not stray from the modesty that Gerhard received as an authentic part of her character, she drew him nonetheless into the subtleties of her sensual nature. The lavender fragrance with which she had scented her body, the silky blueness of the dress that clung to the contours of her slim figure, the grace that attended her every gesture as she poured more wine into his glass and lit his cigarette, and her innocent smile as she brushed against his body while for the first time sitting next to him on the sofa —all these things became part of her strategy for seducing him.

The words she chose to bring him under her spell were another strategy.

"I am glad that you have stayed," she said. "There is something important that I must ask you."

At once she roused his interest. But he waited for her to say more.

"I need you to help me," she began. "You are the only

person who can."

"It will please me to help you, if I can."

"My cousin, Jean-Claude Jourdan, has been captured by the Germans. He is a pilot who flies with the Free French Air Force. A few months ago, my father and I received news that he had been killed. For all those weeks and days, we were grieving privately. But last week brought us a ray of hope. We learned that Jean-Claude is alive. For how long, we don't know. The Germans have brought him to one of their prisons where they interrogate and torture their enemies. You know what that means. They are eventually going to kill him."

Simone began weeping. Her tears appeared heart-felt, and sorrow shadowed her lovely face.

"I am sorry for you and for his family," Gerhard said. "It is a hard thing to lose someone that you love."

She hurried to say more. For the first time, she called him by his first name.

"We haven't lost him yet, Gerhard," she said. "He is alive, and you can save him, if you are willing to take the risk."

He was looking at her intently now. His name upon her lips was a new intimacy between them.

"How do you propose that I do that?"

"You are the clever one. You can find a way."

"You are asking me to do something that cannot be

done," he said. "The Germans regard Jean-Claude Jourdan as one of their most formidable enemies. The Allies have used him as a poster-boy to convince themselves that they are going to win this war. When the Germans captured him, they caught a big prize, and they will never set him free. Our war machine will advertise Jean-Claude Jourdan's captivity. His being our prisoner underscores the probability that we will win this war."

She would not allow his matter-of-fact words to deter her.

"If you love me, you will try to save Jean-Claude."

"You know that I love you. I would do anything for you, if it were possible."

It was now that she confessed her own love for Gerhard.

"I love you, too. I'll never love any other man. But our future together depends on your saving Jean-Claude."

Her words made him pause and brought to his brow the trace of a frown.

When he answered her, his voice carried regret that to her ears sounded both genuine and troubled.

"There is nothing that I can do for him. His fate is sealed."

"I refuse to believe that," she said, carefully modulating her protest within the safe perimeters of decorum. "As long as Jean-Claude stays alive, there is a chance that he can be rescued. I have to help him. He carries the same blood that I do. In his own way, he is like you. He is not afraid to take tremendous risks. He fights bravely. And he is willing to bend the rules if someone else's safety depends on his doing so."

Still Gerhard resisted her pleas. But he maintained his courtesy toward her and his respectful regard of her genteel manner. Even against his will, her loyalty toward the man he believed to be her cousin touched him. But in this awkward matter he felt it important to express an even greater loyalty to his military training, with its Prussian and Nazi subtexts. Of course, he did not want this business of the captured French pilot to damage his relationship with the exceptional woman who had won his love. As wily as he was politic, he began to make an abrupt departure, neglecting neither his courtly bow to her, nor the warmth of his smile.

It was in these crucial moments that Simone committed herself to a course that was to haunt her afterwards in unexpected ways. Believing that she had all but lost the game of rescue into which Marc had drawn her, she now played her strongest card. She asked Gerhard not to leave.

"You know that I am in love with you," she told him, while placing the soft touch of her fingers upon the rough skin of his right hand. "You also know that war may not give us time to be married or to share our love. We could be killed, or the world we know might be lost."

She paused, while moving gently away from him and weighing her next words even more carefully. She had roused Gerhard's attention, just as she had anticipated.

"We can enjoy our love before you return to the war," she said. "We may never have another chance."

He moved closer to her and allowed his big athletic hands to hold once more the tips of her delicate fingers.

The press of his warm hands upon her fingers disquieted her. Though his touch was gentle, she felt his strength nonetheless. This nearness to him, an altogether new sensation, intensified his presence. Her eyes wakened to the full reality of him—to the heated blood that was rushing through the hands that held her own, to the blue eyes that with careful intimacy brought her into his regard of her, and to the full-bodied masculinity that was himself, so suddenly exciting and predominant.

She hurried past these feelings and with words both precise and matter-of-fact played out this scene that she had willed herself to devise.

"Oh, I know that sleeping with you before we are married goes against my principles," she explained. "But I've had such bad dreams lately. The war has destroyed so many lovers. Let us make use of our time while you are out of its reach. We may never have another chance."

Still he held the tips of her fingers. Still he studied her refined loveliness and her well-measured poise. There was in her precise intonations the tinctures of sadness as well as yearning. She saw that the words she chose, anchored as they were to the charm and the surprise of who he thought she was, excited him. But he responded cautiously nonetheless. He intended (she imagined) to keep her consent of him free of his own urging or persuasion.

"Are you really sure that you want to be with me before we are married?"

She heard in his voice an excitement that his clipped words and his husky timbres could not conceal. Again her unease rose up as if it would overtake her. There was a fear in her that, once she set her plan in motion, Gerhard would take control of it. But without even a pause she held herself steady. She was determined to go forward, even though her plan altered in a radical way the steps that Marc had outlined for her to follow. Encouraged by Gerhard's response, she took the step that she regarded as most necessary.

"I am very sure that I want to be with you," she said. "But I have one condition. You must find a way to set Jean-Claude free."

She was bargaining with him—her body for her cousin's

life. She was also gambling. The openness of her negotiation might dismay him and might compel him to believe that she had far more experience of the world than she led him to believe. But she was counting on the genuine love he felt for her. A love like his gave no quarter to dismay or distrust. He would not think of her as a whore. Instead, she imagined, he would tell himself afterwards that she was an extremely clever woman.

"I'll find a way to save your cousin," he said. "Then we can enjoy our love for all the days that I am on leave from the war."

The next time she saw him, Gerhard told her what he had done to accommodate her wish.

When he returned to his unit, he spoke with his commanding officer about a plan to free Jean-Claude Jourdan in exchange for Major Wilhelm von Trotter, a much-admired pilot who had fallen captive to the Allies after they shot down his plane outside London. A friend of von Trotter, his commanding officer listened quietly to Gerhard's plan. Then, with the cold detachment and disciplined objectivity he brought to all his evaluations, he approved it. Within a few days, the High Command in Berlin also approved the plan. Returning Major von Trotter to the war was, the High Command remarked, more important than keeping Captain Jourdan as their prisoner.

In this way the exchange of prisoners was accomplished.

Several days before the exchange took place in late March 1942, Gerhard met Simone in Lausanne, as they had planned. He was on a ten-day leave. He had told her that, to prove her trust in him, she must share his bed before Jean-Claude Jourdan was set free.

She accepted his terms.

Only during the sleepless hours she endured on the night before she was to make her way to Lausanne did she permit herself to confront her doubt and her apprehension. That she would of her own free will share her body with a Nazi unnerved her. Never before had she given herself to any man except Marc. Generous and proficient, Marc always brought her pleasure, and he always eased her spirit. But to allow Gerhard to enter her body was a different matter. He had bombed Allied cities and had at the same time killed thousands of innocent people. In spite of her courteous regard of him and of the civilized persona that he smoothly crafted while he was in her company, there was a part of her that still leagued him with all the savages who called themselves Nazis. Sex with Gerhard carried tawdry implications. She wondered whether the experience would leave her feeling forever contaminated. Yet, if she backed out of her agreement to have sex with this Nazi, Jean-Claude would surely die. In these sleepless hours just before she activated her dangerous pact with the well-spoken

German who seemed more mysterious to her now than ever before, she found herself wishing that there were a way for her to telephone Marc or to cable him or to send him a message on her wireless transmitter.

"To save Jean-Claude, I will have to sleep with Gerhard," she might have told him over the telephone or through a coded message. "There is no other way. Do you really want me to do this thing?"

If the decision were Marc's, then she need not bear the guilt and the shame that might haunt her afterwards. But she could not telephone Marc or send him a cable. Nor could she transmit to him a coded message. All around her there were double agents, paid assassins, and malevolent strangers. There was Gerhard, too, who believed in her because thus far she had not miscalculated the effects of her actions upon him.

She, not Marc, had to decide what to do.

So she told herself as the shadows of the wretched night that had stolen her peace slowly disappeared or lingered still like vague apparitions in distant corners of her room, here in the apparent safety of her father's house. Leaning into the scented white pillows that had brought her no comfort, she lit her tenth cigarette and watched the vaporous rings of smoke rising about her. A crisp breeze hurried through the partly open window and pushed the silk curtains into eerie motion. At the same time, the first light of dawn peered into the room and revealed in ambiguous fragments the objects that lived familiar and whole in her memory and that would be clarified when the full light of day overtook the room.

It was now that she drew once more from the hardened part of her nature the determination to carry her plan forward. If war had made Gerhard a killer, that same war had made her one, too. She had killed many people, most often face-to-face. She had shot them or strangled them or stabbed them or poisoned them. When she did not face these enemies directly, she had blown up the trains or buses on which they were passengers. Or she had dynamited the buildings in which they were at work or in hiding. Her unflinching awareness of who she was pushed her forward into the journey that she had already begun. She had, she told herself, to be that Simone. She had to be the militant woman who did not hesitate to kill her enemies and who, though she had never yet done so, slept with a Nazi and made him believe that she enjoyed him. She must continue to do what the rules of war required of her. She must go on being ruthless.

She did not anticipate how much Lausanne would change things for her. She did not yet understand that her ambivalent feelings for Gerhard were the uneasy stirrings of love.

During their first day alone together, without her father or her devoted staff hovering about them, Gerhard became before her eyes someone else, someone different from the militant Nazi imagery that she had taken to be his accurate personhood. Dressed in the clothes of a casual civilian, he looked even more ruggedly handsome. No longer constrained by his lock-step militarism, he was free to inhabit the persona of a young, cosmopolitan gentleman. It was a role, she thought, that suited him admirably. There was in him at times a debonair manner, a witty engagement with the world, and a muted sensuality that suggested the bright fires he had discreetly banked.

Wary at first of her favorable impression of him, she studied him with a gaze as careful as it was congenial. On one occasion, she took special note of his cool assurance when a formidable Swiss banker confronted the both of them at the door to their suite of rooms.

"The hotel has always assigned these rooms to me," the banker said. "The clerk made a mistake. These rooms belong to me."

The banker was a middle-aged man, apparently used to having the people around him fulfill his every need. She had met his type before. Tall, silver-haired and burly, his patrician background did not soften the rough character of his face or his arrogance.

Gerhard eyed him directly. If he disliked this man, he made no outward show of his feelings. To the banker's demand that he give up the rooms, Gerhard responded through words that tempered their cutting edge with a natural buoyancy.

"You are traveling alone," he said. "But these rooms need the company of a good woman. Bring your wife next time, and the door will fly open to you."

The banker was fuming.

"Don't take it so hard, old sport," Gerhard told him. "Come in and have a drink."

Grim-faced and disapproving, the banker turned away without replying.

Together, both of them watched the banker hurry into the elevator nearby.

"Too bad," Gerhard said to her. "He could have enjoyed these rooms for at least a half hour."

She liked Gerhard's irony and his self-control. He reminded her of Marc when he confronted a disgruntled rival in a polo competition in Argentina three years earlier and when, only a few weeks before the Germans overtook Paris, he devised sly responses to a French magistrate who berated him for not supporting Hitler.

There were other occasions when she noticed Gerhard's

quick-witted reactions and his generous nature.

One morning, while they were having breakfast in the hotel dining room, a nervous young waiter brushed against a glass of water that spilled upon Gerhard's hands. Not a whit annoyed by the accident, he quickly put the waiter at ease.

"Well," he said, "that's one way to clean my hands."

Once again she thought of Marc and the sense of humor he brought to any scattershot mishap (a dislocated shoulder during a rugby match, for instance) or to an unexpected complication (a wrong turn on a rain-swept country road). He knew how to laugh at his fate and still keep it as an ally. In this respect, he and Gerhard were brothers under the skin.

On a different morning, another episode acquainted her even further with Gerhard's character. She and Gerhard had just emerged from the hotel and had entered the chauffeured limousine (a rented Lamborghini) that would bring them into St. Moritz, which was one hundred fifty miles away. There, during a three-day excursion, they would enjoy more skiing, snowboarding, and tobogganing, and Gerhard would participate in a horse race on a frozen lake. They were about to begin their journey when they saw— outside the mini-bus that stood twenty feet in front of their car—two rugged young men arguing with each other. Paired with their wives, who waited uneasily near them, the men were on the brink of punching one another. Each of them was claiming the remaining two seats on the mini-bus that was also headed for St. Moritz.

As they observed the scene more closely, she and Gerhard recognized the taller man and his wife. They were Dieter and Bettina Keller, a newly-married couple from Munich. Dieter was a surgeon whom the German army had assigned to one of its hospitals there. She and Gerhard had met him and his wife only a few days earlier. In that brief time, though, she had noticed that the war had made Dieter tense and brought to Bettina's sunny disposition shades of apprehension and of dismay.

"My wife and I bought our tickets before you did," Dieter was shouting. "You will have to wait for a later bus."

The other man wouldn't budge from his place at the door of the bus. Nor would he listen to the mild-mannered driver who was trying to resolve the problem.

Now Dieter clenched his fists and looked as though he was about to swing his first punch into his opponent' face.

But, stepping out of the car, Gerhard called out the words that made both the arguing men look his way. Their wives and the driver looked, too, and so did the men and women who had already boarded the bus.

"We are going in the same direction, Dieter," Gerhard said. "You and Bettina will ride with us, of course."

The Kellers took only a moment to reflect upon the meaning of his words. Then, smiling broadly, Dieter answered him.

"We will gladly ride with you."

They hurried toward him and toward the waiting limousine from which she was watching Gerhard as well as them.

When he entered the Lamborghini with the Kellers, she joined their conversation with an energy that was both cordial and refined. She did not stiffen when his long athletic leg pressed against the slimness of her own. She was not in the least dismayed when the Kellers, who were seated opposite them within the spacious amenities of the car, continued to perceive Gerhard and her as a married couple. Nor did she draw away from Gerhard when, eager to discover her responses to his words, he brought his face so close to hers that their nearness to each other became intimate and almost thrilling.

For a long time afterwards, Simone recalled these occasions. But not until several days after they occurred was she willing to admit that, in each of these incidents and with extemporaneous and accurate responses, Gerhard had revealed something important about himself. She was learning to admire his good-natured humor and his sense of fair play. She was learning as well to like his generous spirit and the courtly manner in which he escorted her to a dining table or to a waiting car or into the ski lodge where he so easily drew her with him into the general merriment. Now she accepted the warmth of his hand upon her own as they sauntered across the hotel courtyard to peer at the crescent moon and the snow-capped mountains that gleamed like phosphorescent bodies. She accepted as easily the touch of his face against her own as his body leaned into hers while they were dancing. She welcomed his embrace when he placed his rugged arm around her waist so that, when they were ice-skating, she could maintain her balance as they approached the swerve of an intricate turn. Always before, whenever she had seen him in her father's home, Gerhard had been a strong physical presence. Here, during these days and nights in Lausanne, he was even more vivid, because in her eyes he was no longer a Nazi.

What impressed her most of all was the sensual hold that he was beginning to have upon her. She enjoyed being with him. At the hotel where they stayed as man and wife, they swam in the blue-green waters of the heated pool as if they were long-time partners who had perfected their synchronous movements. One time, while they were cavorting in the water, she happened to touch the smooth skin of his chest. The touch, which was more like a caress and lasted only a moment, excited her. If she closed her eyes, she might have believed that she was touching Marc while they were swimming or were in bed together. This time the thought did not disconcert her. Rather, it persuaded her that in many ways Gerhard was an intriguing variation of Marc.

Her bond with Gerhard deepened. They skied in mid-afternoon while journeying in similar unison across the wide span of snowbound hills and the dangerous curves of icy slopes. Always compatible and always collaborating on this new partnership between them, they dined on salmon in Champagne sauce and danced in the later hours of that same evening. Through all of their hours together, she felt her spirit reaching out to him. He, in turn, reveled in the sheer wonder of being alive with her beside him.

"You've given me new life," he said. "I feel re-born. And yet I feel the same—not as I have been in these war years, but as I used to be when I was a student who thought he could make a very happy life building planes or becoming a surgeon or making films."

The tremendous change that was taking hold of him thrilled her. How human he was. How extraordinary. How self-contained and magnificent. It lifted her spirits to watch his masculine assurance and to listen to his clear-sighted remarks about music, painting, and aviation. Nor did he require that she merely listen. Eagerly, he sought out her view of things.

Together, they collaborated within dialogues that were as crisp as they were original.

That they were well-trained pianists who often played classical music made her feel even closer to him. One of their conversations about music drew from each of them comments about the emotional intensities of Claudio Monteverdi's opera *The Return of Ulysses*. Both she and Gerhard admired this opera about Ulysses because it centered on an individual who, having fought his way though ten years of war, went on to surmount tremendous obstacles when he returned to find that corrupt men had overtaken his homeland. In Monteverdi's portrayal of him, influenced as it was by Homer's epic poem, Ulysses was an extraordinary man who identified himself bravely to a hostile universe.

"Monteverdi is the Italian Homer, and Shakespeare, too" Gerhard said, "because of his understanding of human nature."

"Yes," she agreed. "Monteverdi makes us understand that there are no certainties even for wily and heroic men like Ulysses. The world is filled with violence and betrayal and unbearable sadness."

On some afternoons she and Gerhard discussed the Symbolist prints of Edvard Munch. He was a Norwegian artist who was famous because of his portrayals of the conflicted relationships between men and women. Until the war came,

Munch had often visited her father, whom he regarded as a loyal friend. They had first met many years earlier when her father attended an exhibit of Munch's art in Stockholm. With her father and sometimes with her, Munch shared lively conversations whenever he stayed with them for a few days. He was a white-haired rangy gentleman whose presence dominated a room. His brown eyes glowed behind wire-rimmed glasses, their quickened gaze drawing into their awareness the persons and the objects before him. Even then, when he was in his seventies, his sculptured demeanor retained a worn handsomeness. But his large, strong hands were his most memorable feature. They were hands that were inspired by a first-rate mind. During his long career, they had created thousands of prints, paintings, watercolors and drawings, as well as hundreds of copper plates, lithographic stones, and woodblocks.

She remembered fondly Munch's discussions with her and her father about his Symbolist art. For him, the very elements of the material world such as a tree, the sky, a bed, or a face were signs or correspondences of underlying moods, emotions and ideas.

Here in Lausanne, her memory of that time did not allay her tension or persuade her to forget why she had come to Switzerland with Gerhard Hauptmann. But Gerhard's respect for Munch's art held her attention nonetheless.

One print in particular drew Gerhard's special praise. It was called *Consolation*. Munch had composed its imagery in drypoint and aquatint, which he then printed in black on Japan paper. The narrative it suggested involved a nude man embracing a nude woman on the edge of a bed. The woman is weeping. Perhaps, the man is leaving her, or she is remorseful after having given in to passion.

As she studied the print in the company of Gerhard, Simone became uneasy. Against her conscious will, she was sexually roused as she looked at the naked couple that Munch had brought to life in his print. Yet it was not the print alone that roused her. It was the presence of Gerhard and the influence of his body next to hers, there within the plush comforts of the sofa. Once again, his long leg pressed against her leg, and his blue-eyed handsome face touched her cheeks as though he intended to kiss her.

She thought of Marc and quickly tried to push away her guilt so that she could take the next steps needed in this scenario that he had devised to save Jean-Claude.

The next step involved her commenting upon Munch's print.

"If I hadn't met Munch and enjoyed many conversations with him," she said, "I might be surprised that he is so honest about the role of the woman in a love affair. Few men, I think, admit the truth of their relations with women. In this print, Munch exposes the vulnerability of the woman. It is she who loses most in a love affair. She is the one who compromises herself and risks being punished by society."

Again she thought of Marc. The intensity of his love pleased her. But his love for her, which had become an obsession, was problematic. Her knowledge of him, drawn from their seven years together, convinced her that he would never forgive her for sleeping with any other man. Her body was a private territory that he had claimed for himself. But she loved him no less. She saw his proprietary hold upon her as a sign of his insecurity. He feared losing her. That fear was a weakness that stirred her love of him and her pity.

Gerhard took gentle hold of her hands now. He was, she felt, thinking about her words that told him how much women lose in their relationships with men. If he detected the bitterness in those words, he gave no evidence.

"It won't be that way with us," he said. "That is a promise."

"I believe you," she said. "I think you are different from most men."

For a moment, he held her in his gaze. Her words did not influence him to smile, perhaps (she felt) because he regarded those words as an essential part of the love that was growing between them. Instead, he raised her hands to his lips and kissed them.

The gesture filled her with awe. There was so much love in this man, and he was drawing her into its powers.

Now he proceeded to say what he thought about Munch's print.

"I like its indeterminacy," he said. "I also admire the artist's subtle use of shadow to portray an environment that is as ambivalent as it is sensual. We don't know why the woman is weeping or whether her relationship with the man is ending or beginning."

"Not even the man or the woman may know that," she said. "That is part of their mystery."

Now Gerhard did smile.

"For a woman who has spent most of her life in her father's home," he said, "you know some of the important things about men and women."

"Sometimes I know," she said. "But generally I make my way through the dark, as do most people."

She was moving through the dark right now, and with ingrained wiliness she was keeping her fear at bay.

At dinner a few evenings later, they spoke of aviation. That she had learned to fly a plane pleased him immensely. She had been a pupil of the renowned racing pilot Michel Detroyat. After he listened to her experience of flying a Mauboussin M.200, Gerhard praised her adventurousness and her skill. She perceived in his words a genuine empathy for all that she had been telling him.

"You must be very good," he said. "Detroyat works only with pilots who demonstrate an exceptional skill."

"I think that he took pity on me. I wanted so much to be a good flyer. But at that time I was so awkward and uncertain."

"Oh, I imagine that he saw more than that. He saw your adventurousness and your courage."

His praise moved her. Marc had often praised her flying, but in an understated manner. Whatever proficiencies she achieved as a pilot, he took for granted. Nor did he find extraordinary her work as a Resistance agent or her decision to become a pilot in the Women's Air Transport Auxiliary later that year. She was a part of the Allies' war team. She wasn't doing anything that other capable agents and pilots had not already done. There was in his attitude, she felt, a genuine respect for her work. He did not want to single her out for praise that he accorded to no other agents or pilots that he knew. To do so would be to treat her as if she were an amateur who needed encouragement.

She liked Marc's attitude. Never did he condescend to

her. Always, he treated her as an equal.

Yet she saw in Gerhard's praise of her an empathy that Marc sometimes lacked. Though he had known her for only a few months, Gerhard was more sensitive to her need for praise. He was also more willing to share with her the plans that would make his life after the war both creative and useful.

It pleased him to tell her of his dream of designing a new plane that might be a more advanced brother to the Siebel Si.202 Hummel.

"As a sports plane, the Hummel has proved itself to be very effective," he explained. "It is a small low-wing cantilever monoplane equipped with side-by-side seating for two and designed to accept a variety of single engines of nine cylinders or so. At its best, the Hummel can attain a speed of ninety-six miles per hour. But the sports plane that I am designing will be made of metal rather than wood. It will have a larger wing span, and it will be powered by a jet engine."

Once again, Gerhard's knowledge and enthusiasm impressed her. Once more, Simone imagined that he must have been a very fine man before the war, when he was very young and could enter the world on his own terms and with unstinted hope. Even as he believed that he was becoming someone new in her presence, so also did she tell herself that she was turning into someone else. No longer was she the familiar young woman with whom she had made a well-examined acquaintance. That woman belonged to Marc. With Gerhard, she was someone not herself—a stranger free to be drawn into an intimacy that lived at the cusp of danger.

Toward this intimacy, she moved with a tension that Gerhard mistook for her lack of experience. He did not mind when, on their first night together and at the moment that he began undressing, she seemed to withdraw from the agreement she had made with him.

"I'm not ready for this," she told him while her voice became a tremulous whisper. "I need more time."

"I understand," he said. "Don't worry about it."

But she was worried. She wondered whether she had gone too far. Marc had sent her here to save Jean-Claude. He had not asked her to sleep with a Nazi. She wondered, too, whether Gerhard would force himself upon her, once she slipped into bed beside him. Or, possibly, his manly presence would rouse her and, with no inhibitions to hold her senses taut, she would open herself to receive him.

She need not have worried.

That first night together, Gerhard did not make love to her. Instead, he lay beside her—his blond handsomeness and naked body caught in the glow of the lamps that flanked their bed and lingered by it, as if watching them. His blue eyes gleamed as well, and his penis hung distended. Still, he would not touch her. She saw that he wanted her to become at ease with his rugged body beside her. He wanted her to have the chance of backing away from their agreement, if it was her wish to do so. At the same time, he was testing his own capacity for self-willed disciplines. Though he was eager to make love to her, she realized that he would on this night continue the game of celibacy that he had been playing for her. For a half hour and more, while they softly spoke of the travel they might experience together after the war and after they were married and of the homes they could share in Berlin, Paris, and Buenos Aires, he studied the lovely curve of her figure, which was clothed in a white silk nightgown. Her beauty, her soft skin, and her fragrance roused his desire for her. But he would not touch her. Then, because he had passed whatever test he had devised for himself and because he had given her a chance to lie next to him while studying him in his nakedness, he turned away from her and, after switching off the lamp near him, fell into sleep.

A new dismay lived in her now. Lying next to his nakedness and observing all the details of Gerhard's well-endowed muscularity had aroused her. The affection that she had suppressed during his many visits to her father now flared up before her conscious awareness. Guilt overtook her, and the fear that she was betraying Marc stung at her pride and her self-respect. It was this guilt that gave her pause, struggling with her to hold her excited senses still. But her guilt, tentative and confused, was not strong enough to alter her feelings. She was relieved that the night had not tested her fidelity to Marc or incited her need for Gerhard. Yet she was also disappointed that Gerhard had not made love with her. The desire that had taken hold of her was urging her with raw and familiar intensities to bring him, naked and erect, inside her.

All through the rest of that week, though, Gerhard did make love with her. Everything between them seemed new and extraordinary. Even the simple act of squeezing the end of a condom between her forefinger and thumb and placing it over his erect penis thrilled her. He had cast a spell over her. She was a woman made new by the ecstasy of their love-making. Vigorous yet gentle, he drew her willingly into that ecstasy.

"You know more than I thought you would," Gerhard said, as they lay back against the ample and comforting pillows of their bed after this second night of making love. He felt, she could see, as sated and renewed as she was. That she appeared to be a more experienced lover than he was anticipating did not disturb him. His manly self-possession persuaded him, she imagined, to attribute her ease and her versatility to his prowess as a lover. The clue that her careful words now threw out to him was, she felt, just as convincing an explanation.

"Why should my knowing how to behave with a man in a bedroom surprise you?" she began. "I had a mother, after all. She was a wonderful woman. She was artistic. She was educated. She was genteel. She loved my father very much. She told me what I needed to know. She once said that, if I wanted to keep my husband happy, I must leave modesty outside the door to the bedroom."

Her explanation, which she imparted with precise and cool-headed intonations, drew from him none of his own words. But he studied her with new interest, all the while offering her an enigmatic smile.

By the third night of their lovemaking, she was responding with furious sensuality to his every move. He was an accomplished lover who played upon her body as though it were a musical instrument. Now she gave herself freely to him. Neither her troubled awareness of what she was doing nor the self-loathing that haunted her in solitary hours afterwards held her back. She longed for his touch, whether it was vigorous or gentle. She yearned for the spermatic scent that was a part of his nakedness. She craved the erotic gestures through which he brought her to multiple and extended orgasms.

By the final days of their time in Lausanne, she felt that her body and Gerhard's completed each other. When they made love, no matter the sensual techniques they used to fire their blood, their bodies were in perfect coital alignment. She felt this way with Marc as well. As vigorous a lover as Gerhard, Marc also made her feel complete and whole—in and away from their bed. She saw the two men as competing dualities. They were different, yet in so many important ways—in their intellect, in their courage, and in their sexual prowess—they were similar. In their sensual relationship with her, they might have been fraternal twins or spirit-brothers. So she willed herself to imagine, finding in that thought a temporizing judgment—a verdict that appeased her guilt and excused her wartime aberration. Now she began to tell herself that she loved Marc and Gerhard equally. She could be happy only if the two men remained in her life.

At the moment, Gerhard was very much a part of her life. So intense was her desire for him in these last days she was sharing with him in Switzerland, that she brought a nearly reckless abandon to their lovemaking. Each time he mounted her, in the morning or in early afternoon or all through the night, she consented to him completely. Always, she consented to the push and thrust and swell of his rhythms, firing as they did her need and her eagerness to collaborate with him to achieve a nearly perfect symmetry.

Never in the last days of being with Gerhard in Switzerland did she think about Marc. Only after Gerhard had returned to Berlin and after she had gone on to London did she think about her husband. Once more her guilt rose up to accuse her, leaving her as unhappy as she was uncertain about her future. She loved two men and would have gladly lived with both of them. But that was not possible. Her matter-of-fact understanding of things made her see clearly where she stood with each of them. From their perspective, her loving both of them could only bring all of them to grief.

There were other problems.

Gerhard did not know that she was married to Marc Roussillon. Nor was Marc aware that, to save Jean-Claude, she had slept with Gerhard.

Chapter Three

Marc, Simone, and Gerhard

A few days after arriving in England, Simone joined Marc at his parents' country estate in Derbyshire, about one hundred fifty miles outside London. His parents were not there. Having withdrawn from their careers in classical music because of the war, they were giving themselves completely to the fight against the Nazis. Marianne was ferrying Hawker Hurricanes, Spitfires, and Avro Lancasters from factories in the Midlands and Southern England to Fighter Command squadrons in Glasgow, Manchester, West Sussex, and Normandy. Henri was flying in bombing missions over Berlin, Dresden, and Munich. They would return in two days.

For all that time, she and Marc would have the house to themselves, though the housekeeping staff and the gardeners would be a part of the scene.

When she arrived, Marc was waiting for her. Rarely had she seen him so elated and so certain of himself in this new happiness that random chance and her calculated risk-taking had given them. Whether the emotions that were charging his spirit held him to a silence that seemed like a momentary awe of her or whether it was his need to hear first of all everything that she had to tell him, she did not know. She saw only that he was waiting for her to speak.

"Everything is fine," she assured him. "Your plan worked."

She was conferring with Marc in the privacy of Marianne's rose garden. All around them the warm April flourishing of hybrid tea roses and floribundas was a flare of red, lavender, cream-white and pink. A long hedge of potentillas, sun-yellow and orange and red, was another flare upon their senses. Two spotted thrushes, with white eye-rings and orange-brown napes, were trilling fluted notes as they winged their way onto the branches of a golden robinia.

Marc had drawn her to the blue-rimmed well, where—breeze-stirred and compatible—she stood with him in the spring sunlight and watched him return her smile. His brown eyes gleamed with love for her. She knew well how to read the language of his eyes. He was delighted to see her—not only for who she was, but also for what she had accomplished.

"You've done it, Simone," he said. "You've saved Jean-Claude."

His happiness and his love for her gave her the clues that

she needed. She began to play this hour alone with him in the same keys. She did not need to fake her love for him. But her happiness with him now seemed a blemished and devious thing. No longer did he alone influence it.

Carefree and glowing—or seeming so, she chose words that played the right keys. "It was your plan that saved him," she said. "That was the thing that made everything work the way we wanted it."

"It was you," he insisted. "It was wonderful and courageous you. You are the hero of the day."

She felt his strong arms enclosing her and felt as well the warm lips that kept kissing her mouth and cheeks and eyelids.

"I love you so much," he said. "You are wonderful. You are everything that I could want you to be. I didn't think that there could be any more love in me for you. I thought that you already had all of it. But there is more. I have so much more love for you inside me."

This very openness, drawn from his authentic feelings for her, quickly dispelled her certainty that she could give to their relationship all that he gave, anchored as it was to an ingrained honesty. The words that he now spoke unsettled her.

"I've needed you for such a long time," he said. "You are what I need most of all. You are the only real happiness I've known."

"I feel the same way about you," she answered him.

She was grateful that he did not notice her unease. Instead, he smiled. Her words were the ones he had expected her to say. But his warm regard did not ease her guilt. It intensified her understanding that she could no longer be completely honest with him. His love was so real that it made her conflicted love of him seem small and synthetic. Her guilt stayed with her day after day, stealing her peace and teaching her its harsh lessons. Even if she and Marc and Gerhard survived the war, she could envision only a lifetime of furtive meetings and secret pacts with the other man that she loved as much as she loved Marc.

She must, she told herself, do everything to conceal this other love from Marc.

Now in his company for an extended period in these days right after she had lived out her tryst with Gerhard, she could not bear to meet Marc's inquiring glances or—with charm and self-possession—to share his light-hearted remarks. During her days and nights with Gerhard in Switzerland, something new had been given her and something important had been taken away. Gerhard had given her his love and, by so giving, had humanized himself. The thought excited her and conferred upon their relationship a profound significance. But she was determined to resist the spell that Gerhard's love had cast upon her. She kept insisting to herself that her feelings for Gerhard were no more than a schoolgirl's excited response to unanticipated love.

What she had lost was her fidelity to Marc. No longer did she feel at ease with him. She loved him still, but without the purity that in her mind had made of her his extraordinary partner—a woman who never allowed any man to touch her except her husband. She thought herself too much a realist to disdain any woman simply because she had slept with a man who was not her husband. Sometimes, that sort of thing worked out very well, especially if it represented for the woman an awakening—spirit-driven or carnal—or an entrance onto a new and essential path.

That, until her arrangement with Gerhard, it had not happened to her had much to do with her having fallen in love with Marc when she was a girl in her teens. Each of them became the other's obsession. Each of them found in one another the only partner who could be authentic. Though Marc had slept with other girls before he came to her, she was not dismayed. By the time he was sixteen and sleeping with her for the first time, he was an experienced and generous lover. He taught her how to find joy in her sensuality and how to make their hours together a passionate experiment.

Now, six years later, she regarded herself as a sophisticated woman. In this new cycle of her life, she had fallen in love with another man. The experience troubled her. But it also awakened her to the joy of being in love with two men. She wanted "to seize the day." She wanted to take possession of her good luck and of the more complete version of her womanhood. At the same time, because she carried uneasily her tattered loyalty to Marc, she was suffering a remorse that she had not yet learned how to elude.

In the weeks that followed their conversation in Marianne's secluded garden here in Derbyshire, she was careful to engage in the light-hearted repartee that gave special pleasure to Marc. She also answered with clipped and understated inflections every one of his questions about the days and nights in Switzerland that she had spent with Gerhard. Her words made him believe that she regarded her time there as an ordeal. She had passed through it effectively because of her emotional detachment from the experience. The war, she reminded him, had made cool-headed detachment her stock-in-trade. She had learned well how to distance herself from the violence swirling around her, from the killings that she had perpetrated, and from the plots that she was activating. Only in this way could she be this other woman that the war had made her. In this way only could she do all the things that the assignment involving

Gerhard Hauptmann demanded of her.

"My living outside myself," she said, "as though I were an altogether different person, helped me to save Jean-Claude."

Her words carried a conviction that seemed natural and extemporaneous.

"I knew that I could count on you," he said. "You are one of the best on our team. You have guts, and you have a good brain. You can tell when a risk is worth taking."

His belief in her brought her new shame. There was a purity in that belief that she could no longer emulate. Now her guilt overtook her even more furiously. She could not bear to meet Marc's good-natured inquiries or his abiding trust in her. Though she had rescued Jean-Claude, she had broken the bond with her husband that had made their love very special, indeed.

It did not take long for Marc to notice how she turned away from his glances, whether his discerning eyes were probing her muted discomfort or studying her with his familiar, sensual need. He noticed, too, how—whenever he caressed her shoulders or touched the delicate skin of her arms or held her close to his body so that he could breathe the fragrance of her hair or fondle her ample breasts or lightly kiss her lips—she would stiffen, held taut by what she now received as the surprise of his intimacy, as if he were a stranger.

Once, after she had pulled away from his embrace of

her, he drew her back. She had no choice except to turn around and face his careful regard of her.

"What's wrong?" he asked. "Why are you so tense?"

"Don't mind me," she said. "I've had a few bad nights. Some of my war experiences have come back to haunt me."

"Let them go," he said. "Push them back to the past where they belong. Forget all of them."

She faked a laugh which he appeared to accept as the real thing.

"I wish that I could," she answered him. "If I could forget them, I would be a much happier woman."

The frown that lightly touched his brow told her that he was concerned about her. He wanted her to be happy. She recognized as well the sly wit that he injected into his next remark and that brought a grin to his face.

"Don't think about the war. Think about something else—or someone. Think about me."

"I will," she said. "You will be the answer to my prayers."

The grin left his face. He pondered her words before calmly throwing out a question that, she felt, suggested his own unease.

"Haven't I always been the answer?"

"Of course," she said. "You always have been."

If he saw through her artifice, Marc gave her no sign. But for the rest of that day and for many days afterwards, he went on watching her. She felt his enigmatic glance taking her in. She saw love in those eyes, and she saw uncertainty. The eyes were studying her carefully, as though they were observing a stranger. She guessed at what the mind behind those eyes was thinking. She was a new version of the Simone about whom he had always believed that he knew everything that was essential. She was no longer the same woman. She was different.

Even when he made love to her now, she was different. No longer was there between them the longed-for symmetry, the smooth and natural rhythms of their bodies together, their teasing and constant momentum, and the protracted joy of their climaxes. Their intercourse became a shared and enigmatic tension. Whatever pleasures remained were part of an unsentimental biological act. Gone was her roused elation when, naked and erect, he would enter her—vigorous, spermatic, and adept. Gone, too, was her belief that she belonged to him alone.

Marc did not see that she loved him no less. Nor did he see that it was herself that she could not love. With her husband, she could never again be authentic while she concealed the truth of her relations with Gerhard. Those relations were anchored to the perversity of her having taken pleasure with Gerhard.

Through all those secret days and nights with him, she had enjoyed his love. This thought tormented her and drove her guilt as if it were some furious revenge that Gerhard had enacted upon her.

To Marc's searching eyes, her appearance of guilt convicted her. Whatever had changed between them involved Gerhard. With each day and night that passed uneasily between them, he grew certain of that.

"There is something wrong," he insisted. "You have to tell me all of it. Never again can there be anything real between us if you are going to go on concealing the truth from me."

So he reminded her day after day. As if they were in a courtroom and he was a lawyer challenging her to defend herself, he began to confront her with abrasive questions and a refusal to be satisfied with her evasive answers.

One question in particular became the familiar preface to his punishing interrogations.

"Why," he often demanded to know, "did Gerhard agree so quickly to arrange for Jean-Claude's release?"

Grown weary of his rapid-fire questions and the lacerating bluntness of his accusations, Simone usually answered him in a warm, natural-sounding voice. He knew that she meant to conciliate him. If she maintained her self-possessed manner and the fluencies of expression that suggested she was at ease with herself, he might perhaps accept her words as authentic. The understated smile she offered him was still another expression meant to dispel his brooding interpretation of all that she represented.

"I promised to marry him by the end of the year," she sometimes said. She was careful not to mention Gerhard by name for fear that apparent familiarity might rouse her husband's tautly-harnessed anger.

Like a panther circling his prey, he would—with penetrating glare—study her quietly as, with the rugged authority she had always admired, he moved about her. Never, in the beginning, did he raise his voice or unsettle her with the driving intensities of his suspicion. Yet, as self-controlled as he was blunt, he knew that in her eyes he was becoming somebody else.

"Did you allow him to kiss you?" he frequently asked, matter-of-fact yet insinuating.

Once, for just an instant right after he first surprised her with that question, he thought he saw apprehension in her eyes. But the moment quickly passed. Her glance upon him became as calm as it was direct.

"I had to," she said. "He thought I loved him."

"How many times?" he hurried to ask her. "How many times did you let him kiss you?"

"I don't remember," she answered him. "It isn't really important."

"Did you enjoy it?" he wanted to know. His voice was low now and nearly an insistent whisper.

"I had to pretend to like it," she said. "I had to make certain he liked me."

"What did you do when you were with him in Lausanne?"

"We swam in the hotel's heated pool. We skied and skated. We went riding in a sleigh driven by a team of white horses. We socialized with other Germans who were also staying at the hotel. We dined, and we danced. And that was all of it."

Still he glared at her. Still he insisted that there was much more to the days that she had spent with Gerhard in Switzerland than she was willing herself to tell.

"You slept with him," he often began. His quick words rode on the air like the quiet taunt he meant them to be.

For many days, she avoided telling him the truth.

"No," she kept saying. "That never happened."

He did not believe her.

"You slept with him, and you enjoyed it."

Now she protested his distrust of her. She made her voice stern and hurt at the same time.

"How can you imagine I could do such a thing?" she asked him.

"I can imagine it," he answered her. "I know how much you enjoy sex."

She would turn away from him then, tight-lipped and furious or at the brink of dismay that withholds its tears.

Sometimes he let her go, to the activities that held her to her proper course. Perhaps she and his mother then rode their favorite Tobianos across the undulating hills of Derbyshire. Or she prepared him a favorite meal with the assistance of their cook. Or she worked on the portrait she was painting of his parents as the strong-minded couple that he used to believe that Simone and he were emulating.

On other days, he grabbed hold of her arm and drew her back from her hurried departure from the room. Then, because he stood so close to her, she could see—palpable and dis-concerting—his furrowed brow and haunted brown eyes and the full lips which were twisted by the angry words that he spewed through his teeth without ever raising his voice.

He began once more, compelling her to admit the truth that she was concealing from him.

"When he was with you, how many times did he come?"

"You mustn't go on like this, Marc," she would say. "You'll ruin everything that is important between us."

She would break away from him, and he—sickened by his tormenting of her and wary of his emerging self-hatred—would let her go.

On those days when with his sternest self-mastery he willed himself to suppress his doubt of Simone, he would join his parents and her on the brief excursions which had always before called him back to the favorable personhood he had been cultivating through all the years of his life. With them, he canoed on the quiet lake behind his parents' large Georgian house. In the distance, there at the edge of the sun-tinted forest that stood apart from the lake, he saw Chilean willow trees, Scotch elms, and blueberry ash trees bringing flares of excited color to an otherwise tranquil afternoon.

On a favorable Sunday at the end of May, still with her and his parents, he cycled along the picturesque Monsal Trail in the Derbyshire Peak District. With light-hearted camaraderie (or its plausible appearance), he stood at the top of Monsal Head and looked out upon a blue-mist greenery of hills beyond hills, cloud-laden implications of mountains, and the sun-spotted expanse of corridors of space wheeling freely around and below and above him.

On other days when he had harnessed his energies to equally permissible scenarios, he—with her and his parents—

would hike briskly through the various trails that drew them away from their comfortable home into the painterly villages and towns that served them as affable neighbors. One extraordinary time, they climbed the Derwent Edge, which is a Millstone grit escarpment that lies above the Upper Derwent Valley within the Peak District National Park. The guide accompanying them explained that glaciers in the last ice age had scraped away most of the grit-stone which had originally covered the Peak District. Raw nature, as predominant here as it was arbitrary, had—through centuries of wind, rain, and frost—formed oddly-shaped crags or tors. The one which Marc noticed was called The Coach and Horses, because the grit-stone that formed it resembled a coach and horses on the horizon. Though he recognized the shape, he was less impressed by the surprise of the imagery than by the stone's having endured a long wilderness of centuries.

The imagery put him in mind of his own resilience, as willful and time-trapped as that was. In a world of uncertainty and violence, his capacity to withstand brute adversaries and wrenching betrayals was, he felt, his most essential weapon. The stark message he took from the stones eased his senses more profoundly than even the rare and colorful beauty of the earth that surrounded him.

He could not, of course, ignore that beauty. Across

much of the moorland around Derwent Edge, there lived—vivid and charismatic—the Eurasian golden plover and the red grouse, as well as the kinetic individuality of the ring ouzel and the mountain hare. Species of plants as various as they were rare included common cotton grass, mountain strawberry, and crow-berry. In former days, when his happiness was authentic, his sighting these remarkable specimens would have quickened his scientific curiosity and his satisfaction. But in this period, when his doubts about Simone's relations with Gerhard were slowly burning away his soul, he could summon merely a modulated enjoyment that was anchored nonetheless to a disguise of his unease while in the company of his parents.

When—after each day's excursion—they returned to the house in Derbyshire, he would on some late afternoons linger, solitary and brooding, in his mother's garden. There, with his scientist's unsentimental perceptions, he observed the lavender-blueness of South African plumbago and the dark burgundy and bright green leaves of the Fijian fire plant. But not even their natural splendor could rouse his botanical aptitudes. Nor could the tupelo's canopy of sweeping branches and its graceful flares of orange and red hues content his musing mind that in no new way at all had resolved his festering distrust of Simone.

Only his being called to a new bombing sortie kept him from confronting her once again with brute accusations and rapid-fire questions. Piloting a Hawker Tempest fighter while flying alongside the Royal Air Force with the hunter squadron Alsace, he brought his brooding hatred to strafing raids over strategic bases, factories, bridges, and rail lines in Germany. On this mission, he bombed Berlin, Munich, Stuttgart, and Mannheim. As he eluded the firepower of the enemy and invoked his own conflagration upon them and upon their cities, his cool-headed poise and wily calculations renovated his spirit. His possessing the moment, vigorously and unconditionally, gave him back the formidable self he knew and respected.

For a week or so after that, he kept at bay his distrust of his wife. If he found her strangely pensive or withdrawn too deeply inside the subtleties of her melancholy, he told himself that she was worried about her father. That estimable gentleman, sensing that the Nazis were about to force him to join them in Berlin, had left Sweden. He was now busy at Bletchley Park, about forty miles from London, working with other scientists—most of them British—to build an atomic bomb. He was, she knew, being treated supremely well. He had, in fact, been asked to tea on several occasions at the home of Winston Churchill and his wife. Recently, the King and Queen had invited him to a dinner which honored His Majesty's officers, physicians and nurses, and scientists who were bringing their invaluable skills to the war effort. As a guest of the prominent mathematician Gordon Welchman and his family, Knut Bergman had adapted to his Bletchley residence with the easy-going precision that had always been his most defining characteristic. But Simone was nevertheless concerned that her father might become overworked or heedless about his sometimes-frail health.

The few times when she mentioned her father to him, he told her not to worry. Her father would do all the things that needed to be done, and he would enjoy what he was doing.

On other occasions, he attributed the muted intricacies of her melancholy to the worry that he or Henri might be killed during one of their bombing missions. Or he convinced himself that she missed her work with the French Underground Resistance. Now that the Nazis would probably discover her father's and her involvement with the Allies, the leaders of the Resistance advised her to stay out of France and Sweden.

But one evening, when he was dressing for an elaborate dinner which his parents were hosting for their London friends, he came upon a diamond ring in a drawer where he expected to find his handkerchiefs. Simone must have placed it hurriedly beneath the handkerchiefs, believing that she was concealing it inside the drawer that held her own handkerchiefs. He imagined that his unexpected entrance into their bedroom earlier that day may have compelled her to hide the ring as quickly as she could. Made tense and perhaps apprehensive by his sudden appearance, she had not taken time to verify that the drawer she chose was the correct one. While he was away on business in London, she must have enjoyed the embrace of the ring about her finger. She'd had the whole morning to savor the impress of its reality upon her skin.

The thought maddened him.

A few minutes later, she entered the room adjusting her diamond earrings and reviewing in the long mirror at the side of a Louis XVI armoire the glamorous image she inhabited while wearing a black chiffon evening dress. This night she appeared to be once more the epitome of self-possession. The modulated serenities of their most recent days had disarmed her. She believed that she had won back his trust.

Tight-lipped and bitter, he glared at her. The grimace that overtook his handsome demeanor stopped her in her tracks. The harshness of his glance reinforced her startled awareness that something was wrong.

Then, opening the palm of his right hand, he showed her the ring that she had concealed from him.

If he had expected her to turn pale and tremulous, he would have been disappointed. In this tense moment, she revealed no fear of him. Instead, a blush vitalized her already vivid beauty, and an enigmatic smile poised itself upon her lips.

An objective observer might have seen in that smile a worldly resignation or a hint of philosophy. What he saw convinced him that she was going to admit the truth of the ring and her willful possession of it. There would be within her responses neither petition nor tears.

He was too personally involved to see anything except her guilt and her defiance. With a gesture as stinging as his whiplash rebuke, he stepped in front of her and placed the ring in her hand.

"Is this what Gerhard paid you after he fucked you?"

Simone disregarded his words. They were (she knew) the weapons which, for the moment, he was using to hurt her.

"So you found it," she said, crisp and assured as she covered the ring within the palm of her hand. "I suppose my keeping it was a mistake. But I plan to sell it and donate the money to the Red Cross."

Very carefully, she returned the ring to her jewelry box and, with graceful and nearly balletic movements, placed the box inside a private drawer in her dresser.

By maintaining her calm, she hoped once again to draw him away from suspicion and jealousy. But he would not let go of the doubts that were plaguing him.

"You haven't answered my question," he said, as he followed her to the dresser. He might have been a hovering nemesis or an implacable Spirit planning to punish her. "You haven't told me why he gave you that ring."

She had kept her back to him, even after she had returned the ring to its proper drawer. Whether her reluctance to expose her guilt had compelled her to hide her face from him, he did not know. There was, he sensed, a new hardness in her parrying his remarks. That, along with the clear-headed decorum she quietly imparted as if it were the armature protecting her, roused his anger to a new level. Now he grabbed her roughly and brought her face to face with him.

"Tell me the whole thing," he demanded. "Tell me first why you accepted that ring from him."

Still Simone remained calm. Still she allowed herself the hint of a smile, so that she might persuade him that the ring had no real importance to her. Both her calm and her smile came, he felt, from the hardened place inside her heart.

"Of course, I accepted the ring," she said without hesitation. "Gerhard and I had become engaged. How else do you think I could have carried out your plan? What other way was available to me for saving Jean-Claude?"

His anger coiling itself nonetheless about his regard of her, he would not accept her words. To his ears, the words sounded carefully rehearsed and clever.

"He gave you that ring because you let him fuck you,"

he said. His deep voice stayed low and insistent, as he snarled his words out to her. Yet, even though their brooding timbres held themselves at the rim of understatement, his words sounded threatening. "Tell me that and I'll believe you."

He saw that she was weary of him. He sensed that his doubts and his accusations had made him mean-spirited and tiresome. He knew his wife well enough to understand that she wanted him to be the man he had always—until this ambiguous episode with Gerhard—been for her. His realism had been his ballast against confusion. A shrewd detachment and a cosmopolitan sensibility had quickened his perception. Because of them, he had avoided emotional displays as well as inaccurate readings of the reality unfolding around him. She wanted that Marc Roussillon. This stranger standing here before her, with his festering anger and his anguished doubts, was some other Marc—an inauthentic variant, an abrasive and arbitrary man.

At last, after all these uneasy weeks, he had taxed her patience. Her furrowed brow and her brusque inflections told him so.

"Do we really have to go through this scene again?" she asked him. "Are you that uncertain how things are between you and me?"

"I'm very certain how things are between us," he said.

"I'm very certain that you don't love me—at least not in the same way. You love Gerhard."

"If you really believe that," she answered him, "then there is nothing more to say. You don't want the truth. You want to be right, even if your thinking falls so wide of the mark."

"Tell me what went on between you and Gerhard. Tell me that he slept with you. Tell me! Tell me!"

Now, as he kept shouting his words to her, he grabbed her by the shoulders and shook her so hard that the clasp of her necklace broke open, the gleaming cluster of diamonds falling across the Aubusson carpet. She tried, without avail, to pull away from him.

"Don't do this," she screamed. "Don't do this to us."

She was fighting his hold of her now. She began to punch his chest and to scratch his face with the long fingernails which she had just polished, so that they would enhance her glamorous appearance at the dinner party.

He grew even more furious because she had refused to tell him what he wanted to hear and because there had been unleashed in her defense of herself not only a rebellious spirit, but also a new contempt for him. So he began to slap her— again and again. He hit her so hard, that she might have fallen across the floor or onto the bed. But he held her tautly in front of himself, pinioning her as if she were his captive.

"Tell me the truth," he kept demanding, until his shouts had become a raspy whisper and his anger had spent itself upon his harsh slapping of her face and her upper body.

Only when he noticed that she was bleeding did he draw away from her. Only then did he lean against the bedpost, his rugged shoulders slumping as if in defeat and his entire body, with its muscular textures and well-honed powers, relaxed and untypically diminished.

By then, Mrs. Dowling, the good-hearted housekeeper, was knocking—fearful and importuning—on their locked door. She had heard the shouting and, perhaps, even the slaps that were like punches. She and her husband, a tall and lean cavalry officer from the First World War who, here in this sequestered place, was both a wise manager and the primary groundskeeper, had served the Roussillons for two decades and more. It was they who oversaw a staff of six well-trained persons. The Dowlings' meticulous capacities continued to bring to the Derbyshire estate excellent care and a renovative, aesthetic ambiance.

Mrs. Dowling, gray-haired and motherly, called out to him and Simone, even as she went on knocking on the door.

"Is everything all right?" she inquired. "Is there any way that I can help?"

His head bowed and his body still slumping within the masculine confines of his self-hatred, he said nothing.

Still Mrs. Dowling knocked—this time more rapidly. The silence was a fuse to her apprehension.

"It's all right, Mrs. Dowling," Simone now assured her. She nearly succeeded in making her voice sound natural. A smoky tremor brought a new gravity to her inflections. "Everything's all right."

After a moment, they heard Mrs. Dowling going away.

Now he left his place at the bedpost. Still in her eyes a tall and impressive physicality, he stood by the French doors that he had quietly opened. The early summer evening breathed its own cool vitality upon him, perhaps recognizing him as a kindred Spirit. The brisk air quickened his pulse and quickened too the life of the room, touching everything in it with crisp breezes and the fragrance of blooming flowers. The glow of the moon hurried in, as well, lingering about him as if it meant to watch him.

The bracing air revived him, though it could not appease the shame he felt at having struck his wife. He had lost control, a sign of weakness he would have disdained and even loathed in any man. He had failed himself and failed her. But he was going to tough it out. He would put this hour behind him and go forward.

When he turned to face Simone once more, he saw her seated before her mirror. She was not weeping, nor had she withdrawn to the bitter privacies of regret or guilt or sorrow. That, he knew, was not her way. She also was going to pass through this hour, tough-minded and pragmatic. Already, she had willed herself to make repairs to her appearance. Her face was bruised, and her hair and her dress were disarranged. To lift her arm so that she might readjust her earrings cost her some pain. He wondered whether, as she fought against his hold of her, she had sprained it or even fractured a bone. But she did not wince in anguish or pause with uncertainty during this careful refashioning of herself. Though a discreet application of cosmetics would conceal most of the bruises his rough hand had wrought upon her face, even the most proficient make-up could not hide the swelling beneath her left eye and cheek and the lacerations upon her neck.

If his parents' dinner guests asked about her injuries, she would—he imagined—tell them that she had been thrown while riding a Tobiano that was new to her.

Observing her in this moment, he was aware how—with her steadfast realism and her refusal to pity herself—she had smoothly summoned her poise and whatever equally essential capacities she needed in order to meet the evening before her. He admired her spirit. He loved her beauty, her courage, her razor-sharp intellect. He wanted her all for himself. He could not live easily in a world that harbored any other man who might be her lover.

But he did not want to lose her. His wily instincts warned him that, in this complicated matter of Gerhard, he must not on this evening commit himself to reprisal or to any other action. If he did, he would lose the only woman he could ever love.

With these thoughts in mind, he crossed the room to the dressing table and mirror before which she was seated and was artfully restoring her beauty.

"I'm sorry," he said, not without genuine compunction or the profound affection that made his words authentic. "These last weeks, I've been a beast. I couldn't stop myself, though I wanted to."

She turned to him and, at first, said nothing. He was glad that she could see how wretched he felt and how difficult it was for him to let go of his doubts. That he was making so strong an effort impressed her. It was now, he guessed, that she realized that the only way they could save their marriage was to face the truth together. So she willed herself to say all the words that needed to be said.

"I did it to save Jean-Claude," she said.

Her remark, clearly enunciated within the ambiguous

layers of her quietude, was an explanation more than a plea.

The words caught him by surprise. For a moment, he hesitated before their ellipsis and their indeterminacy.

"You slept with Gerhard," he said, calling forth the words she had not spoken.

"Yes," she answered him, all the while observing how carefully he was disguising his sorrow and his bitter heart. She also saw that he was effectively invoking once again the militant self-discipline that had always been an essential part of his character. His temperate response encouraged her to say more.

"I did it so that the Germans would free Jean-Claude and he would go on living."

He stood within the mysteries of new silence now. If her words disconcerted him, he allowed neither a frown nor a tight-lipped grimness to influence his regard of her. Nor did he care to choose any words that might draw him away from the quieter path he had just entered.

Instead, Simone used the moment to remind him how things were with them.

"If we are to go on together—and I want to go on with you—you will just have to make the best of things. I did what you asked. I saved Jean-Claude, and I am not sorry for it. I would do it again if I had to."

Still he stood near her, his rugged manliness having risen over her, as she sat by the mirror recomposing the imagery that the Roussillon guests were to receive as an accurate reflection of her personhood. Still he held himself in silence. He was not brooding and, in fact, allowed a thin smile to cross his lips. He meant to reassure her that no new words she told him would anger him or throw him off his proper course.

Simone probed further.

"Would you have wanted Jean Claude to die?"

Before her question, he hesitated. He used that moment to weigh her words carefully and to calculate the value of Jean Claude's life. He also guessed at the weeks and months and years it would take to forget that she had slept with Gerhard.

But even that uneasy moment passed. Then he answered her question—straightforward and matter-of-fact.

"No," he said. "You did what you had to."

On this evening, they had, he felt, survived a crisis. Now he began to believe that they were going to be all right together, after all.

For a time, all was well with them.

In this period, he and Henri flew many combat missions and, miles away from London and from Derbyshire, shared a barracks life with the officers in their squadron. Away from Simone and in the company of his friends as well as his father, he rallied. Although he had not adequately resolved his anger and doubt, he was able to displace them. The dangerous intensities of his missions and the necessity of maintaining a lethal precision in combat compelled him to focus on the actions that would punish the enemy and preserve his life as well as the lives of the men in his squadron. Self-aware and ascetic, he immersed himself completely in the performance of his military duties. Never did he allow himself even a scanning thought of Gerhard and Simone together. Nor did he tell Henri of the unease and anger and sorrow that he kept, like himself, a prisoner of his heart. To save his friend, he had—he felt—compelled his wife to sacrifice the purity that she had always offered him. No, he did not speak of his sorrow to his father. Nor did he remind himself of its origin or of its permanent place in his history.

Only when—on a rare weekend leave from combat duty—he was alone with his wife, did his suppressed anger come back to disarrange his careful efforts to be forgiving and conciliatory. Yet, even within the hidden recesses of his festering rage, there glimmered—stark and incriminating—his grudging awareness that it was himself he could not forgive. He had sent Simone on a dangerous mission, persuading her to use every strategy to save his friend. She had slept with the enemy so that Jean-Claude, who was an essential person in their lives (though more essential to his life than to her own), would go on living. She had saved Jean-Claude. She had accomplished the mission on which he had sent her.

On any one of those days that Simone spent with Gerhard, he might have discovered that she was working for the Allies and that she was married. During every hour that they were together, there hovered about her this risk of being exposed and of being tortured and murdered. Never, before the tremendous odds that confronted her, did she hesitate to carry forward the plan to rescue Jean-Claude. She had been steadfast. She had been courageous. She had been true. All these things made her authentic. The thought of them, recurring only fitfully, constrained his anger even as he told himself that his distrust of her was spawned from schoolboy jealousy and from his goading suspicion that she had enjoyed sleeping with Gerhard.

During the weekend through which they had just passed, he sensed nonetheless that, beneath their cool-headed exchanges and their well-measured reciprocal courtesies, he and Simone still carried between them a muted enmity. Even when he was swimming with her in the heated pool within the west wing or sailing with her on the sun-touched waters of a July sea, or when—at one of the extraordinary parties that his parents hosted—he was dancing with her on the south terrace while piano and violin and trumpet played riffs upon the melodies of

Cole Porter and Irving Berlin, or when he joined her and two friends in a game of tennis, they withheld themselves from each other. They held back, that is, the intimate gestures and responses that had always before—in happier times—appeared as natural as they were extemporaneous. Now, to his eyes at least, his relationship with his wife seemed contrived and even rehearsed. Nor did Simone's reactions to him anchor themselves to the casual and the authentic.

He saw in her what others could not see, because they did not know how to read the enigmatic language of her face, her voice, and her gestures. They saw and heard only surface expressions. They missed the hidden layers of her existence. They did not perceive, as he did, the raw tension that bound her tightly to its ordinances, as if her unease were born out of anguish or despair or guilt.

Her secret unhappiness, he was convinced, yoked itself to her guilt. Not only had she slept with a Nazi. She had also fallen in love with him. It was her willingness to love Gerhard that, in retrospect at least, disgusted her. Guilt kept feeding her sorrow. Of that, the pensive stillness that sometimes hovered about her and the determined smile that resisted the outward show of melancholy assured him.

Now he decided to use Simone's feelings of guilt to draw her into another dangerous plan. He must persuade her to work with him to destroy Gerhard. Only in that way could she be clean again. In that way only could he absolve himself from having unwittingly sent her into the bed of a Nazi.

Chapter Four

Simone's Guilt

A conversation between Simone and Marianne became an essential influence upon the way that Marc's scenario of vengeance against Gerhard played itself out.

In spite of the pledge that she had made to herself to keep silent about so personal a matter, Simone found herself telling Marianne almost everything about her tryst with Gerhard.

She confided in her mother-in-law on a cool Sunday in July, right after Henri and Marc—at the end of one of their rare three-day leaves—had returned to their air force base and to the combat missions that awaited them. Within a late hour of that afternoon, the large Derbyshire house seemed lonely all over again without them and without the fourteen guests from London that Marianne had invited to stay with them for that week- end. Those guests, as well as ten others who lived in the area, had returned to their own Derbyshire homes or to their obligations in London.

Within the festival atmosphere that Marianne and she composed, the guests enjoyed horse riding and hiking and sailing. They enjoyed as well a chamber concert within the Roussillons' splendid music room. Actors from the National Theater played scenes from Shakespeare's *Twelfth Night* and Bernard Shaw's *Candida.* In addition, Henri and Marianne surprised all the guests with their first public performance in nearly two years. They were, Simone admitted as she took wary notice of them, an impressive couple. Time had been kind to Marianne, negotiating with charming subtlety this mature rendition of herself. Her dark hair, brown eyes, and alabaster skin made her even now an extraordinary beauty. Henri was a tall man whose gaunt appearance only partially diminished his well-trained ruggedness. Marianne stood next to him, ready to ease this moment before they entered the solitary realm of their separate performances. Through the grace of her gestures and her lovely assurance, she appeared to be his ideal partner. The formidable look of him—his dark hair with its modulated flecks of gray, his broad forehead and aquiline nose, and the chiseled bones of his well-worn handsomeness— enhanced rather than eclipsed her presence. Her being so precisely there next to him seemed a natural thing. She completed him, because she was his equal.

Extraordinary violinist that he was, Henri enthralled his audience with the pure melody and the poignant longing of Rachmaninoff's *Vocalise*. Marianne's piano conveyed with an equal conviction the emotional and spiritual distance of Schubert's *Piano Sonata in B-flat*. As a capstone to an occasion that contrived to be celebratory and carefree (the better to withstand the time's dangers and sorrows), there was a banquet within the expansive greenery of the south lawn. In these war years, some of the food that the Roussillons served their guests was grown on their own property, and their wine had been stored in their cellars years earlier. If, Simone told herself, the splendor of this party did not glow quite as luminously as it had during the parties they gave before the war, the Roussillons succeeded nevertheless in subverting the gloom of war time. Actors and musicians, a Spanish poet and an American playwright, a French diplomat and a British foreign minister, and a Swedish scientist (her father) accepted the stylized construct that kept at bay—for a weekend at least—their awareness of the tumult raging through cities and towns, on sea and on land and in the suddenly palpable corridors of the sky.

Marianne and Henri and she and Marc mingled as if light-hearted and buoyant not only with their friends of long standing, but also with the talented musicians and actors who enhanced the glamour of the occasion. All went well. Only in the early hours of that Sunday did the news from the radio that the Nazis had bombed some of the most populous districts within or near London dispel the general merriment. But she helped Marianne and Henri host their banquet nonetheless, and the guests did their part to make the closing hours of their weekend both gregarious and memorable.

When the hour arrived in which Marc prepared to return to his air force base in Lincolnshire, which was about a hundred miles away, she had forgiven him his beating of her two weeks earlier. It was not difficult to forgive him. She felt that she deserved the beating. In fact and perversely so, the beating appeased the guilt which continued to haunt her. Never before had Marc struck her. She could not imagine his assaulting her in the future. His moment of violence against her had cost him harsh penalties, including an aftermath of shame and a loss of self-respect. Besides, he loved her too much to risk hurting her again in any way or to forfeit the love that she still felt for him.

"This weekend gave you back to me," he told her just before he pressed his lips upon hers in a parting kiss.

He was standing with her in their bedroom, where she had helped him pack his luggage. The intimacy of being there with him in these hurried moments pleased her. She was aware that they also pleased him and moved him to speak other soft words to her.

"I saw the colored lights again—the ones that only you and I can see when we are together."

"I saw them, too," she said while placating his need to believe that everything between them was as it had always been.

The words were true, yet they carried her ambivalence. Her three days and nights with Marc had brought her joy. But the emotional colors of that joy were, for her at least, muted and blemished. The Marc of this weekend was the Marc that she had always known. He was a generous and caring lover. He was a quick-witted and good-natured partner. The intensities of his love still thrilled her, though not as before. Marc was in love with a woman who did not exist. He loved the ideal that she no longer accurately personified. In spite of her ambivalence, though, she accepted the weekend as a harbinger of future happiness between them. The camaraderie and the sex that they had shared quickened her confidence. It strengthened her determination to make things work for Marc and her. She had already begun teaching herself to maintain her love of him, even while Gerhard became more and more essential to the secret part of her life.

If the weekend gave her back to Marc, it also gave her back to herself, though only intermittently. She was learning how to live with her guilt. But she still had much to learn about dispelling or eluding temporarily the unhappiness that kept coming back to haunt her.

Now, late on this Sunday afternoon after the weekend guests made their way to their own homes or—like Henri and Marc—to their war-time obligations, Marianne came in search of Simone, though not before instructing her staff to begin the complicated process of dismantling the ornamental props of the banquet and of bringing the south lawn back to its more traditional order. From time to time during this festive-seeming weekend, she sensed what her guests may not have noticed. Simone was very unhappy. She knew her well enough to perceive the sorrow that was tightly binding her within its mysteries. Marianne was also aware that her rescuing Jean-Claude created problems for her relationship with Marc. She and Henri—from their suite of rooms nearby—overheard their son's quarrel with her a few weeks earlier. But, because Mrs. Dowling assured them that all was well with Marc and her and because they did not care to interfere in the problems of their son's marriage, she refrained from asking intrusive questions.

When, several weeks ago, she first sensed that there was a rift between them, she wondered whether Marc had been unfaithful and whether, for this reason, she was keeping him at bay. Years ago, in her own marriage (she told Simone months earlier), she had kept Henri at bay, once she grew weary of his many infidelities. Even now, the memory of that time yielded only dark images. But after she overheard the intense quarrel between Marc and Simone—heard, that is, Marc's accusatory voice riding upon a spate of abrasive words of which she had deciphered mere fragments—she began to imagine that Simone, not Marc, had been unfaithful.

All during this weekend, which wore holiday colors and stylized exuberance, Marianne saw that beneath her daughter-in-law's glamorous appearance, there lived—as if it were a variant imagery or a will-o'-the-wisp that disclosed its nature only in temporary flashes—a sorrow that melded itself to both guilt and remorse.

It was this same imagery which she noticed upon finding Simone standing pensive and solitary at the blue-rimmed well in her rose garden. All about her were the harmonies of floribunda and hybrid teas, delicate rosemary and damask and blue-moon surfaces. Cloistered there, within the shadows of late afternoon, Simone appeared tentative and melancholic, silently debating perhaps whether she would pause there a while or return quickly and unobtrusively to her room. Not even the orange, yellow, and white splendor of rhododendrons and the red, lavender, and cream petals of camellias could dissuade her from her sorrow. Nor, Marianne imagined, could the golden-yellow leaves and glossy, rounded red fruits of the pomegranate tree ease her daughter-in-law's troubled awareness that the confident woman she had once been had now become—to herself most of all—an uncertain stranger.

"You'll catch a chill if you stay out here too long," Marianne told her, intending to make her sudden appearance there in the garden seem both pertinent and natural.

In search of her daughter-in-law, she had—while passing through the southwest wing of her home—discovered her standing alone in the garden, enveloped by the blue- gray mist of the oncoming night. She could see, even from the dusk-laden distance that separated them, that Simone was lost inside sullenness and recrimination. Rather than intrude upon her too abruptly, she devised a pretext for joining her in the garden. With the smooth poise that gave to her carriage a grace both straight-back and feminine, she hurried to Simone's room and afterward to her own room to fetch the clothing that would keep them warm while they conversed in the breeze-touched, secluded garden.

When her mother-in-law entered the garden, wearing a white ermine jacket over her cobalt-blue gown and carrying to her a black cashmere coat, Simone was surprised but not displeased to find her there. She allowed herself a grateful smile as Marianne helped her into the warmth of the coat. Then they took their places on a comfortable bench not far from delicate topiaries of a doe and her fawn. For a few minutes, they sat together without uttering a word. To a casual observer, they might have appeared as two stylish women who had come to the garden to breathe the crisp air and to savor the variety of colors that, in their scanning glance, wore the fleet emphases of a montage or the imagery within a kaleidoscope. Before their contemplative eyes, the oncoming night was changing the colors of flowers and ferns and of trees and shrubs, disguising in subtle ways the reality of their forms. A soft wind with tactile energies animated these forms even as the fading light kept translating them into eerie and watchful presences.

Or so Simone allowed herself to muse, for that moment regarding the imagery around her as an ambiguous play upon her senses. Only after that did she turn to observe her mother-in-law as she sat beside her, taut within an interior stillness that held her to its steadfast ordinances. Sorrow worked as a shadow upon her mature yet ethereal beauty, redefining the intricacies of her poise and of her pensive manner. Usually austere in her responses, Marianne was (she could see) moved by the nearly imperceptible hint of anguish that she was struggling to keep at bay. Her mother-in-law's unease at witnessing that struggle pushed her forward now while she dispelled the silence that had held them inside its powers.

"I've been noticing how unhappy you are," she said. "Perhaps you would like to tell me why. Sometimes it's good to bring these secret things into the open."

Before her gentle manner and her equally gentle words, Simone at first remained silent. Very carefully, she was studying her mother-in-law and, at the same time, weighing the consequences of telling her about Gerhard. She trusted Marianne, aware as she was that in all of their exchanges her mother-in-law had expressed a well-considered discretion and a quick-witted realism.

So she told her nearly everything that she felt needed to be said about her involvement in Marc's plan to rescue Jean-Claude. Only when she described her sexual relationship with Gerhard did she pause in her telling. Although Marianne and Henri were aware of her importance to the rescue plan, neither she nor Marc had told them that, to save Jean-Claude, she had slept with Gerhard.

Marianne nudged her forward.

"Go ahead," she said. "Tell me all of it. I'm not brittle. The truth won't break me apart. Nor should you allow it to break you."

In any other crucial moment, Simone was to say later, she would have drawn strength from her mother-in-law's tough-minded detachment. She, too, had expressed the same tough-mindedness through every test or battle into which the war had drawn her. But now her complicated feelings for Gerhard confused her. To her mind, they were more formidable than any danger or violence that the war had shown her or that she had perpetrated. She could not persuade herself that even so cosmopolitan a woman as Marianne could forgive her for having fallen in love with a Nazi.

She began by assuring her mother-in-law of what she had not lost.

"I still love Marc," she said, "in spite of what he and the war compelled me to do."

With cool poise, Marianne waited. Simone sensed that her mother-in-law saw in her remark both a petition for her understanding and a preface to the more problematic aspect of what she needed to tell her.

She proceeded cautiously.

"But, to save Jean-Claude, I had to sleep with Gerhard," she said. "And I loathe myself because of it."

In the face of her wretched news, Marianne remained impassive. Her composure startled Simone.

"You are not the first woman in this ghastly war who has had to sleep with an enemy to save something or someone important," she said. "It's not so surprising that the war has used you in that way."

Simone wanted to tell this hardened woman more. She wanted to tell her all of the truth. She needed to admit to someone other than herself that she had enjoyed sleeping with Gerhard. She needed to say clearly and without hesitation that she was in love with him. But an ingrained contempt for herself overrode her need. So she said nothing. As if she were hovering at the rim of a precipice, she stood very still while Marianne hurried forward with new, trenchant remarks.

"You mustn't punish yourself," she said. "You did the thing that needed to be done. There's nothing wrong with that."

With casual-seeming ease, Marianne took from the pocket of her ermine jacket a gold monogrammed case and offered her a French cigarette. Simone readily accepted it, pleased to focus her attention upon the case and the slender imagery of tobacco and the stylish manner in which her mother-in-law brought her own cigarette to her pursed lips. She focused as well upon the gold lighter that Marianne used to ignite their cigarettes. She noticed, too, how this formidable woman held her in a steady and probing gaze.

"Be thankful that you have not fallen in love with Gerhard," she said. "There have, after all, been more than a few Allied women who have fallen in love with Nazis because they make good bed partners."

Confronted by these incisive words, Simone stood very still. She wondered whether her mother-in-law had rightly perceived her sullen constraint as the armature of a mind and soul guilt-ridden and perverse. Allowing herself the hint of a grimace, she now chose the creditable words that might appease Marianne's roused ambivalence.

"Gerhard has killed so many of our Allies," she pushed herself to say. "There isn't a reason in the world why anyone should love him."

Marianne kept watching her, enigmatic yet searching.

"Gerhard is a Nazi and that, of course, makes him monstrous," she said. "But he also has a human side. In Lausanne and, before that, in your father's home, you saw his human side. You could easily have fallen under his spell."

Though she could not say the words that would accurately define her relationship with Gerhard, Simone would not—within the seclusion of this late afternoon—permit herself to lie. Instead, she met her mother-in-law's remarks with her own enigmatic temperament.

"Yes," she agreed. "I might easily have fallen under his

spell."

Marianne probed further.

"That sort of thing has happened more times than you might imagine," she said, her inflections both studied and cautionary. "And the women involved in the mess have often ended badly. Some of them have killed themselves, and more than a few have been killed by the people they betrayed."

While she was speaking, Marianne continued to observe closely the influence of her words upon her responses. Never before had her mother-in-law perceived this uncertainty in her. She imagined that Marianne saw it as a fault-line in the emotional armor that her conflicted experiences had taught her to wear. Older and even more cynical, her mother-in-law understood that whatever had happened with Gerhard and her had subverted her certainty and, possibly, her realistic priorities.

As if with idiosyncratic nuances she were answering her mother-in-law's oblique inquiry, Simone casually inhaled the perfume fragrance of her cigarette. Just as casually, because she wanted to imply that she had been listening to a problem that did not concern her personally, she offered her own appraisal of the women who had fallen in love with the enemy during a time of war.

"There must have been at least a few women who did

not regret that they had given everything for love."

Marianne pondered the thought, calculating its implication for all that she herself had been asserting.

"I wonder," she said. "It must be a terrible thing to know that you have betrayed your country and all the good people who are fighting for freedom. And for what? To satisfy your carnal appetites."

Simone noticed the contemptuous edge in Marianne's voice and the searching glance that was taking her proper measure. She was also aware of Marianne's ambiguous language that with its use of the second-person pronoun might be including her in the group of traitorous women. Before the possibility of that intention, she did not flinch. Instead, she hurried forward to say what she felt needed to be said.

"Those women were human. They were in love. They were lost. Besides, real love knows no politics."

"You're too soft on them," Marianne said. "But I'm glad that you are hard on yourself. You understand the things that we can forgive in war and the things that we can never forgive. The only way a woman can exonerate herself from the crime of falling in love with the enemy is to fight more fiercely. She must work to be the instrument for killing as many of the enemy as she can. Only in that way can she belong to her country again."

Simone was not surprised at the intensity of her mother-in-law's hatred of the Nazis. Not only had they overtaken France; they had also sent many of her friends and some of her relatives to the gas ovens. To express any sympathy for those women who had fallen in love with Nazi soldiers and spies was indefensible.

To dispel her mother-in-law's worried regard of her as well as her own doubts about the episode with Gerhard, she offered to her the words meant to reaffirm her own allegiances.

"All that you've said is true," she told her. "They are the things that my life has taught me to believe."

Suddenly she felt very cold, though the wind was stirring only slightly. She trembled and felt her ghost waiting beside her.

Marianne, noticing her shiver, rose from her seat on the bench.

"We had better go inside," she said, "or we'll catch a chill."

Simone agreed. Rising from her place, she looked once more about her. Darkness was falling around them, concealing trees and shrubs as well as flowers and foliage. Only the pale moon permitted them to see—as discolored fragments or ellipses—the summer splendor of the garden.

As they were moving toward the French doors that would enable them to re-enter the southwest wing of the house, Marianne had more to say. Through words that were as terse as they were direct, she was pointing the way back to the correct path.

"In war, you do not have to worry when you have done the right thing," she said. "It is, however, essential that you do whatever needs to be done, no matter how cruel or distasteful it may seem to you. The important thing is never to feel too deeply. In war, feelings can be traps. Don't let your feelings trap you."

If she had any regrets at having opened her heart to her mother-in-law, Simone gave no evidence. Summoning a well-practiced poise and confident inflections that disguised her unease, she made her reply seem both persuasive and strong-minded.

"You needn't worry about me," she said. "I know the things that need to be done."

If she knew the things that needed to be done, Simone did not act upon that knowledge. The clear-eyed detachment that had always informed her response to a problem had eluded her. Gone, too, were the austere energies that had worked as a fuse to her accurate judgments of herself, as well as of the people around her and of the circumstances that brought them together. Try as she had, she could not dispel her longing for Gerhard or her memory of the happiness they had shared during the week that they spent in Lausanne. Her yearning to be with him had become an obsession. On those days when her realism prevailed, she dismissed her love of Gerhard as a perversity of her will—a self-defeating repudiation of her familiar life with Marc. It was on these days that her feelings disgusted her. She had permitted herself to love a man who was fighting on the wrong side of all the laws that honored freedom and justice.

But there were all the other days when she was haunted by Gerhard's handsome face, by the montage of imagery involving their skiing and swimming and dancing together, and by the remembered ecstasy of their love-making. On these days she convinced herself that the ordinances of war had compelled him to act as a savage. Yet this man who had killed so many of her countrymen and so many more of their brave allies had, under the influence of her love, become once more human. With her, he had recovered his best self. He had treated her as though she were not only extraordinary. In his eyes, she was peerless. With understated pleasure, he had accepted the demure imagery that she had composed to represent herself. He was, she felt, very pleased indeed to find within the subtle traceries of her individuality all the ideal qualities he sought in a woman. She, in her turn, accepted the danger of her loving him.

But she could not accept herself. On most of the days when her obsession for Gerhard haunted her every thought, flashes of truth—called forth, perhaps, by the news that thousands of embattled allies had joined the newly dead or by her memory of the Jewish friends whom the Nazis had sent to concentration camps and to the gas ovens— revealed her to herself. By loving Gerhard, she was betraying not only her husband. She was also betraying the cause for which she had been fighting. She was betraying the souls of all the men and women who had died fighting the Nazis. She was betraying her country and her lost Jewish friends and her fellow allies who continued to fight the enemy. She was betraying herself—all the strong-minded ideals which had driven her aspirations and all the evolving scenarios that had beckoned her into worthy exploits and unforgiving risks.

The hairline fissures of her uncertainty grew longer, and her self-loathing became more insistent. Not even her volunteer service as a nurse at the 28th Station Hospital in Sudbury, Derbyshire, could release her from her guilt. If anything, the sight of the wounded, mutilated, or dying soldiers, airmen, and navy personnel intensified her guilt.

One night, nearly drained by the long hours that she had

been on duty at the hospital, she stayed with a seventeen-year-old Anglo-Irish youth in the last hour that he lived. His name was Liam Evans. Blond-haired and rangy, he had lost one of his blue eyes and his left arm at Dunkirk. But it was the injuries to his skull and to his lungs that were taking his life from him. When she first met him, she thought, upon sighting him from the distance while she hurried into the ward that held twenty-two other beds, that he was Gerhard. He had the same sculptured features and the same light-skinned complexion. Whenever she and the senior nurse removed the dressings from his head, she saw the blond hair that was growing back weeks after his surgery, and she thought about Gerhard. Even Liam's profile and the curve of his lips as he began to smile put her in mind of Gerhard.

For months thereafter, she worked with the surgeons who were trying to save Liam. Always, whenever she was assigned to the ward where he lay dying, she would bring from Marianne's kitchen the homemade ice cream that he craved. On his better days, when he seemed to rally, she read to him magazine articles about his favorite rugby team, and she drew from him many anecdotes about his own recent days of being the captain of his school's rugby team. He also spoke of his days growing up on a farm in the Yorkshire Dales. Sometimes, even when she was not assigned to his ward, she would find an excuse to visit Liam. She noticed that he looked forward to these visits. His spirit revived when she approached his sickbed. Though his head and the place where his left eye had been were bandaged, his flash of brightness when he looked up and saw her brought back some of the handsomeness that the war had stolen from him.

"You are so beautiful," he told her on the day before he died. "I've never before been this close to a really beautiful woman."

"You are very gallant to say so," she said.

Knowing that he was going to die within a matter of hours, she found other words to comfort him.

"And just to show you how pleased I am to be in your company, I should like very much to kiss you and to hold your hand. But only if you want to."

"Oh, I want to, very much."

Leaning forward to meet his lips, which were parched from heavy medication, she felt him press gently against her mouth. His right hand cradled her face, and his eye gleamed with excitement.

"Was it any good?" he asked afterwards. His voice was husky with the pleasure of the kiss.

"It was very good, indeed," she assured him.

In the last minutes before he drifted out of consciousness, Liam's grieving parents and the sympathetic senior nurse allowed her to hold him in her arms. As his final breath left him, he kept her in his gaze. Though he was smiling in his acceptance of things, a tear trickled out of his eye and flowed upon his pale cheek.

For weeks, she carried with her the memory of that hour. Over and over, she told herself that Liam was not Gerhard. Liam Evans gave up his life fighting Nazis who were like Gerhard. The thought haunted her. It never left her, condemning her to uneasy days and sleepless nights.

Conscience-stricken, she worked even harder at the hospital.

With Marianne, she spent whole days and sometimes weekends administering to these brave and suffering men and women who had given their courage and their skills unconditionally in battles fought on land, at sea, and in the air. Whether she was assisting a team of physicians in the hospital surgery ward or washing battle-scarred bodies in convalescent rooms or feeding a patient his lunch, she was awed by the faces of these wounded. Some of them were tight-lipped and determined, others bitter yet willful, and a few carefree and jaunty or seeming so.

Before the stoic detachment which enabled her to confront their losses even as she tried to console and nurse them, her steadfast will sometimes faltered as she observed the ongoing anguish of her patients. One Navy ensign especially disconcerted her. His name was Gareth Wilkinson. He came from the Midlands, and his father had trained him to be a carpenter. But that was all behind him now. The Germans had torpedoed his ship and, though he was one of the survivors, his hands had been blown away and the shrapnel that had pierced his chest was lodged in a place just inches from his heart.

"Look at what they've done to me!" he sometimes yelled out to her, when the pain of his wounds was shooting through him and before the dose of morphine that she had injected into his veins began to lull his senses.

His black hair, slightly upturned nose, and brown pleading eyes gave him a boyish look. His scrawny physique made him appear even more vulnerable. As she was giving him morphine, he recognized her even in the crazed awareness that had become his burden. No sooner did he remember her, than he raised his arms and the bandaged stumps that had once been attached to his hands. Once more he cried out to her, this time more intensely. His words were an appeal as much as they were a lament.

"I want my hands!" he yelled. "Make them give me my

hands back!"

She could not find the words that might ease his sorrow. Were there any such words? Instead, methodical and capable, she propped up the fresh pillows against which he leaned his head and, with a cool compress, washed his fevered brow and cheeks. She checked his pulse and, before the morphine drew him into a merciful sleep, she coaxed him to drink some water. Her heart was filled with pity for him. But she gave him no sign of it, so inadequate did she regard her pity while in the presence of his bleak reality.

Night after night after that, in the darkened privacy of the restlessness that no longer allowed her to sleep, she thought of Gareth Wilkinson and of Liam Evans and of all the other grievously wounded and dying men. Over and over, as if she were at a military tribunal that was determining the cause of their deaths or of their having been maimed, she heard a voice speaking to her conscience.

"The Nazis destroyed these men. Gerhard Hauptmann destroyed some of them, too."

But, in spite of her sullen perception that, by loving Gerhard, she was making a mockery of her patients' sacrifice, she refused to submit to private and tearful recriminations that might leave her feeling insufficient in the face of her patients' steadfastness and their anguish. The war-hardened part of her did not permit her self-reproach to undermine her confidence and her usefulness as a nurse and, should her country call her to new assignments, as a Resistance fighter. She was doing all that she could for the wounded and the dying. That, she felt, might count as some form of expiation.

Still her guilt tormented her. Still her disarranged heart compelled her to love Gerhard.

Chapter Five

The Savage

Whenever he was home on a weekend pass or for a week's furlough, Marc continued to notice that Simone's ambivalence and her uncertainty had not left her. On these occasions, though, he was no longer the prisoner of his anger or of his jealousy. Instead, he activated a strategy as wily as it was subdued to draw her into his plan to destroy Gerhard.

He began by planting in her mind a self-questioning that yielded incriminating answers. They might engage in casual-seeming remarks while they were skeet shooting in a colorful summer field behind his parents' home in Derbyshire. Or they might, after cantering across hills and alongside teeming orchards, dismount from their Tobianos to pause and converse at the foot of the white cliffs that rose higher and higher into the fleece-clouded blue sky. In these moments that were meant to be solacing, he would tell Simone that once again he had been plagued by sleepless nights and by deep-seated guilt.

"I feel contaminated because I sent you into the bed of a

Nazi," he would say. "My pushing you into such a compromising situation was selfish and rash. I'm to blame for the terrible thing that has happened to both of us. We are no longer clean. I bear the guilt of having involved you in a reckless and dangerous mission. You carry the guilt of having slept with a Nazi who has killed many of our allies, including close friends and relatives who have been part of our life experiences."

Simone, made tense once more by the very mention of her episode with Gerhard, would answer him with matter-of-fact inflections.

"We saved Jean-Claude. There is nothing for which we need to blame ourselves."

"Oh, but I do," he would tell her. "I should have followed you to Lausanne. Once the Germans freed Jean-Claude, I should have killed Gerhard, there at the hotel where you were staying."

Brooding, or seeming so, he would walk slowly to the field where their horses were grazing.

"There wasn't any way that you could do that," she would remind him while hurrying to catch up to him. "The Nazis released Jean-Claude only after I spent the week with Gerhard."

She was telling him what he already knew. But, as he

had anticipated, she was imagining that his guilt at having compromised her status as an honorable married woman had revised the sequence of scenes that had actually occurred. As quick-witted as she was, she did not yet perceive the path toward which he was leading her. By saying that he should have killed Gerhard in Lausanne, Marc was revealing the central action of the plot he was devising.

On some nights, he would toss and turn in bed beside her, moaning with furious anguish. Only when his uneasy body had wakened her would he rise from his pillow and, apparently caught in a nightmare, punch the air with his clenched fists as if he were subduing an opponent.

"I'll kill you," he would yell. "I'll kill you."

Simone would call out to him, her voice tremulous in spite of its control.

"Marc," she would say. "It's all right. There's nobody there."

Then he would appear to waken, though he had been awake all along. And always, just at the moment when she might imagine that he was fully conscious now and aware of the familiar room and of her beside him, he would say the words that condemned both of them.

"We're lost," he would tell her. "We're lost and unclean."

His pretended nightmares, invoked by a determination to draw her to his will, became as harrowing as they were frequent.

Invariably, she would turn on the light of the lamp on the table beside their bed and coax him back to an awareness of the safe room where they had been sleeping. He would rise from their bed and pace back and forth, his tall and athletic frame—with hair- trigger aptitudes—held taut and threatening.

"We're lost," he would keep saying as long as he knew that Simone had stayed there in the room with him and had not hurried away to bring him warm milk or the brandy that he preferred. His sorrowing voice, with its husky timbres that she heard as the bewilderment of a man who had always been strong, left her dismayed and anxious.

On other weekends, she remarked about how gaunt Marc looked. A weary pallor had overtaken his ruddy handsomeness, and a leaner frame—even while retaining much of its formidable muscularity—made him appear more vulnerable. His anguish, she told him, was burning away not only his soul, but also the athletic solidity that had always defined him.

During this summer of 1942, he would begin these weekends in a nearly hopeful mood. Having returned from flying a series of combat sorties against German aircraft, he created the appearance of having reclaimed some of his former jauntiness and his ease with himself as well as with others. To her when they were alone, he would mention how tremendous it felt while being at the controls of a Spitfire or a Hawker Tempest fighter. During this period, as in recent months, he and his crew, flying with the hunter squadron Alsace alongside the RAF squadron of pilots with whom they had trained, were involved in dogfights and fighter sweeps over Berlin, Mannheim, and Stuttgart. Just as often they flew strafing and dive-bombing attacks on V-1 launch sites on the French Coast.

No matter, Marc said, that during each mission he lived on the cusp of death. His bombing Nazi pilots and their cities now loomed as the primary reason for his existence. It was a way of exonerating himself from the crime of sending his wife to a Nazi officer's bed.

"There was no crime in what we did," she would assure him. "In war, one does what one must do."

"You're right, I suppose," he would concede. He was careful, nevertheless, to wear a slight frown. He wanted Simone to imagine that he was struggling toward a new perception about all that had happened with Gerhard.

Then he would go forward with her to the weekend parties and the gregarious activities that included hiking, canoeing, and horse riding.

By the close of each weekend that he had returned home on a military pass, though, he would—before her inquiring eyes—have fallen into more brooding and recrimination. By the time he gave her a good-bye kiss, its passionate intimacy still a bond between them, he was struggling visibly with brooding thoughts of the episode involving her and Gerhard. He would leave her with brooding thoughts of her own and an emerging anxiety that he might be right. Perhaps, by rescuing Jean-Claude, they had lost their honor or, at least, their belief in themselves as clear-sighted individuals who refused to be morally compromised.

On those days when she heard news that the war was not going well for France or for England or for any of their allies, she suffered most of all. He imagined what she was going through. That she still loved Gerhard and spent much of her free time remembering his keen insights and his courtly manner, as well as his vigorous love-making, brought her both elation and shame. She would (he guessed) also remember, with the admiration she always conferred upon extraordinary achievers, the visionary remarks he had made about the aircraft he was planning to build. Yet he sensed that she was finding it more difficult to defend her love of him to the anguished self that she concealed. The news of the war made her association with Gerhard seem the crime that, at the height of one of their bitter arguments, he had called it.

During the next months, he noticed a change in her. She, too, wore a weary pallor—an appearance he at first attributed to the long hours she spent as a nurse at the 28th Station Hospital. Now, whenever he reminded her of the burden they carried because of her involvement with a Nazi, she grew very uneasy. It pleased him to believe that her guilt was overtaking her secret passion for Gerhard.

On one of these weekends, he altered the role he had been playing for her. Now he became more assertive in setting forth his plot to win back their honor. Even when they were out riding their favorite Criollos, he spoke the words that insisted they must activate the plan that would release them from the burden of guilt which they carried.

On this crisp September afternoon, after they dismounted from their horses not far from a meadow behind his parents' home, he stood with her by the cedar fence that enclosed a paddock where their horses began grazing in movements as supple as they were contented. Seven other horses were there (Criollos, Tobianos, and Kentucky Saddlebreds), either grazing or walking or cantering. The fleecy clouds that appeared to wait, languorous and perfunctory, in a soft blue sky; the ornamental grasses that swayed in precise unison and gave to the meadow graceful dancing rhythms; and the distant flare of golden robinias and crimson tupelos—all these painterly images brought to the moment a solace that soon revealed itself as transitory and deceptive.

His brooding sorrow and his urgent words now dispelled whatever fleet happiness the day had been granting them.

"The only way we can make ourselves clean again," he told her, "is to kill Gerhard."

He observed her carefully while she held herself inside a wary silence. Her blue eyes flashed with an anger that was yoked to fear. He knew her well. She was going to wait before she told him what she was feeling. So he hurried to say more.

"I've made a plan that will work," he began.

"You must write Gerhard a letter, telling him that you were unaware of your father's activities against the Nazis. Tell him that you knew nothing about your father's helping the British and the French to decode German military correspondence. Reassure him that your love for each other has nothing to do with your father. To prove your love of him and your allegiance to his cause, tell him that you are prepared to give him information that is vital to the German war effort. Convince him that you have discovered cryptographic codes which the Allied countries use in their military correspondence. Knowing these codes will enable the Germans to anticipate the military strategies of their enemies. 'Surely,' you must write, 'the codes will help the Nazi regime to win the war.'"

Now Simone found the words that challenged the complicated scenario that he was devising.

"I can't do this thing," she protested. "I'd never get away with it."

"Of course you can," he insisted. "You have fooled the Germans before. You can fool this German, too."

"I can't, I tell you. I can't do it."
He ignored her refusal.

"In your letter, be sure to tell him that you will meet in Lausanne, because that is the place where you were so happy together. Remind him that the two of you can enjoy days and nights of pleasure before he returns to the war. Tell him even more than that. Say that you will also join the war, as a nurse or as a pilot. England and France have already allowed women to participate in aerial combat. Germany must do the same. Point out that you are a skillful pilot and can be of some value to the Nazi party. Say all these things to Gerhard when you write to him."

Her look of dismay, poised as it was within a frown, did not hold him back. So swiftly did he speak, that he gave her no chance to dissuade him from his plan.

"The letter that you write will draw Gerhard to Lausanne," he said. "You will already have arrived there, in the event that Gerhard decides to trace your movements a day or two before you are to meet. It may please him to know that the beautiful young woman he loves is waiting for him on the fourth floor of a luxurious hotel within the suite of rooms that in their previous visit they made so memorable.

"Gerhard will not know that I too will be there, in that same suite of rooms waiting for him. I'll be the one to finish him off. But your setting him up for me will make you clean again."

Of all these things, Marc spoke in clear and understated language. Yet the hatred he felt for Gerhard was palpable. Palpable too was his confidence that they would succeed in this new and important mission. Now he paused, observing even more cautiously the effect of his words upon Simone. He was aware that she had noticed his rigid self-control and his mastery over the telling of his plan. He knew how she thought. She was clever and intuitive. She would surmise that he had been devising his revenge scenario for many weeks.

In spite of his earnest belief in a successful outcome of his plan, Simone did not yet agree to become a part of it.

Even more intensely now, she challenged the realism of his expectations.

"This is madness," she protested. "Even if I were willing to be a part of your plan—and I am not—our killing Gerhard cannot be done."

He met her protest quietly. But his temperate manner did not undermine his determination.

"It can and will be done," he answered her.

Very gently, with his large, adept hands, he was stroking her flushed cheeks now. There was genuine love in his direct gaze of her and an intimacy of touch that she received as the emblem of the bond between them.

"Don't you see?" he asked her, while the timbres of his husky voice played on sounds both melancholic and petitioning. "It's the only way that things will be good between us again."

He paused, studying the influence of his words upon her. Both his petition and his melancholy stirred her with emotions that surprised her. He wondered what she was thinking. Were her feelings compelling her to admit that he was still the most essential person in her life? Or did the thought disturb her that, by capitulating to his words, she would be the catalyst of Gerhard's death?

Once more she resisted his plan.

"There is too much uncertainty in it," she told him, "and

too much reckless danger. We wouldn't accomplish anything, and we'd probably get ourselves killed."

Still he petitioned her. Still his voice played upon his sorrowful memory of the shame to which he said he had brought them because of their association with Gerhard. His forthright expression lent even more conviction to all that he was asking of her.

"If you really love me, you'll help me make this plan work," he said.

Again she resisted him, her voice maintaining the same understated timbres that held both of them to a quiet path.

"I tell you that your plan will not work," she said. "The whole thing is wishful thinking on your part."

He was wise enough not to push her further.

"Think about it," he said. "It's the only way we can save ourselves."

Now, when she answered him, there was melancholy in her smoky voice, too. But the sorrow it conveyed was authentic. There had been genuine sadness in his inflections. But he had complicated that sadness with wily contrivances meant to draw her into his will.

"We are lost, you and I," she said. "But your plan is not the way to find ourselves."

"Think about it," he answered her. "My plan will free us from shame."

They were walking into the paddock now, where they quickly retrieved their horses.

Because he had finished saying everything that he needed to say, he mounted his Criollo. Then, signaling his stallion into a cantering gait, he hurried across autumn-flecked hills and dales and on to the long riders' path that would guide him through the tree-shaded forest.

As he rode swiftly away from her and while she lingered by her own stallion, Marc could not then guess at Simone's thoughts. She was staring at him, bitter man that he was, until he disappeared inside the forest. At once, the image disconcerted her. It left her with the uneasy sensation that he was disappearing from her life.

On this day and on the days that followed that weekend, Simone hesitated before the conflicted mandates of her will. She loved Gerhard too much to accept a plan that would destroy him. Yet Marc's insistence that her involvement with a Nazi had brought dishonor upon them continued to give her pause.

Still, she was no fool. As close as she was to this problem about her relations with Gerhard, she could even now interpret with incisive accuracy both her motives and her deeds.

By sleeping with Gerhard, she had saved Jean-Claude Jourdan—a heroic ally. She did not regret having done so. Nor did Marc regret the part he had played in rescuing Jean-Claude, his best friend whom he loved and respected as if he were a more-than- ordinary brother. Hadn't he often referred to him as his twin?

Nevertheless, in the aftermath of their rescue of Jean-Claude, both she and Marc were suffering. Marc, she believed, was suffering not so much because she had slept with Gerhard, but because she had fallen in love with him. She, in turn, was suffering because she had betrayed not only her husband. She had betrayed the cause for which she and Marc and all their relatives and friends were fighting. And, yes, she was suffering because the life that she expected to live without Gerhard would always be incomplete. Her need of him would live unrequited, and the consummation of the desire that had been a fuse to her new happiness would never fire any of the hours and days or weeks and years that she was to be condemned to live without him.

That she might one day meet Gerhard again, should he survive the war, placated her uneasy heart. At these times, she reminded herself that, according to the rules of war, Gerhard had done no wrong. He had fought his enemies bravely. He had fulfilled all the commands that his superior officers had told him were essential, if his homeland was to win the war. Though war had made him a savage, it had rendered him no different from his fellow soldiers or, for that matter, from the men and women who were fighting on the side of the Allied nations. After the war, Gerhard would become himself again. The creative spirit that had in peacetime always defined him would influence him to build new airplanes and to bring together people of different nations.

So, in solitary moments when she defended her love of Gerhard, did she tell herself. During the next two weekends when Marc, on a well-earned pass, came to his parents' Derbyshire home to share with her what always started as solacing time, she continued to resist the quiet words that would throw the two of them into his plan of revenge against Gerhard. She refused to accept any scenario that would make her a catalyst in the killing of Gerhard. She wanted him to stay alive so that he could prove to the world that his existence was a special value. Killing him, she was convinced, would be equivalent to killing her future happiness. It might even kill her future with Marc.

She did not want to fall out of love with Marc. Their years together had intensified her need of him.

She well understood Marc. Once more she told herself

that she loved his courage, his tremendous energy, and his rugged ways. She loved his ability to sacrifice himself for a cause he deemed worthy. She loved the originality of his thought. She loved his trust in her courage, and she loved his loyalty. She knew that it was not easy for him to send her into missions that carried formidable risks and dubious outcomes. In so many important ways, he treated her as his equal. Coming from a man who was the epitome of brave and well-calculated risk-taking and whose honed-sharp mind experienced the world as an ongoing and tremendous experiment, his respect for her own diverse capacities was no small praise in her favor.

But his possessive love of her had become claustrophobic. She wondered whether he also had felt, at least occasionally, that their love for each other was an imprisonment, a symbiotic arrangement that consumed the partners it represented. Marc's brooding distrust of her feelings for Gerhard did not surprise her. Nor was she surprised by his sexual envy of Gerhard's prowess as a lover whose dangerous sensuality had captivated her. Those were a realistic man's responses. She respected his realism, even as she disdained its conventionality. There was in her a desire to love whom she wished. She did not care, of course, to be promiscuous. Too many of the young women whom she knew from her school days had complicated their lives by entering one casual relationship after another. They learned nothing from these relationships except, perhaps, to exploit their lovers even more than their temporary partners exploited them. The women who played this shallow game with mock seriousness or with an amused irony were, in the end, only a little less unhappy than those whose playfulness concealed a desire to find one man who was willing to share their fidelity.

She believed that she was not of their kind. She wanted to be free to love both Gerhard and Marc—and to love them at the same time. But she did not want to make a game of love. Chance had brought Gerhard into her life and her happiness had become two-fold. That she could love two different men so completely exhilarated her. She knew herself well enough to be convinced that her love for each of them was genuine. When the wretched war was over, she might collaborate with the both of them to make life and love dynamic and memorable experiences. Marc need not know that she and Gerhard were fulfilling their desire for each other. Nor would she be repudiating her desire for Marc. She would love both men equally.

Marc, too, she told herself, should share his love with another partner. A different (and ancillary) woman might be good for his spirit. She should be as sophisticated and stylish as she was self-reliant. Marc didn't need a leaner, though he might—like many arbitrary men—go in search of one. For the most part, she had learned not to be a leaner. But a truly independent woman could liberate him even more than she had from his arbitrary codes and from his brooding ways.

Marc's volatile response to her association with Gerhard, though understandable from a conventional viewpoint and even inevitable, reaffirmed her previous conviction that his relationship with her was as self-centered as it was passionate. She had to admit that at first his jealousy did not displease her. A woman likes to believe that her husband wants her only for himself. But all through her years with him, there had been underpinnings of her submissiveness to his will. Was it pity that persuaded her to defer to him whenever a conflict loomed between them? She wondered, understanding clearly how Marc's troubled relationship with Henri, the father whom he worshiped, left him feeling like an outsider. In his adolescence, especially, Marc had suffered because of Henri's cold withdrawal to a life scenario that kept his son at a distance. At Le Rosey and later, she had been the only one, except for Jean-Claude, from whom he was willing to receive an encouraging word and who, simply by being a tried-and-true presence, had coaxed him away from bitter and self-defeating thoughts.

Now, years later, Marc's obsessive love frightened her, even as it brought her the joy of his fidelity and of his regard of her as someone extraordinary and indispensable. Nor did obsession belong to him alone. She, too, found him indispensable. Her need to be with him had become an obsession. She needed the pleasures they took from each other in the privacies of rooms made memorable because they were there together. She needed as well the risk and thrill of their adventuring together in the wider world that kept unfolding around them.

Yet she needed Gerhard as well. He also was her obsession. In her divided heart, she did not want to be free of him.

Her resistance to Marc's plan to avenge himself against Gerhard might have prevailed. But during one of the weekends in November when he was at liberty from his military duties, news reached them from Sweden about the Nazis' massacre of forty-two of the hundreds of Jews whom her fellow Swedes had rescued from Nazi-occupied Denmark. A team of hardened German soldiers had also killed eighteen of the Swedes who had been involved in the rescue and in other underground activities that meant to subvert the German war effort. That these German commandos were attached to Abwehr, a militant unit known for sabotaging large cities and for torturing and killing whole districts of people, heightened Marc's grim telling of the events. Because Gerhard belonged to the same murderous unit, he too, Marc now insisted, must have taken part in the massacre.

"Gerhard is no longer human," Marc told her. "He is a savage. He has killed innocent women and children, as well as decent men who were citizens of a neutral country."

"He couldn't have been there," she protested. "He belongs to the Waffen unit. They need him to fly combat missions."

"He was wounded in one of those missions," Marc said. "The Nazis reassigned him to Abwehr."

"I tell you that I know him well," she said. "He spent weeks as a visitor in my father's home, speaking of the things that are really important to him. I know him. I know him nearly as well as I know you. He's a man filled with a love of music and science and art. He wants to create. He intends to build aircraft that will dissolve the distance between people. He loves people, I tell you. He could never kill in cold blood or face to face."

Marc noticed how tense she had become and how uncertain. There was in her voice a tremulous petitioning, because she was asking him to perceive Gerhard as she did. Yet, even as she made her petition, her belief in Gerhard was faltering before the realistic possibility that he had indeed been a part of the massacre.

Nevertheless, she defended him once more.

"At heart, Gerhard is not a Nazi," she said. "He's a brave German trapped by the wretched politics of his country."

"He was there with those other killers," Marc said, his husky voice a bitter snarl upon the air. "He was one of their leaders."

Now Marc repeated all that he had told her about the massacre. This time, Simone found the narrative even more horrifying.

Repelled by these ugly details in Marc's repeated description of the atrocities, she fell silent. Gerhard and his fellow commandos, disguised as marauding Russians, had slit the throats of some of their victims. They had raped the younger women and then strangled them. They had disemboweled the minister who had been a life-long friend of her and her father, and then they set his wife on fire with gasoline they had poured on her. They machine-gunned eight of the Resistance workers who had earned reputations as the most daring freedom fighters. They buried alive ten Jewish children and their mothers.

All these terrible things Marc told her without flinching. He might have been a prosecuting attorney offering a judge his closing evidence against the infamous Gerhard Hauptmann.

Only after she had completely fathomed the gravity of Gerhard's alleged murderous acts did she say the words that, for weeks, Marc had been waiting for her to say. By then, he had told her that two of her distant cousins, as well as her father's loyal housekeeper and that good woman's husband, had been among those persons either shot or hanged.

"Gerhard is not fit to live," she said, spewing through the teeth her angry judgment. "He fooled me into believing that he was an honorable man. He's not fit to live."

So distraught was she made by all that Marc told her that she began to weep. Never before had he seen her weep. Always, she had prided herself upon being resilient and stoical.

In that moment, Marc wanted to reach out to her. But a wise intuition held him back. He understood her well enough to know that she would resist both his touch and his commiseration. So he stood inside the stillness that separated him from her, though she was seated only a few feet away in the ample Louis XV sofa that dominated the south corner of their living room.

But he was pleased that she allowed herself to weep for no longer than a few minutes. Rather than go on weeping, she listened carefully to his new words that hurried the two of them forward to the scenes their fate had in store for them.

"We must kill Gerhard as soon as possible," he said.

His words increased her tension. They drew her to a silence that he interpreted as her acquiescence.

By then, she was offering him one of her Parisian cigarettes even as she drew from her gold, monogrammed case one for herself. With a gentleman's practice, he lit her cigarette and then his own, as well. Light from the afternoon sun floated its radiance with Indian summer airs past the French doors and past the Renoir observing them from the pale gold wall. The radiance included them in its ambiance, softening their tautened features and almost concealing the furrowed brow of each of them and, at the rim of their mouths that held their cigarettes, the tension of their grimaces.

The light also revealed the sheen of a Derringer pistol. It held a place on the delicate Louis XV table that stood to the left of the sofa. Marc had set it there, having hurried into the room from the workshop where he had been cleaning it. It was while he was in his private workshop that he had learned, from a message transmitted from London via his Siemens and Halske teletypewriter, that Abwehr commandos had wreaked havoc upon sixty people in Sweden. Now, with a muted satisfaction, he watched Simone as she caught sight of the pistol. He imagined that she was noticing, too, that its harsh sheen and its vivid reality occupied only a small space on the table. But, while autumn light revealed it, the Derringer dominated the room.

Simone could not know that Gerhard had not participated in the massacre. Her assumption that he was more essential to the German Air Force was correct. Marc had seized these moments of her sickened reaction to the news of the massacre that had taken place in Copenhagen and on the island of Scania to plant in her mind grave doubts about Gerhard. He felt no compunction in misleading her. He told himself that he was fighting to save their marriage. He also told himself that, had the German High Command ordered Gerhard to lead the massacre, he would not have hesitated to do so.

He felt charged with new energies as he began to activate his plot against Gerhard. The planning filled most of his time as well as his thoughts. Its movements were swift. Like the subtle mechanism of a Swiss clock or like the intricate workings of the teletypewriter that informed him daily of the enemy's strategies, the plan unfolded as smoothly as he could wish. Within a week, Simone had sent the letter to Gerhard that invited him to Lausanne and, in turn, the German hero had accepted her invitation. She had registered at the hotel as Mrs.

Gerhard Hauptmann and had been given one of the largest suites, with the luxuriously appointed rooms usually reserved for royalty, for government and military leaders, and for guests whose backgrounds defined them as patrician or as immensely wealthy. Mrs. Hauptmann would be the first to arrive. Her husband, she had advised the hotel management, would arrive a day later. That the Hauptmann family was patrician, as well as military and wealthy, made the placement of Gerhard and his wife in a magnificent suite of rooms both apt and inevitable.

Simone was going to activate even the smallest details of Marc's plan.

She would be traveling with a concealed handgun. With him, she had carefully pondered the advantage of carrying her FN Browning 6.35mm Vest Pocket pistol. After weighing the liabilities of being caught with it, she had at first reminded him that she must not give Gerhard any reason to suspect her motives for being there in Lausanne with him. The demure young woman whose persona she embodied would not be carrying a weapon. But without the weapon, he told her, she was going to be more vulnerable. She increased her risk unnecessarily. It was then that they decided that she must carry the pistol with her. She placed it inside the secret pocket of her sealskin jacket.

Neither Simone nor he had any way of knowing whether

Gerhard had discovered that they were married. Gerhard's eagerness to see her may have had more to do with his wanting to avenge himself against her. He might have learned that she had assisted her father in decoding important messages concerning the Germans' latest strategies of war. He might want to kill her not only for that reason, but also—even if he believed that she had not been a part of her father's espionage—for Knut Bergman's betrayal of the Nazis' trust of him.

"Even while carrying a pistol, you could get yourself killed," Marc warned her.

"I can take care of myself," Simone said. "Besides, you'll be shadowing me all the time. Of course, you'll have to move faster than Gerhard."

"I will," he promised her.

He appreciated the toughened spirit she was showing him. He noticed too a harder edge to her voice and the hint of bitterness upon her still-lovely face. With no discernible hesitation, she was playing the killer game to which he had with wily effort persuaded her. He had won her approval not without some cost to his self-respect. He was not proud that he was exploiting her guilt because she had given her love to a Nazi. Nor was he proud that he had lied to her about Gerhard's involvement in the massacre of the Danish Jews and their rescuers.

But he did not want to lose her and he wanted her all to himself.

These weeks when he had become aware of her passion for Gerhard had left him unhappier than he had ever imagined he could be. He had known unhappiness before. Early in his life, as a youth whose definition of himself was still tenuous, he had discovered that Henri did not love him with the same attentive care and paternal intensity that had previously solidified their relationship. Not even then, during the long, bruising years of his feeling emotionally banished by the father he had come to love so completely, had he believed himself so betrayed and abandoned as in this new anguished time, when Simone had—with feminine subtleties—turned her attention to another man.

There had been one other time when she had appeared to direct her subtle attention to another man—or, rather, to a youth like himself who was a student at Le Rosey. That sixteen-year old athlete had in various ways declared himself a rival, whether they were on the rugby field or skiing or boxing or swimming. His name was Hubert Binoche, and he was most impressive. First in their class in terms of his academic standing, he was exceptional as well in his height, his muscularity, and his handsomeness.

When he had faced her with his accusations, while—not far from Le Rosey's winter campus—they were on their way to an afternoon of skiing in Geneva, Simone denied having any special interest in Hubert. He was, she explained, a boy whom she respected for his versatility and for his charming manner. She admitted that, casually, they would from time to time engage in banter that some might perceive as flirting. But there was nothing wrong in that. The lightness between them pleased her, perhaps because it was a welcome change from the always-serious exchanges of their own relationship.

That day, Marc regarded her lightness differently, especially because she had shared it with his rival. As far as he was concerned, there was nothing light about a teammate's betrayal of his friendship and, on her part, about a breach of decorum. Weren't they, after all, going steady?

Wary of his roused anger, she had at first fallen silent. Familiar with his moods, she knew the inadequacy of coaxing him to another subject or of treating as unimportant something that he regarded as very important.

When she did speak, she made a promise that she felt might conciliate him.

"I won't joke with Hubert anymore, if you don't want me to," she said.

Her soft blue gaze and her warm smile eased his anguished distrust of her. With her delicate hands, she had cupped his searching face into her fragrant palms.

"I'll always be the girl you want me to be," she said.

He remembered that they had walked hand-in-hand to the cabin next to the ski lift, where they would collect their skis and go forward to the crisp brightness of a Swiss afternoon in January.

Simone kept the promise that she had made to him. She remained courteous whenever she saw Hubert. But never again did she exchange any lighthearted or personal remarks with him.

Her fidelity to her word didn't matter, though. Within a week after their conversation about her good-natured exchanges with Hubert, Marc challenged him to a boxing match. Though Hubert fought well, he gave him a vicious beating. Even when Hubert, exhausted and thoroughly battered, had fallen against the ropes, he kept punching him. Not the bell signaling that the fight was over or the referee's rugged attempt to separate him from his opponent or the wild, ambivalent shouts of the spectators compelled him to stop. The boxing coach and two other referees had to jump into the ring to pull him away from Hubert, who by this time was unconscious.

Hubert suffered a concussion, but no damage to his

reputation. His teammates, in fact, stood somewhat awed by his stoical acceptance of things and by the rumor that beautiful Simone had taken pleasure in the affection he had expressed for her. These teammates also admired his refusal to make a formal complaint against his adversary. After a private conference with his father who had visited him during his brief stay in the campus hospital, Hubert had played the gallant gentleman. His fight with Marc, his father reminded him, had been ignited by an affair of the heart.

"I think," Hubert's father told him, "that young Roussillon is one of those men who will not merely fall into love. He will fall into obsession. I cannot say that I envy him."

Days later, Marc heard about this remark from his teammates. They looked at him with special interest and even envy. Monsieur Binoche's prediction suggested that he was going to lead an exciting romantic life.

The dean of the school, he now recalled six years later when he and Simone were preparing to return to Switzerland so that they could confront Gerhard, was not as lenient as Monsieur Binoche. Though he was not expelled, he was not allowed to box for the rest of that year.

Now Gerhard had become his sexual rival. There was in his compulsion to destroy this German adversary neither a military nor a political motive. Though he might lie to Simone and to others, he was at all times honest with himself. The Gerhard problem had reawakened his fear that the person whom he regarded as most essential to his happiness was going to betray him. Henri had done so. And Marianne, with her meticulous focus upon her music career and her understated withholding of herself, had also betrayed him. They had not loved him as he had loved them, unconditionally and intensely and warmheartedly. All over again, as if he were reliving the darkest hours of his childhood, he was enduring long, sleepless nights and the unabated conviction that Simone, this beautiful woman, this soul-mate and wellspring of his existence, was turning away from him. That, even now at the age of twenty-two, he should fear being abandoned left him startled and baffled. So also did his jealousy baffle him. Ever since their marriage, Simone, he had to admit, had never given him any cause to be jealous. Always, whether they were horse riding or skiing or attending a concert or a party, they enjoyed one another's company. In bed, their passion was as exciting as it was mutual.

Only Simone's attraction to Gerhard had disturbed the honesty of their happiness.

He and Simone could recover their happiness if they worked together to destroy Gerhard. Simone's complicity in his plan of revenge was, he believed, essential to their being able to go forward together. Her willingness at the last to assist him in the killing was a good omen for their marriage. By this act of revenge, the two of them would reclaim the honor that he felt they had lost.

To advance his plan, he would be carrying a Beretta 1934 semi-automatic pistol, which possessed a very reliable feeding and extraction cycle. It was made of very few parts and was easy to maintain. He would also be carrying a Colt Model 1903 Pocket Hammerless pistol, which was relatively small and easy to conceal. Despite its name, the pistol did have a hammer, which was hidden from view by the gun's slide. He would carry a Colt Model 1908 pistol, too, which was also small and concealable. He could easily tuck it into his vest pocket. There would be on his person as well (worn low on his leg for easier access) a V-2 Stiletto.

He wanted to be free of this burden of having to avenge himself against his rival. He wanted to be certain that this privileged Nazi, this hero-seeming fighter of wars and killer of enemies, this romantic man who had slept with Simone and had won her love, would no longer be alive in the world. In that way only could he be certain that this Gerhard Hauptmann would never again sleep with Simone.

He was not proud of this plan to destroy his rival. It was the plan of a sadist. It was the plan of a disarranged man who was not playing by the honorable rules that he had always represented. Its success was meant to subdue the mad reaches of his jealousy. But it would not diminish the contempt he felt for himself. On each morning when, shaving before his bathroom mirror, he stared back at the bitter face peering upon him, he knew how much of stranger he had become to the earlier and honorable version of himself, an imagery he could perceive only in his memory. In this altogether different year, he intended to kill an enemy who was not armed and who had no chance to survive the attack he would make upon him. At the same time, he was placing Simone in jeopardy. He was using her as a decoy. With wily lies and ill-defined purpose, he had stirred her willingness to help him kill Gerhard. There was in him a reckless dismissal of how much this journey into revenge would cost her. That she loved Gerhard, he was certain. That she would suffer for the rest of her life after they killed him, he was equally certain. Her private suffering would be adequate payment for having betrayed the love that, for as long as he had known her, he had always given her. He had denied himself so many equally beautiful women who had entered his life and then, because he had not collaborated with their desire, moved on.

Simone, he wanted to believe, had been as faithful. Except for her schoolgirl infatuation with Hubert Binoche, she had never violated the pact between them. It was Gerhard who changed everything. It was Gerhard whom he intended to shoot. Because of the revenge he had devised, Gerhard's life-blood would swiftly drain away.

He hated himself for dishonoring that better self whose imagery he had always emulated. But he was determined to go through with his plan, as malevolent and as heinous as it was. That he would loathe himself forever after would be part of his suffering. But, he believed, he would gradually accommodate this new version of himself. In the same way that he had looked upon the most repellent experiences of war and had nonetheless endured, so he would look upon his self-to-be. Eventually, he would accept the callous man that he had become, his mind with ruthless aptitudes having adjusted to the tarnished imagery.

.

Chapter Six

The Real Gerhard

From the beginning, Marc's plan to destroy Gerhard played itself out differently from what he had anticipated. The difference shadowed not only Simone's movements, but his own activities as well.

He had expected, first of all, to be on a week's leave during the period when he would arrive in Lausanne to put in motion his slow killing of Gerhard. That he would be on leave at that time was not an unrealistic expectation. Flying Halifax bombers, Avro-Lancasters, and Hawker Tempest fighters, he had recently participated in eight combat missions within a span of twelve brutal days. He had earned new leave-time. At the last, though, the Alsace squadron of which he was a prominent member ordered him to additional missions over the ports, railways, airfields, and industrial districts of Berlin, Hamburg, and Cologne. The bombings of the cities were especially punishing. They caused spiraling firestorms and left tens of thousands of Germans dead.

Two weeks must pass before he received his leave.

So he told Simone when he telephoned her the news about the change in their plans.

"Don't worry," she said. "I'll find a good reason for postponing Lausanne. I'll phone Gerhard today. I'll tell him that it will be two weeks before the hospital administrators will approve my leave from my nursing duties."

Her brisk words carried both determination and ingenuity. He saw that she was on his side and that she was going to do everything to make their plan work. Even her parting kiss seemed more intense. They were, he felt, on their way to recovering what they had lost.

Not only Simone was on his side. Luck was there, too. Only a day later Simone telephoned him some good news. Gerhard's own plans were changed. He, too, was being sent into more combat missions. Because the Germans were losing many pilots, the Luftwaffe was assigning him to new aerial battles. Gerhard promised to meet Simone in Lausanne in fifteen days.

"Perfect," Marc told Simone. "Things are working just as we want them."

"I'll meet you in Lausanne in two weeks," she said. "We'll have time to review your plan before Gerhard arrives there."

That he would have to wait fifteen days before he killed Gerhard might have unsettled a different kind of man. But Marc stayed in control. The personal disappointments that hovered about his life and the rigorous military experience that kept testing him had not only sharpened his perceptions. They had made him a hardhearted man. But those experiences did not persuade him to love Simone any less. In fact, he loved her with the same brooding passion that he had always brought to their relationship.

In fifteen days, he was going to kill the man who had slept with his wife. He could be patient when he had to be. He could wait. After he killed him, Gerhard would be dead forever.

During these intervening days, while summoning rigorous self-discipline and a clearly-focused awareness of his military mission, he did not permit himself to think of any essential problem except the strategies that he and his squadron would need to activate if they were to prevail over the enemy. Now in these bleak days of December, when he returned to his barracks exhausted from the tense hours of night flying, he half-listened to his buddies' camaraderie and to their carefree words, which he recognized as a willful flouting of the chaos and death that had hovered about them while they were in the sky, fighting their adversaries. Flippant and tough-hearted, he parried their remarks. He shared a cynical understanding of his squadron's peril and the likelihood that some of them would not survive their next aerial encounters with the Nazis. Brothers in spirit, they compelled themselves to laugh in the face of the death that might be waiting for them. Only at these times, when with his comrades he expressed a gallows-humored contempt for death, did he allow his thoughts to drift to a concern about his wife. It was a concern which, with hard-hearted aptitudes, he had suppressed all through his bombing missions. Now, as he sparred verbally with his friends, he thought about how much he missed her.

But it was in the private moments, when he felt free to think upon the unhappy dilemma involving Simone, Gerhard, and him, that dismay and resentment returned as emphases implicated in his roused bitterness. Then, austere and enigmatic while in the officers' large public washroom he studied himself in the mirror shaving or when he was running briskly along the path on which he and his co-pilots and other crew members often raced one another, he thought about Simone. Sometimes, rather than guide him to an acceptable calm, his thought of her roused his fury. If he died in battle, she would be free to marry Gerhard.

Most often, though, whenever his free time permitted him, he worried about Simone. He wondered whether his drawing her into his plot against Gerhard would throw her in harm's way. Had Gerhard discovered her complicity with her father in their furtive code-breaking of the Nazis' cryptic war messages? Had he learned that she was married? Was Gerhard joining her in Switzerland only to kill her?

If, in the event that his own combat assignments wounded or killed him, would Simone—alone in Lausanne—use the pistol inside the secret pocket of her sealskin jacket to kill Gerhard?

Or would she use those unexpected days with Gerhard to test and to revel once again in her passionate love of him?

He wondered, his anguish nearly as intense as his need for revenge.

Unknown to Marc, both Simone and Gerhard were already at the Beau-Rivage. Only a day after he told her that the Luftwaffe was assigning him to new air battles, Gerhard found that his commanding officer was giving him the leave that he had been promised.

"We must meet in Lausanne immediately," Gerhard cabled Simone from Norway. "It will be a long time before I have another leave."

She cabled him back, agreeing to meet him in Lausanne within two days. But she did not inform Marc. She did not want to worry him. He needed to direct all of his energies to the battles he was fighting in the air. There was nothing he could do to help her. She had to make her own way. She had to go to Lausanne alone. Once she was there, she would have to kill Gerhard.

She arrived at the Beau-Rivage a day before Gerhard. Her fashionable wardrobe, with its discreetly colored fabrics and its prestigious labels, identified her as a young woman who was accustomed to the luxurious appointments that the hotel was offering her. Her soft hair, which was pulled away from her face to form a glamorous coil at the nape of her neck, also collaborated with her blonde beauty to impart a carefully wrought patrician sensibility. Poised and subtly remote, she drew the favorable attention of even the most world-weary guests whenever she entered a room. Government officials and military officers, as well as lovely brides, precise matrons, and entitled dowagers watched with approving eyes as she moved gracefully into their presence. That she belonged to the Hauptmann family by marriage enhanced her appeal and validated their belief that she was a more-than-ordinary young woman.

Her refined manner and her engaging conversation gave no evidence that she had come to the hotel to participate in the killing of the very Hauptmann to whom she appeared to be married. She was, after all—or so she had said—a von Sydow. She was the third daughter of the estimable Tomas von Sydow, the utilities magnate and investment banker who had made a fortune in the United States. It was, she told herself, favorable chance that had made her Tomas von Sydow's niece. She knew all about his background and the years that he had spent in Sweden as a privileged youth who had always been kind to his sister. That sister later married Knut Bergman and eventually became her mother. But nobody there at the hotel knew her connection to Knut Bergman. A few of them merely recalled that Tomas von Sydow had married a lovely French woman who had given him three daughters and a son. That he and his family had rarely returned to Sweden was understandable. His immense wealth permitted him to travel around the globe and to replenish the sum of who he was through international business investments and by means of gratifying associations with persons nearly as affluent as he.

To those guests at the Beau-Rivage, the union of a Hauptmann and a von Sydow was both appropriate and commendable. That she had won their favor on her very first day at the hotel, while she was skiing or dining with them, gave an unobtrusive conviction to the scenario that Marc had devised and that she was playing out. Nor did she rely on their approval alone. As focused as she was wily, she had—on the very first day of her being there—enlisted a locksmith to make a copy of the key to the suite of rooms which she and Gerhard would share at the hotel. The locksmith's shop was located in the central part of Lausanne, on the gregarious rue du Petit-Chêne. In Marc's original plan, it was essential that he have a key to their apartment, so that on the night he intended to kill Gerhard, he could conceal himself in their bedroom and wait for him to return there with her, from the romantic hours when they had dined and danced and made promises for the future. On the chance that Marc's squadron commander did grant him his leave in the next day or so, as Gerhard's commander had done for him, she left a copy of the key in Marc's apartment. That was an important part of the plan that Marc had devised. She did not want to alter it.

But, as much as she kept hoping that Marc would arrive within the next few hours, her realistic sense of things persuaded her that Marc was not coming to Lausanne. He would not be hiding in the apartment that she and Gerhard were sharing, a Beretta pistol in his hand as he waited for her to return from that first evening's dinner with Gerhard. She was on her own. She was the one who must kill Gerhard.

She had also used her first day in the hotel to make

certain that Marc's luggage had been securely placed in the suite of rooms across from theirs. Although she was carrying her favorite Browning handgun to kill Gerhard, she thought of using Marc's Colt Model 1903 Pocket Hammerless pistol, which he had packed into one of his suitcases. The Colt was smaller than the Browning and easier to conceal. She made a mental note about the Colt. If she needed it, she knew that it was here.

Marc had reserved the rooms in the name of Julien Deneuve and had given London as his current address. Who Monsieur Deneuve was and what he did for a living did not especially matter to the hotel management. Nor was it essential that he be pro-Nazi. Switzerland was, after all, a neutral country. Besides, Marc had paid for the rooms in advance and had reserved them for a three-week visit. His luggage, he had informed the maître de l'hotel, would precede his arrival.

From the start of her visit to the Beau-Rivage, Simone's self-possessed manner suggested that she was a cultivated woman used to making efficient requests of her reliable house staff. In fact, her making a request of a hotel porter who was assigned to the south wing where she was staying seemed as natural as it was pertinent. Her courteous manner, married as it was to imperious inflections, persuaded the porter to open the suite of rooms where Monsieur Deneuve would be staying. She wanted to see these rooms, she told the porter, so that she could determine whether they were larger and more luxurious and had a better view of the mountains than the rooms that she and her husband would be sharing.

"I would be disturbing no one," she said. "Whoever has reserved those rooms has not yet arrived."

"As you wish, Mrs. Hauptmann," the porter said.

Once inside, she ascertained that a large trunk was standing near two suitcases. In the trunk, Marc told her, would be some of the weapons he would use in the unfolding of his plan to kill Gerhard. She imagined that the trunk held all the familiar weapons that her training for the Resistance had taught her to use. They would be concealed inside the thick lining of ski jackets and within specially designed boots with detachable leggings that could be quickly converted to look like civilian shoes. A French Resistance fighter had transported the weapons from the Roussillons' chalet in Geneva. He was, he told the maître de l'hotel, Monsieur Deneuve's chauffeur.

It pleased her that everything was as it should be. The weapons had arrived safely and without the worry of mail clerks checking the baggage at postal stations or of security guards discovering them at the endangered borders spanning London, France and Switzerland.

Satisfied that the essential luggage was there, she moved out of the apartment with composure both straight-backed and understated. Only after the porter had locked Marc's suite did she give him a handsome gratuity. His respectful bow indicated that her generosity impressed and pleased him. She doubted that he would mention the incident to Gerhard. If he did, because Gerhard might make inquiry of the neighbor occupying the rooms across from theirs, she would make a lighthearted thing of her visit to the apartment. She knew exactly what she would tell Gerhard. She simply wanted to verify that, as a Hauptmann, he was being given one of the best apartments in the hotel. She would have felt unhappy if the rooms across from theirs had been superior. She wanted him to have the best.

If chance required her to say those words, she knew that Gerhard would believe her. So smoothly would she conceal her hatred of him, that he would not doubt whatever she told him. Yet, in spite of this confidence in her powers to deceive him, she found herself uneasy before this new desire for revenge. She could rightly tell herself that the killing of Gerhard was justifiable because of the heinous crimes he had committed against the unarmed and the innocent. But she was unable to connect the Gerhard that she had come to know during his visits to her father's house in Sweden and within the week she had spent with him in Lausanne to the image of the savage Nazi whom Marc had called forth in his summary of Gerhard's massacre of the Danish Jews and of the compassionate Swedes who had at first rescued them. The Gerhard Hauptmann whom she had come to trust and to love was human and empathetic. He was the type of individual whom her professors at the Sorbonne used to call a Renaissance man. Surely, the broad range and the profound depth of his learning had influenced him to cultivate his humanity. He had been drawn into the war because he was an earnest patriot, not because he had a need to kill.

Now, when she believed herself only a day away from murdering Gerhard, she hesitated before a returning uncertainty that pushed itself forward from the most secret workings of her mind. Once again, a discrepancy between the Gerhard of Marc's corrosive narrative and the Gerhard of her personal experience confused her. By willing herself to echo the words which Marc had taught her to believe, she tried to elude the memory of her more affirmative experience of Gerhard. But the occasions they had shared together still lived, vivid and satisfying, within the complicated folds of her recollection. It was on this first crowded day at the Beau-Rivage, when she felt alone even while an impressive company gathered around her, that she told herself that she must not think of that other Gerhard, the heroic and romantic man with whom she had fallen in love. She must think of him as the cold-blooded killer of women and children. She must keep in mind that he was with the commando unit that also killed her three cousins, her beloved housekeeper, and that good woman's husband. She must impress upon her memory the brutal image of Gerhard as a savage, as a traitor to his best aspirations and—yes—to all the promises he had made to her.

On that first night in the hotel, she lay sleepless inside the flowing space of her solitary room where the slanted light of the moon peered through the panoramic window and illumined her unhappy face. She was leaning within a galaxy of upright pillows when she vaguely noticed the fragrant smoke wafting in vaporous unison from her cigarette. As was her habit when bitter thoughts and rancorous calculations of her losses were assailing her, she felt her ghost lingering near her, watchful. To dispel the ghost and the disarranged sense of her self that made her feel that she was utterly confounded, she turned on the lamplight by her bed and crushed the remnants of her cigarette in a convenient ashtray. The room, with its Second Empire opulence, stood waiting to receive her while, leaving her place within the ample bed, she gathered a light blue, flowing velvet robe and matching slippers to her tall, sylph-like frame.

With the nearly balletic movements that gave to her carriage a natural elegance, she hurried to the moonlit window and to its panoramic view of the night. Not only light from the full moon that was radiant upon the window, but also the lights that were burnishing the solitude of the hotel grounds comforted her. In the palpable distance, the ellipses of villages and towns flared their homespun identities, and snow-capped mountains wearing the dark cloaks of sentries—guardian and proprietary—stared back at her, only partially illumined yet no less monumental.

From this familiar imagery, she located her proper bearings. She would allow neither ghosts nor hesitation to push her from her necessary path. Nor would she permit her memory of her love for Gerhard to dissuade her from her mission. She promised herself that she would not think of Gerhard at all. She would keep telling herself that this man whom she was going to kill was a stranger. He was a Nazi who needed killing. Only in this way could she go through with her husband's plan.

Every so often, while she was alone in the flowing space of the suite of rooms where she was staying, she strengthened her resolve by fingering the FN Browning 6.35mm pistol that she had concealed within the secret pocket of her sealskin jacket.

She understood with grim awareness that, because Marc was delayed, she was the one who must kill Gerhard. The thought appalled her. But the savage part of her nature, which the war had sharply honed, compelled her to keep thinking of Gerhard as an enemy. He was a Nazi. He was a murderer of women and children. He was a monster.

But early the following day, when Gerhard came back to her as buoyant and hopeful as he was passionate, she wavered once more before the mandates of Marc's vengeful plan.

"We're in it again—you and I," he said as he kissed her in the privacy of their hotel apartment. "Right this minute we are making the future that will belong to us together."

She had not anticipated being so surprised by him. His eyes glowed with love for her, and his voice was husky with emotion. Even in these first moments, her heart leaped with the thrill of him. This charismatic man, this generous and warm-hearted spirit who openly declared his love for her and his dreams of their future together, was the same Gerhard whom she had come to trust and to love in Sweden.

She wondered whether Marc had been misinformed about Gerhard's involvement in the massacre of women and children. She began to doubt the accuracy of the information that Marc had given her. She wondered whether he had lied to her.

Now she found herself relieved and even grateful that

Marc had been assigned to a series of combat missions which would delay his arrival in Lausanne for two weeks.

Before Marc came to Lausanne, she intended to put Gerhard to the test. She wanted to discover the hidden facets and the convoluted mysteries of his character. She wanted to learn whether this man, under the guise of a dutiful allegiance to the creeds of his belligerent country, was capable of murdering innocent men, women and children. If she discovered that he had, indeed, participated in the killing of the Danish Jews and her fellow Swedes, she would no longer hesitate to kill Gerhard. But, should she learn that Gerhard was innocent of that massacre, she would find some plausible excuse for persuading Gerhard to leave Lausanne before Marc arrived.

As cautious as she was discreet, she gave Gerhard every indication that she loved him. Whether they were reveling in the activities of the ski resort where they were staying or conjoined in the ecstasies of their lovemaking, she tried at first to believe that she was an actress playing a fictional role.

During these uncertain days and nights, she stood, willful and detached, outside her life. She was, she told herself, not that Simone who was married to and still loved Marc Roussillon. She was some other Simone, whose complicated military assignment required her to be both tough-minded and devious.

In the beginning, there was in her a furtive tension, a suppressed fear that Gerhard might be playing with her. He might be using these days to take his pleasures with her before he admitted that he knew who she really was. He might, somehow, have uncovered the plan that was meant to destroy him. He might, in turn, have devised his own plot against Marc and her. Perhaps, she imagined, Gerhard was waiting for Marc to appear, so that he could kill the two of them at the same time.

Hardened by her own experiences of war, she kept at bay the uneasy intricacies of her fear. Instead, with convincing energies and a wholehearted belief in the truth of the episodes she was sharing with Gerhard, she transformed herself, as she had done when he visited her in Sweden, into that other Simone, that demure woman who loved a Nazi. Here in Lausanne she called the same Nazi her husband. So immersed did she become in the enigmatic character of this woman, that only vaguely and in subtle increments did she permit herself to admit once again that she and this other woman, this fictive creation, this alternate whom she had invented, were one and the same.

If Gerhard also was play-acting, she never fathomed his dissimulations. His blond, rugged handsomeness and his vivid physicality were a fuse to his exuberant reacquaintance with his beloved Beau-Rivage and to his sheer happiness at being there with her and being as he was, on leave from the wretched war.

"I want to experience everything here again," he said, as he embraced her at the balcony just beyond the fluent space of the living room within their apartment. "I want to feel as free and as hopeful as I did when I was a student on leave from school and when there was no war."

He had made similar remarks during their previous visit to Lausanne. This time she noticed how he pushed his voice into the words, as if his clear enunciation of each of them would give both heft and credibility to his stated intention.

"I'm going to do everything to survive this rancid war," he said. "It will take me a while to find the way back to myself. But I'll do it. I'll be myself again, you'll see. I won't let the war destroy my good dreams."

His words quickened the belief in him that she had been suppressing.

She had been leaning her head against his chest, at first reminding herself that she was acting a part. She was surprised nonetheless at her willingness to accept an intimate proximity that she might have easily eluded. But, enfolded within his rugged arms, she savored her quickened contentment at being there. Hearing his words, she hurried to collaborate with his optimism. Already, within the first hours of their being together, she was beginning to believe in him again.

"You're going to do tremendous things," she said. "Whatever you do will always be tremendous."

With her, he was observing a constellation of cirro-cumulous clouds that appeared to be floating near the blue-gray amplitude of mountains. Their whiteness made small puffs and flakes and streaks that kept floating and vanishing and reappearing. The mackerel sky, sun-tinted with pale green and azure properties, was another amplitude upon their senses. The curves of steep snow-covered hills and ski runs, a maze of spiraling ascensions and jagged passages, leaped before their scanning glances. The plangent waters of the breeze-stirred lake and the red-tiled roofs of rows upon rows of terraced houses wore painterly idiosyncrasies. Below the place where she stood with Gerhard on the hotel balcony, young couples—as exhilarant as they were athletic and proficient—boarded the sleek Beau-Rivage bus which would bring them up the first level of the mountain to the comfortable lodge and to the hut near the lifts where they would gather their skis.

"We'll be joining those skiers this afternoon," Gerhard told her. "You and I are going to have a very good time here."

For ten days she did enjoy herself with him. They skied on the white-capped Savoy Alps. They hiked in the Sauvabelin

Forest. Hand in hand, they sauntered along the shaded and lakeside promenades in the park-like districts of the city. They danced in the glamorous ballroom of the Beau-Rivage and in a nightclub in the town of Flon. Often, they were with new friends that they had made at the hotel, young men and women from affluent backgrounds like their own who accepted them as the persons they said they were: a married couple.

One of these couples, Karl and Johanna Röhm, had known Gerhard during his student days in Berlin and had liked him very much. Gerhard and Karl had not seen one another for a year or two, probably because their wartime assignments had brought them to different locations in Europe. But Karl and his wife knew Gerhard as a man of the world and as a romantic idealist. They did not find themselves surprised by his telling them that he had recently married.

Like Gerhard, Karl was on leave. He was a storm trooper, drawn into that murderous cadre by his father, a bellicose Army captain who had recently made the stormtroopers a paramilitary organization. The Karl Röhm who stood before Gerhard was a different incarnation from the life-affirming youth he had known in school. So Gerhard was to tell her later that evening when she was alone with him. This variant Karl, this reinvented analogue to the original youth he had known, was blunt and cynical. Of medium height and hard, wiry frame, he did not look Aryan. His dark hair, olive complexion, and aquiline nose hinted at a family history that included Algerians and Jews. Karl never before had admitted to such a genealogy, nor would he have reason to admit to that history now, when the Nazis were hunting down Jews and Algerians and working to make Germany exclusively Aryan. On leave from his brutal assignments, he was—for the most part—shrewd enough to avoid any talk of politics or of the war. Only once, when he and Gerhard were sharing a drink at the hotel bar, did he mention the war. They were there with Simone and Johanna, enjoying a cocktail before going forward to an evening that included a dinner with Cordon Bleu propensities and hours of dancing in the sumptuous hotel ballroom.

"This is Germany's time," Karl said, swallowing his second whiskey as efficiently as he had his first. He had been speaking of the Germans' recent successes against their adversaries in North Africa, in France, and in Great Britain. There was in his demeanor a haunted look and the hardened creases of care-worn grimness.

Subdued yet incisive, Gerhard pushed him to say more, all the while challenging his too-easy assessment of their country's status.

"What time is that?" he asked. "What time belongs to

Germany?"

"A time to conquer," Karl answered him. "A time to make the world our own."

Johanna, with her light brown hair, pale skin, and blue, inquiring eyes, smiled with enthusiasm. Her gleaming white teeth and her moist, painted lips punctuated the smile. She looked older and harder, Simone imagined, than the schoolgirl Gerhard remembered. Yet the hint of a tremor in her smoky voice and her excessive drinking of wine belied the confident manner she had imposed upon her immaculately-groomed appearance.

"It's a wonderful period for us," she exclaimed. "It's wonderful to be young and to be German."

To this apparently light-hearted remark, Gerhard lifted his whiskey glass in a respectful gesture of salute.

"To Germany," he said.

But he quickly changed the subject. Clearly (she noticed), he did not care to hear the Röhms speak of the war. Instead, while addressing himself to her and to Johanna, he began to speak of the years in which he and Karl, while on summer recess from their rigorous obligations at a military school, had explored the world in the company of two or three other classmates. With a smooth cordiality that subverted his ambivalent feelings about his former schoolmate, he was careful to draw from Karl comments about their travels that she found as vivid as his own.

During that period, the two of them—with three other friends—had shared adventures that lifted their spirit and validated their masculine proficiencies. Together, they had traversed the Larrapinta Trail in Australia. For fifteen days, they had hiked for one hundred thirty-eight miles along red ridges and through deep gorges of the West MacDonnell Ranges. They encountered emerald-and-blue parrots flashing through the gum trees. They also saw rock wallabies, sacred Aboriginal sites like the Fish Hole, and the kangaroos that the Australians called euros. During a later summer, he and Karl and the three other youths had hunted snow lions in a remote corner of northern Mongolia. Days afterward, in the grassy valleys of the Arhangay region, they participated in a festival of wrestling, archery, and horse racing. More recently, from a ninety-seven foot yacht, they had dived and snorkeled in the Galápagos Islands of Ecuador. On those days, they swam safely with hundreds of scalloped hammerheads and eagle rays.

As the two men spoke of their adventures to Johanna and to her, she noticed that—with quicksilver aptitudes— genuine happiness was transforming Gerhard's face. His blue eyes gleamed, and the laughter that was a fuse to his expression was as exuberant as it was spontaneous.

That evening, while she suppressed her guilt at having enjoyed so completely an hour of love with him in the heightened privacies of their hotel bedroom, she learned even more about the person that he had once been. Outside the capacious window, the moon with its profusion of light hurried past the French door that opened to the balcony and hurried, as well, into the exquisite symmetries of the room. As if they were stipples of color quickened by her glance, the elliptical imagery of canvases on the wall, richly upholstered sofas and chairs, and an Aubusson carpet rose before her seeing. The light of the moon revealed more completely Gerhard's supremely masculine nakedness and the delicate contours of her own nakedness, as well. They were leaning against a galaxy of pillows, there in the ample bed, smoking French cigarettes and musing languorously after their vigorous lovemaking.

"I was free then," Gerhard said ruefully, as he recalled once more the years in which, as a keen-minded and athletic student, he had enjoyed life-loving and adventurous summers. "The whole world was a wonderful promise. But I've lost all of it. The war has robbed me of nearly everything."

"In war, you do the things that you are told to do," she said.

She spoke the words with gentle conviction, though she was not yet certain that she should believe in him.

"What I have been told to do is to kill," he said. "Not because I want to kill, but because my country tells me that it is necessary."

Hearing his confession, she remained very still. She could not find the words that would push her to ask whether he had killed women and children and Jews.

"When I have to fire upon enemy pilots during combat missions, I try not to think of them as human. I think of them as metal targets. I imagine that they are things and not men as young and as trapped by the war as I am. It is not good for one's soul to watch human beings explode as their bombed aircraft falls apart."

She saw that the pleasure he had felt during and right after their intercourse had left him now. The sheer joy of love was being displaced by his conflicted feelings about the war and about his ambivalent participation in that chaos.

Not even the fragrance of her body next to his or his casual inhaling of the cigarette brought him comfort. They were, she thought, nearly invisible reference points for the sullen moments he was experiencing. Now she compelled herself to speak the words that might persuade him to tell her more.

"You are not the first man to fight a war in which you do not believe," she said. "There are many men who have fought not because they believe in a war, but because they believe in their country. Perhaps you are one of them."

He leaned silently into his pillows and watched the smoke of their cigarettes float in vaporous rings about them. He was, she guessed, reflecting upon her words and weighing the sum of their truth.

"I believe in Germany," he told her, "but I do not believe in Hitler. At heart, I am not a Nazi. I do not think that it is necessary for my country to take over the world."

She wanted to ask him whether he had killed Jews and other innocent people. But the fear that he might confess to such killings gave her pause. She wanted to believe in his goodness. She wanted a reason for rescuing him from Marc's assassination plan.

Her fear kept her from saying the words that she should have spoken. Instead, she chose temporizing words, words meant to encourage this unhappy man beside her.

"The war won't last forever," she said.

"No," he answered her. "It will end one day. But, if I live through it, I don't know whether I will ever find my way back to the man I was becoming before the war."

He took one last puff on his cigarette and then crushed its remnant in the ashtray on the table by his bed. Summoning a smile, he turned to her and gently kissed her eyes and her face and her mouth. The kisses brought him back to their hour of pleasure. Satisfied by the memory of it, he placed his large, warm hand upon her belly and held it there for an instant. Then, allowing his weariness to overtake him, he turned away and fell into sleep.

With a vague pity and a furtive wish that it would be all right for her to believe in him, she lay beside Gerhard, sleepless and worried. To find a proper reason to save him from Marc's revenge, she would have to find out more of the truth about Gerhard in the days that were too swiftly coming upon them.

She wondered whether her knowing the truth would save Gerhard. She could not know then that, to discover who he really was, she would not have to wait long.

At the end of their first week at the Beau-Rivage, she and Gerhard made a journey to Graubünden. So eager was Gerhard to replicate the memorable experiences which he had known in Switzerland that he persuaded her to make a journey with him to this southeast area of the country, which bordered on Liechtenstein and Austria to the north and Italy to the east and south. They would be gone from the Beau-Rivage only for a few days and would be staying at another fine hotel. She remembered having visited Graubünden years earlier with her mother and her father, when she was a nine-year-old girl. That her return to this place would recall a happier period in her life intrigued her.

Graubünden did not disappoint her. How swiftly, upon seeing its Alpine beauty, did her childhood visits come back to color anew her memories of the place. Its folded landscape of deep, isolated valleys, its sheer rocky summits, and its thick pine forests still possessed, as an imprint on the landscape which was visible now only to her eyes, the imagery of herself with her father and her mother horse-riding or hiking or traveling in a Bentley all around the country. As a child, it had fascinated her to see glaciers oozing from between the high mountains. It was these glaciers, her mother had explained, that launched two of Europe's great rivers (the Rhine and the Inn) on their way to the North Sea and to the Black sea, respectively. On that trip, she had also seen two smaller rivers watering pomegranates, figs, and chestnuts in secluded southern valleys. Those rivers, her father reminded her, were en route to the Po and the Gulf of Venice.

The memory affected her more deeply than she had expected. Though it had given her glimpses of her parents and of herself as an innocent child, the recollection left her uneasy once more. It showed her how much of her best self she had lost. For this reason, she did not care to linger within these scenes of the past, even when they included the picturesque amenities of Graubünden. Besides, her years working for the Resistance had trained her to disdain nostalgia as a self-defeating weakness. She prodded herself now to see Graubünden without the emotional sub-texts that, against her conscious will, were making her feel a complicity with Gerhard's belief that he had lost the only self he cared to cultivate. Instead, she saw Graubünden matter-of-factly. She recognized it as the landscape of her childhood and not as a scene that invited her to calculate her current losses. She had been happy in the years when she had first visited the area. She had been happy later, when she and Marc had spent their winter vacations here. Whether she would be happy again here or in any of the other locations to which chance and fate led her, she did not know. Nor did she need to know. What she needed to know was whether Gerhard had killed innocent Jews and Swedes. Only then would she know the next step she had to take.

On the pretext that she was eager to see more of Graubünden, she influenced Gerhard to go forward to St. Moritz in the Engadine valley, with its undulating ski runs and its tobogganing races on Muottas Muragl, with its polo tournaments on a frozen lake, and with its lilting music festival. She had never before visited this part of Graubünden when she was a child traveling with her parents. Their images belonged to later episodes that had paired her with Marc.

Though contentment and even exhilaration often touched their days here, she sensed within Gerhard a muted forlornness, a pensive stillness that was anchored to dismay and sorrow. Not even his furious game of polo on a frozen lake or the bravura risk-taking of his skiing through the steep-sloping intricacies of the Engadine Valley could ease his troubled mind beyond the swift hours that activated his competitive spirit and his superb athleticism. Nor on the day when she joined him in a tobogganing race or during the evenings when they were dancing at the Grand Hotel did he seem himself. Some burden was weighing him down. A sadness like remorse or unresolved dismay was clouding whatever temporary happiness his leave time had brought him.

"What is wrong?" she gently asked him one morning after she had been awakened by his tossing and turning beside her in bed and by his hastening out of his sleep to cry his alarm and his hostility toward some remembered adversary.

"It's not true!" he shouted as he punched the air with his

rugged right arm and his clenched fist. "It's not true!"

"Tell me what is wrong," she said, her voice hushed by her wary witness of him and by the genteel nature of her petition.

She had risen from her pillows right after he had sprung forward from his place next to her. Only then did she place her hand on his shoulder and speak her soft words to him.

He, in turn, had come fully awake. Glancing at her momentarily as if he needed to be certain of who she was, he at first said nothing. Only when she petitioned him once more, did he answer her.

"Tell me," she said. "Tell me so that I can help you."

"It's nothing," he said. "It's nothing you need to worry about."

"But I do worry," she said. "I love you, and I want to make everything easier for you."

By this time, he had tossed the covers away from his nakedness and was sitting on the edge of the bed, lighting a cigarette. The curve of his strong back and the taut energy of his massive arms enhanced his nakedness. Even in this moment of apprehension, he appeared neither vulnerable nor hesitant.

She hurried from her side of the bed and clothed her own nakedness with a silk nightgown and robe she had thrown over the arm of a nearby chair, which was stitched in needlepoint and complemented the sumptuousness of the room. Then she took hold of the robe he had thrown over the arm of a companion chair and found a sitting place beside him as she helped him to cover himself with the warmth of the robe.

She could see his face now, alert and brooding and self-questioning. As he rose from his place, so that he could allow the robe to envelop his frame, the cigarette dangled from the corner of his mouth. In profile, he looked tough-minded and militant. With hair-trigger proficiency, he had escaped from his nightmare and was ready once again to deal with the world on his own terms.

She believed this was how it was with him, having attained a little knowledge at least of men whom the world had bruised with all manner of betrayals.

She invited him to sit beside her once again at the edge of the bed. Extending her hand to meet his, she drew him to her delicate fragrance and to the warmth of her smile.

"Tell me," she asked him while softly echoing her previous request. "Tell me what has upset you."

"You would not enjoy hearing it," he said.

"I am not weak," she said. "Besides, telling me about it may help you."

He took a drag of his cigarette and silently considered

her willingness to become implicated in his sadness. Then, as he held her in his searching gaze, he began speaking of the memory that called back a bitter sorrow that he had suppressed for many years.

"Seven years ago, when I was training as an officer candidate in the Junkerschule, I made a friend that I came to think of as my alter-ego. His name was Reuben Feld. He looked uncannily like me. He was just as tall, tow-haired and athletic as I was. He, too, wanted to be an aeronautical engineer. In fact, his father owned one of the major aircraft corporations. It was my friendship with Reuben and, eventually my acquaintance with his father, which reinforced my plan to build airplanes, once I completed my military service.

"I thought that Reuben would be my life-long friend. We even spoke of collaborating on the design of high-concept aircraft for his father's company. That happy dream sustained me during my roughest Junkerschule days and, later, during an even more dangerous period when we were selected for pilot training in the Luftwaffe. Neither Reuben nor I wanted especially to be a part of the military. We didn't want to be caught up in the political scene or trapped by the army or air force life that our fathers thought would expedite our later paths to success as civilians. They believed that, if we did not volunteer to be trained as soldiers or as pilots, the Nazi government would eventually compel us to fulfill our military obligations. But Hitler and his henchmen would think far less of us for waiting to be forced into our duty."

Gerhard paused.

She could see that he was debating about whether he should go on with the telling of his story. With the feminine grace and genteel voice that, she knew, he regarded as among her most endearing qualities, she drew away from her place at his side and made her way to the bar in their reception room. She hoped that he would follow her. The ghosts that haunted him on this night in the bedroom would, she imagined, haunt him as terribly in all the other rooms of their penthouse.

"You'll feel better when you have a drink," she said, calling out her words to him just before she left their bedroom. "And so will I. It may be easier for you to say what you want to tell me. And easier for me to listen."

He did follow her into the reception room. But the powers of his will that had worked for so many years to suppress his memory of Reuben Feld now rose to assist him once more.

"It's a story better left untold," he said. "It's a story that you don't need to hear."

She poured him a double scotch and poured herself a

glass of Chardonnay. She was not surprised at the quickness with which he drank his scotch. Nor was she surprised when he poured himself another. Once again she placed her hand lovingly on his shoulder. Clearly, she wanted him to see that she was concerned about him.

"You may feel better by sharing your story with me," she said. "I want to help you. I want to make things better for you. But, before I can do that, I need to know what is troubling you."

Her words, a blend of her ambivalent love and her willful testing of him, coaxed him forward. He trusted her sympathy, because—she guessed—his love for her was not cloaked in disguise or hesitation.

He hurried now to tell her all of the story, translating it through words that were as clipped as they were incisive.

"Even now it is difficult to tell what happened to Reuben," he said. "But the story does not take long to tell. Nor, I suppose, is it unusual, when we consider the political climate in Germany today.

"For three years, Reuben was a fellow cadet, a loyal friend, and an altogether positive influence upon my life. For three years, we navigated the same risks, explored the same essential territories, and pushed our courage and our stamina as far as they could be pushed. Then, as if overnight, he was no longer there. The Luftwaffe leaders expelled him, and I could not understand why. Reuben Feld was unacceptable, they said. When I asked them to explain, they threatened me with my own expulsion.

"'He is unacceptable,' they said once again. 'That is all you need to know.'

"Weeks later, I asked my father whether, as a general in the army, he could discover why Reuben, who was at the top of our class in everything, should be expelled from a military program that had always before recognized his merit.

"'There is no need for me to play detective,' my father told me, disdainful and forbidding. 'I know all about the Feld case—not only about the son, but also about the entire family.'

"We were on vacation in northern Brazil, where on the following morning with eight men from the Araweté tribe we would be tracking jaguars in the rain forests of the Amazon. My father and some of our guides were cleaning and loading their rifles. The sky at sunset kept unfolding its crimson layers, lending an Otherworldly glow to the camp that we had made, there within the rugged terrain along the Xingu River. If my father noticed that sunset at all, he did so indifferently. In that moment when I had asked him why Reuben had been expelled from pilot-training school, he saw only my misdirected sympathies.

"'Your Reuben Feld and his father passed themselves off as uncontaminated Germans,'" he declared. "'But they are nothing of the kind. Their name is Feldstein, not Feld. They are more Jewish than they are German and unacceptable for being so.'

"'It's not true,' I protested. 'It's not true. Mr. Feld has done wonderful things for Germany. He has designed new planes. He has provided jobs for thousands of people. He has donated large sums of money to worthwhile institutions and charities. He has followed all the rules. And so has Reuben. He was the best in all our classes at school.'

"'They are Jews, and there is no place for their kind in the new Germany that we Nazis are creating.'

"'But what the country is doing is wrong,' I said. 'The Jews have been doing valuable things for our country.'

"Seated before a bench-like table that the guides had placed not far from the waters of the river, my father went on cleaning his rifle. Hearing my words, he frowned. Clearly, he was displeased. But he remained understated nonetheless and in militant control of the anger that I might otherwise have roused in him.

"'You're being sentimental and weak-willed. Stop being a fool. You'll only succeed in getting yourself into trouble and endangering my life, too. In the new Germany, you are an uncontaminated German or you are not a German at all. You are a loyal Nazi, or you are not a Nazi at all. That is the way things are. Those are the rules. Remember them if you want to go on being acceptable.'

"This time I frowned. In my heart, I was not a Nazi, and I was a German in a country that was no longer the Germany I knew and loved and respected."

Gerhard paused once more, but only for a moment. He crushed the remnant of his cigarette into a Murano blue ashtray that with geometric curves gleamed on the counter of the bar. Then he pushed himself into new and more abrasive words.

"My father ordered me to forget Reuben. In fact, he gave me an ultimatum. If I ever mentioned him again or expressed my sympathy for any other Jews, he would disown me and then report me to government officials.

"'You would not be worthy to be my son,' he said. 'You would have disgraced our name and destroyed everything that I have built.'

"So I trained myself to forget Reuben and to turn away from the Jewish problem," Gerhard said. "I have followed all the rules. I have been a good pilot and an effective squad leader. I have fought the fight that the Nazis want me to fight.

"But this afternoon, here in Graubünden, it all came back to me. Reuben and I used to ski here whenever we were on leave from school. I have not really forgotten him. He exists still in my soul."

She wanted to know more.

"Do you know what happened to him?" she asked. "Did he and his family leave Germany?"

The stillness that had haunted Gerhard for days took hold of him once more. Only after he had poured himself another scotch and swallowed it quickly did he answer her.

"They never got the chance," he said. "They were arrested shortly after Reuben's expulsion from the Luftwaffe. They were sent to a concentration camp in Belsen, and all of them died there."

She watched the stillness take hold of him once again. Perhaps he was collaborating with the stillness as a way to tighten his hold upon his senses.

"How sad for you," she said. She placed her supple hand within his large and rugged one. Without any other words, she was urging him to tell her more.

He squeezed her hand, acknowledging their solidarity.

"Yes," he said. "Almost everything is sad for me, except you. It is sad that I have lost my best friend. It is sad that I have lost the Germany that I loved and still love, the Germany of great scientists and composers and political leaders. That Germany was often compassionate and respected diverse cultures. At least some of the time, it worked for peace and strove for equality."

It was now, in this uneasy moment when Gerhard was revealing to her the truths about his past that he had tried to hide even from himself, that she said the words which for her subtle inquiry were the most important of all.

"If, to you, Germany has become some foreign country, then the Gerhard Hauptmann that you were creating before the war must also be a stranger to you. To stay alive, you've had to follow all the rules. You've even had to kill Jews."

He glanced at her in a new way, surprised that she would imagine that he was involved in so heinous a crime. But he answered her without anger and without hesitation.

"No, I have never done that," he said. "I've never killed women or children or any other Jew. Nor will I, ever. The Nazis can hang me or shoot me. I will never become a hater or a killer of Jews. I am a pilot fighting to preserve whatever can be preserved for the good Germany in which I believe. I kill enemies who are firing upon me. I am not proud of it. But I cannot be anyone except a German. I am fighting for a future in which Germany will not be altogether destroyed. I am fighting for a future that may never exist."

He took two cigarettes from the gold case that he found in the pocket of his robe. Then, while offering her one of them and smoothly lighting it, he lit the one hanging from the corner of his mouth. Quietly, he inhaled the scented tobacco, all the while studying her sympathetic face. She could see that he was going to tell her even more.

"Parents are traps, and countries are traps," he said. "I've never learned how to escape from their traps. The only thing that I've learned is that I cannot be myself without my father or without Germany. Yet I cannot be myself with them."

She caressed him now and kissed him, touching his lips with her lips.

"You've had a rough time," she said. "But I'm here to make things better for you."

He brought her lips to his once more, this time meeting them with a passionate kiss. Clearly he was grateful for her being there, empathetic and true.

"You're good for what ails me," he said, allowing himself a fleet smile. He wanted to lighten the mood now. He wanted to rid himself of his bleak thoughts.

"Let's leave Graubünden," she said. "Let's leave your ghosts behind. Tomorrow we'll go back to the Beau-Rivage and have a good time."

She was not surprised that he agreed so readily. Nor, on the following morning, was she surprised at the efficiency with which they made their departure from the area. She had greeted the day with a feeling that was close to exhilaration. Gerhard was innocent of the murder of the Jews. Because of that reason and because she loved Gerhard, she must prevent Marc from killing him. Once they returned to the Beau-Rivage, she would find an excuse for hurrying Gerhard away from that scene. She was not apprehensive. The danger for Gerhard had not yet closed in upon them. They were still safe. Marc, she believed, would not arrive for three or four days. A private telephone call that she made to the Beau-Rivage confirmed her belief. She and Gerhard had time to share two more nights together.

She could not know that, by the time she and Gerhard were returning to the hotel, Marc was already there. He had arrived earlier than she had anticipated. At the Beau-Rivage, furtive and murderous, he was waiting for them

Chapter Seven

Marc's Revenge

While Simone and Gerhard were in Graubünden, Marc arrived unobtrusively in Switzerland. He spent the first day of his leave at his parents' chalet in Geneva. There, within the comfortable privacies of a familiar scene, he gave himself over to the sleep that would fortify his physical agility and the hair-trigger actions he would need to put into motion if he was to attack Gerhard effectively.

He was running three days ahead of schedule. He had completed his latest combat assignments in eleven days. He believed that Simone had not yet arrived in Lausanne. She was probably en route from Derbyshire. As they had planned, she would join him two or three days before Gerhard checked into the Beau-Rivage.

No one else was at the chalet, not even the custodial staff who maintained the property while his parents were away. From their modest homes in a nearby village, they came to the chalet on Mondays and Fridays, unless his vacationing parents or their guests were occupying the chalet. Then the staff would offer their services every day. Wednesdays, he knew, was one of the days when the groundskeeper and the housekeeper and one or two others who assisted them were free from their obligations to the chalet.

For fourteen hours, he slept deeply. The unforgiving combat missions that he had navigated and the deaths of three comrades who had perished under enemy fire had taken their toll. Not even his inflexible resolve to kill Gerhard or the brutal scenarios of the murderous scene which he often summoned could keep him from the long hours of sleep that for him had become as necessary as they were reinvigorating.

When he awoke, a few minutes before midnight, he showered and shaved with military precision. The caustic image he saw in the mirror was a way to separate himself from the more acceptable, if enigmatic, face that had usually appeared there. Tonight, that Marc Roussillon did not exist. Nor, in this solitary hour, did his visionary plans to design modern cities or to build extraordinary houses exist. The wilderness that he was entering involved no dreams at all. Only his private enemy lived there, and the woman who had become an anguished obsession. As skillfully as he could and as swiftly, he would rid himself of that enemy and claim the woman once again as belonging to him alone. Malevolent and determined, he forced himself to drink some coffee and to eat a bit of the still-moist holiday fruit-bread that the cook had stored within a cake-tin inside the kitchen cupboard. Then he hurried into the dark folds of night, eager to get on with things.

He drove to Lausanne in an Aston-Martin, which his comrade from the French resistance, Denis Vidon, had rented in the name of Julien Deneuve. He was the same friend who had delivered to his rooms in the Beau-Rivage the trunks that held the concealed weapons which would make his imagined scenario of Gerhard's end a grim reality.

Because he was a cousin of Jean-Claude, Denis found a special pleasure in helping Marc to kill a Nazi. As a pilot in his and Jean-Claude's squadron, he had killed many Nazis in aerial combat. But they had been anonymous enemies, the individuality of each of them effaced by the aggregate power of the Luftwaffe. Never before had he been involved in the killing of a Nazi whose identity was known to him. Though Gerhard Hauptmann had not been one of the Nazis who had tortured and nearly destroyed Jean-Claude, he was a Nazi nonetheless. That he was the son of a general whom Adolf Hitler regarded as an essential military advisor made his murder of Gerhard even more significant. So Marc told him when he first approached Denis about his plan. The murder would be not merely an act of vengeance; it would be an act of justice. Whatever he could do to assist him in the killing would be, Denis told him, a validation of his respect for his cousin, whom the Nazis had beaten, maimed and partially crippled. Before they freed Jean-Claude in exchange for the release of one of their important field officers, they had broken his arms and his legs. Even now, months after he had endured several intricate surgeries on his arms and his legs at a hospital in London, Jean-Claude was not yet able to raise his arms above his head or to walk without the assistance of a cane. Though his physicians promised that one day he might be able to use his arms nimbly and to walk unimpaired and unassisted, he would have to endure many more surgeries and years of physical therapy. Aware of his plight, Denis did not hesitate to enter the dangerous zone in which he would help him, Jean-Claude's best friend, to assassinate the only son of a Nazi general.

By the time he arrived at the hotel, Marc was considering once again the place in Gerhard's body where he would fire the bullets from his Beretta pistol or his Enfield revolver. The thought intensified his anticipation of the moment. He was certain that, when Gerhard arrived at the Beau-Rivage within the next two or three nights, he would kill him.

He was not dismayed nor was he surprised that, when he first arrived at the hotel around two-thirty that night, Gerhard and Simone were not there. Surprise and dismay overtook him several minutes later, as he began questioning the porter.

The young porter, who had accompanied him into the elevator and carried his single traveling bag to the suite of rooms that had been prepared for him, accepted as natural and pertinent his questions about the quality of skiing in this specific week, about the possibility of his joining a team of snow-boarders, and about playing polo on a frozen lake. When they emerged from the elevator and were standing outside the door to the rooms that he had reserved, he asked this same youthful porter the identity of his neighbors across the hall. He asked the question casually, enhancing his inquiry with his speculation that they might be friends of his. Though he had never before stayed at the Beau-Rivage, many of his friends spent weeks and whole months here.

"Captain and Mrs. Hauptmann occupy those rooms," the porter told him. "But they are not there now. They have gone to see friends in Graubünden."

The news gave him pause. Disguising his anger, he gave the youth a handsome gratuity even as he refused his offer to bring him scotch or whiskey or rum, though the hotel bar had closed for the night. He intended to keep sober, so that with keen-minded accuracy he would bring to completion the plot against Gerhard that was already in motion.

There was still one more preliminary step he needed to take. It involved the words that he now spoke to the porter.

"Tell the desk clerk that I do not want anyone to know that I have arrived," he said. "I have so many friends staying in the hotel who would expect me to socialize with them right away. But I need a few days of rest. I'm very tired."

"I understand, sir," the porter said as he took his leave of him. "The management will see to it that your privacy is respected."

The next day, when Simone telephoned the hotel from Graubünden and inquired about Julien Deneuve, the man that Marc was impersonating, the desk clerk abided by Marc's request.

"He is not here," the clerk politely told her. "He has not yet arrived."

Through all of that night and for most of the following day, Marc secluded himself inside the flowing space of the rooms that stood as if watching his every move, a brooding privacy like imminent storm and threatening. While he waited for Simone and Gerhard to return, the idea that Simone had played him false burned into his soul and roused in him even more furiously his need to kill Gerhard. He planned to do more than that. He would force Simone to watch him as he killed the Nazi. A tentative hatred for her flared up in him, drawn from his distrust of her and the darker and more ambivalent subtexts of his obsession. They were drawn, too, from his surprise and anger that she had not killed Gerhard while she was alone with him, here at the Beau-Rivage. She had killed Nazis before, and she had killed the French traitors who were working for them. She could be tough-minded and street-wise, if a dangerous and necessary assignment required her to be so. Before he hurried on to his latest combat missions, he had persuaded her to see Gerhard for what he was. In fact, Simone had hurried into the days that would bring her into Lausanne and to her complicity in the death of Gerhard. He had roused in her a permanent hatred of Gerhard. At least, he thought it would be permanent.

But, when she became aware that he could not in a timely manner join her at the Beau-Rivage, why did Simone not kill Gerhard? Did her love for him, newly influenced by his presence, dissuade her from the plan that they—as husband and wife—had agreed to carry forward?

He wondered, his furious heart beating in rhythms more turbulent even than the ones he knew in combat.

It was in these moments that he became convinced that Simone's withdrawal to Graubünden with Gerhard was the first step in their running away together to Germany. She was content to be his mistress and to inhabit a life of sensual pleasures and makeshift compromises. So enraged was he by this thought, that he nearly persuaded himself to hasten away from the hotel into Graubünden. There, armed with a Colt snub-nosed revolver or a Beretta pistol, he would kill Gerhard very quickly.

But the thought that he might kill him here at the Beau-Rivage, according to the plan that he had carefully devised, checked the trajectory of his rage and this alternate plot, which he now dismissed as both impulsive and subversive of his need to avenge himself against this Nazi.

So he waited quietly in his rooms, listening for the voices that the privacies of the hall would welcome as familiar and as altogether appropriate. Because there were only two apartments in this wing, he expected to hear the mellow voice of a woman and know that it belonged to Simone. He was waiting to hear as well the imagined gravel-voiced timbres of a man he had not yet seen or heard, though he was planning to kill him on the evening of his return.

Simone and Gerhard returned to the hotel around noon of the following day. Marc heard her first of all, there in the corridor outside the door to his rooms. She was laughing lightly, the timbres of her voice fused with her elation and with the poise that had become a defining characteristic.

As he listened to her, resentful and bitter, he recognized her happiness. These days, it was a rare thing for her to laugh so openly. She had not laughed with him for a long time. In this hour, when he knew her once more, her laughter was filled with joy and with love for the man who was accompanying her into the luxurious rooms that they were sharing across the hall from where he stood, an invisible presence, behind his closed door.

"You have become my splendid temptation," he heard her tell Gerhard in a low silky voice that sounded breathless and whispering.

It was now that he heard Gerhard's voice for the first time. It was a deep, husky sound that he heard, even though Gerhard had also kept his voice low. His inflections teased Simone with their intimacy, even though he had softened them because he did not want the porter to hear him. That young man (who sounded different from the youth whom Marc had casually questioned on the previous evening) was in this moment opening the door to their rooms. He imagined that the porter was hurrying ahead of them, while carrying into their apartment the suitcases they had brought with them from Graubünden.

"I'll always want to be your temptation," Gerhard said to her, matter-of-fact yet sensual nonetheless. "Then I will be certain that I have kept some of my mystery. It is the mystery that will hold you to me. As long as you don't fathom it completely, I shall be very safe. You will never leave me while I remain a mystery to you."

Marc heard these romantic words and was instantly filled with contempt for them. They were the kind of words that he had never used with Simone. Before this trouble involving Gerhard, they had always been straightforward with each other. There had been no need to invoke romantic innuendos or to invent a heightened language that made of their love something stylized and artificial. The love they shared required no artifice. A look, a gesture, or a special touch was the only language they required.

Simone laughed lightly once more, the modulations of another of her private endearments beyond his hearing. What he heard was the honeyed texture of her speech as they entered the apartment and closed the door behind them.

So angered was he by the easy and romantic way through which Simone and Gerhard collaborated with one another, that immediately after the porter had left them he would have barged into their rooms and shot Gerhard. But two waiters were suddenly in the hall, bringing lunch and cocktails to the two of them, whom they must have perceived as glamorous and extraordinary. They also brought lunch for two Swiss visitors who may have been friends of Gerhard and who arrived ten minutes after their hosts. That Gerhard was sharing lunch with them in his suite of rooms, rather than in the hotel dining area, suggested that the two visiting gentlemen could have been bankers or lawyers with whom he had to confer about private business matters. His allowing Simone to remain present while he conversed with these men indicated both the trust and the respect he had for her.

Even when he heard these men leave Gerhard's apartment, he thought that he could rush into those rooms and take Gerhard by surprise. But his wiliness reminded him that the night, with its shrouded privacies and its absence of waiters and porters and intrusive guests, would favor his carrying forward his murderous plan. Besides, shortly after Gerhard's business guests had left, he and Simone hurried away from their apartment. Perhaps, they were going to ski or to join a toboggan race or to skate on a frozen lake.

At the thought that they would be enjoying themselves as if they were actually married or because they were such passionate lovers, he bristled.

Brooding anew and wrathful, he summoned the stern

self-control that the disappointments of his early life and the militant training of more recent years had taught him well. There would be time to carry his plan through. He had only to wait a few more hours before he could permit himself to spring with hair-trigger aptitudes upon this enemy who called himself Gerhard Hauptmann. Gerhard might, he thought, better call himself an indoctrinated Nazi and Simone's wayward lover. Just as realistically, he might call himself a man who was nearly finished with time. First of all, though, he should call himself a targeted man.

It was nearly midnight when Simone and Gerhard returned to their apartment. Once more, their voices were excited, but this time their enthusiasm rode upon the air vivid and unconstrained. Concealed by the door to his own rooms, Marc heard them with a fury that he was able to harness effectively only because he was certain that he would kill Gerhard within the next hour or two.

Earlier in the afternoon, shortly after Simone and Gerhard had left the apartment, he had used the duplicate key which Simone had wrapped in a small gift package and, from a postal station in the city, had mailed to the Beau-Rivage. She had addressed the package to Julien Deneuve, the fictive person whose nebulous identity he had embodied upon arriving at the hotel. The package was waiting for him on the evening that he showed a quick imagery of himself to the desk clerk and to the young porter.

That he had not remained in Gerhard and Simone's apartment, once he had successfully entered it, had much to do with his conjecture that a hotel maid might enter the room to turn down the bed covers and, by chance, find him concealed within the walk-in closet or standing in the darkness of an adjoining room. Unfavorable chance might also draw to the room a waiter or a bellhop right after Gerhard and Simone had made their return. Marc did not want to kill anyone except Gerhard, though he would not hesitate to kill others if he had to.

As much as his hatred of Gerhard tempted him to do so, he decided against waiting for him here in the apartment where he would attack him.

But he had put the key to good use. With it, he had entered the apartment and had stayed long enough to survey the particulars of its environment with keen-minded awareness.

He waited, instead, while enclosed within the privacies of his own rooms. Nor was he surprised that, immediately after Gerhard and Simone returned to their apartment, a waiter did arrive with (he imagined) a magnum of Champagne or with a bottle of vodka or scotch.

He waited for two hours, pacing the reception room of his apartment like an angered tiger or like an all-too-human assassin who had primed himself for the murder of an enemy and who was at this time only vaguely sickened by his need to hurry into the murder.

When, at last, he opened his door and peered about the corridor, he saw that the hour favoring his plan had arrived. The luxurious appointments of this flowing space— the plush of a thick carpet, the delicacy of an Impressionist canvas, and the idealized male anatomy of a Roman statue—might ordinarily have satisfied his love of beauty and of order. But tonight he noticed them only as fleet stipples of color upon his senses. He was mainly aware of the stillness that had taken hold of the corridor. That same stillness lived, or so he thought, beyond the closed door to the rooms where he imagined Gerhard and Simone lay sleeping, sated and comforted by their vigorous lovemaking.

With smooth adeptness, he opened the door to their apartment and hurried inside. The full moon illumined the large reception room even more than did the dimly lighted lamp that stood on a table by the sofa. But the semi-darkness did not matter. He had learned much from his secret visit to the apartment. More than a raveling montage, the imagery of these rooms was impressed upon his mind like an accurate blueprint or a clearly defined map.

He was wearing a cobalt-blue shirt, charcoal-grey slacks, and his pilot's bomber jacket that had large exterior pockets as well as pockets within pockets on the inside of the jacket. The brown penny-loafers that he wore allowed him to move soundlessly across the Aubusson carpet. Nor did the weapons he was carrying on his person make any sound. He wore a V-42 stiletto inside a leather sheath that was strapped to the lower part of his right leg. Within the inside pockets of his jacket, he had securely placed a 1908 Colt Vest Pocket semi-automatic pistol and a Colt Cobra .38 snub-nosed revolver. He had chosen to carry in his right hand an Enfield No. 2 Mk I revolver, known for its lighter weight and its minimal recoil. The spurless hammer of this Enfield model could not be thumb-cocked by the marksman for each shot. Instead, the revolver was configured for rapid double-action fire. It was a British gun that used a long and heavy round-nose bullet in a .38 caliber cartridge. Minimally stabilized for its weight and caliber, the Enfield Mk I bullet "keyholed" or tumbled longitudinally when striking a target. It increased the wounding and stopped the ability of human targets at short ranges.

This Enfield would serve him well. With it, he would fire several bullets into Gerhard's body.

He passed like an invisible spirit through the living room and by the first and smaller of the bedrooms that was reserved for any guests that the registered occupants of these rooms had invited to stay with them. The long corridor that he had entered was also dimly lighted by a delicately-wrought lamp that stood upon a Louis XV table at the end of the space he was traversing. The lamp and its light enhanced the mirror above it and clarified as well a pastel wall against which the table was resting.

Only when he reached the master bedroom did he pause. The moon alone illumined the room, allowing him to sight the two of them in an instant. Their bodies languorous in their nakedness, Gerhard and Simone were sleeping peacefully. Though they were not fully entwined, they leaned into one other, as though the touch of each other's skin might ease their fervid sensuality even as it quickened once more their sated appetite.

He entered the room soundlessly and knew again the lamp that stood on a table to the right of him. No sooner had he flicked on its light, than he was upon them.

Simone was the first to waken, her face surprised and then horror-stricken at the sight of him, standing there before the bed and pointing his Enfield revolver at Gerhard. She sprang up, screaming, her right arm held out as if to keep him back.

"Don't do it!" she shouted to him. "Don't do it!"

She jumped from her side of the bed and, with a tremendous leap forward, rushed to stop him from firing his revolver. The swift trajectory of her naked form flashed across his senses only momentarily. To his fleet glance, she looked vulnerable and primitive and aggressive all at the same time. But already he was firing his revolver into Gerhard's chest and into his right arm and into his right leg.

Hearing Simone's scream, Gerhard had also sprung up from his place in the bed and for the first time noticed him. A tall stranger, as sinister as he was determined, was pointing a revolver at him and was going to shoot him. Gerhard leaped from the bed. But it was too late. The first bullet, which ripped into his chest, threw him back against the ample folds of pillows. Blood and tissue and bits of flesh spattered the pillows and the sheets behind and beneath him. He tried to rise, only to be pushed back by the heaviness of his movement and by the searing pain. His body recoiled once more when a second bullet fractured a bone in his upper arm. Again blood sprayed the sheets and the pillows. His entire frame shuddered as the third bullet entered his right leg. Weaving in and out of consciousness, he saw him and, seeing, understood that death had come for him. He, Marc Roussillon was Death—here, in the form of a dark-haired stranger who, without uttering a single word, had shot him again and again. Vaguely, Gerhard noticed that he was still pointing his revolver at him when Simone, having reached the place where he stood, grappled with him. For less than a minute, she held onto the rugged arm that wielded the revolver.

"You mustn't do this!" she screamed. "It isn't right! It isn't right!"

Then, Gerhard lost consciousness.

In this moment, Marc released himself from Simone's hold upon his arm. Quickly, he returned his revolver to its place in the deep, front pocket of his jacket and moved closer to Gerhard. No sooner had he done so, than Simone hurried to him once again, determined to impede his movements. Her face had hardened with its fear and with its rage. Now, as she flailed her hands against his tautened muscularity, he pinioned her arms and punched her so hard that she fell across a chair by the bed. While she swooned as if going out of consciousness, he slapped her five or six times, the blows striking her one after another with staccato rhythms. This time, she did lose consciousness.

His face twisted by an ugly vengefulness and a momentary hatred even of Simone, he turned away from her to confront Gerhard once again. Even when he was beating

Simone, he had not allowed himself to lose sight of Gerhard except for the violent moments it took him to subdue her.

Gerhard lay upon the bloodstained bed, moaning now and semi-conscious. Prostrate and vanquished, he looked nonetheless like an extraordinary physical specimen. The blond hair and the chiseled features, gone ashen and pain-racked, belonged to a heroic man. The long and perfect body, with its rugged chest and its well-honed muscularity, claimed even now—in its wounded and passive condition—a stalwart magnificence.

Was it any wonder that Simone had fallen in love with him and had yearned for the days and nights when she would sleep with him? But after tonight she would sleep with him no more. After tonight, Gerhard would not be Gerhard.

So he thought, as he moved to the side of the bed where Gerhard lay semi-conscious against the pillow. His enemy's solid arms were limp now and devoid of their strength. His long, powerful legs, equally lifeless, were spread apart. A bone jutted out of the right leg, and blood was seeping out of the jagged wound that the Enfield revolver had made as it penetrated a part of the leg just below the knee.

While he lay prostrate and while his mind was weaving in and out of consciousness, Gerhard had begun to die. So, as his killer, he told himself. But he was not satisfied. He wanted to fire bullets into him again and again. He moved closer to the bed while he drew his revolver from the inside pocket of his jacket. Gerhard's penis, which usually hung ample and firm, had gone flaccid. Marc noticed it with contempt and with the bitter knowledge that, only an hour ago, he was reveling in foreplay with Simone. In that hour of pleasure—and well before entering her—his penis stood firm and erect.

This knowledge roused him to a new level of fury. Now, aiming his revolver at Gerhard's body, he fired a wild shot that grazed his right temple and, instantly afterwards, watched all the wounded parts of Gerhard bleeding profusely.

The shock of the bullet grazing his flesh drove Gerhard back into consciousness. He was not at first aware of what was happening to him. Only by lifting himself from his pillow with much effort did he discover what Marc had done to him. Only then did he open his mouth to yell his panic and rage and despair. But no sound would come. Mute and ravaged, he turned his attention to him—to his assassin. Gerhard did not know who he was or why he had come to Lausanne to kill him, far away from the territories of war that he had recently inhabited. Yet without knowing his specific identity, Gerhard recognized him as the agent of his death. Predominant and contemptuous, Marc sneered as he stood over him. He noticed the rings around his cold blue eyes and his bleak, haunted expression. Then, in that instant, Gerhard fell out of consciousness again, no longer able to bear the excruciating pain and weakened by his loss of blood. He heard a gurgle clogging his throat and watched the body shaking with convulsion. Then, almost as swiftly, a stillness took hold of the body. The eyes, half open, became glazed, staring without seeing.

Still firmly clasping his revolver, Marc looked with an eerie stillness upon the ruined body. His contorted face struggled between hatred for this enemy and revulsion for the crime he had committed. But the struggle did not prevent him from calculating the benefits he would receive because of that crime. Gerhard is dead, he thought. Now there is an end to his hold upon Simone.

His wife was only now coming back to an awareness of who she was and why she had fallen across the chair. She tried to get up, but her uncertain body pushed her back. Only after she made another attempt, wobbly and erratic, did she find herself standing near her husband. But in this moment she was not interested in him. Her fearful eyes looked, instead, toward the bed, on which Gerhard lay as if dead, bullet-riddled and blood-smeared.

A scream roared out of her, anguished and disbelieving.

But before she could scream again, he held his large, rugged hand over her mouth.

"Either you are with me," he said, "or you are with him."

He spewed out the words while he tightened his vise-like grip over her mouth. Only after she no longer resisted his hold of her would he release her. He knew that she would not give him any more trouble.

She whimpered now, her soft, jagged sobbing belonging, he thought, to some weak part of herself that she had never revealed to him. As if she were moving through a nightmare, she compelled herself to follow the directions which he issued bluntly and which sounded like military commands. Quickly, she hastened to dress and to pack her luggage. Because she was still trembling and was still unsteady, he helped her gather all her things. He wanted her to leave behind nothing that belonged to her. During this time, not one word passed between them.

Nor, when they were hurrying from the apartment, did she look back at Gerhard's body or at the eyes that stared without seeing her.

When they reached the corridor, Jean-Claude's cousin, Denis Vidon, was waiting for them. He had stood as a sentry outside the apartment while Marc shot Gerhard. Had anyone such as a house detective or an inquisitive guest entered the corridor to interrupt Gerhard, having heard the shots fired from Marc's Enfield revolver, he would have killed them. He would have helped to kill Gerhard, too, if that had become necessary. But Marc had made it clear to him that he wanted to be the only one to kill the Nazi. Because he was unaware that Simone had become Gerhard's willing lover, Denis was surprised when he heard her scream. He was even more surprised when he saw her emerging from the apartment, looking pale and stunned and stifling her low, guttural sobs. It's the female in her, he thought. In spite of her training in the Resistance, she can't tough things out the way a man can.

Dressed like a hotel porter and pushing a sleek, four-wheeled cart, he now entered the apartment and loaded Simone's luggage onto it. He paused long enough to see, with no little satisfaction, the body of the Nazi sprawled out on the bed. Just as efficiently, he left the apartment and joined Marc and Simone in the corridor. With a signal from Marc, he hurried the cart toward Marc's rooms to collect the bags waiting for him there. In fewer than three minutes, he was pushing the cart into the elevator. Marc and Simone followed. For a moment, Simone seemed as though she was going to faint. Her body caved in to itself, in spite of Marc's firm hold of her. But he shook her roughly, as if he meant to keep her awake and fully conscious.

"It's over now," he said. "It's done. Pull yourself together."

Denis noticed her body stiffening. She wants to please her husband, he thought. That she was repelled by Marc's touch never occurred to him. He remembered the many times when he and his wife, as well as Jean-Claude and his latest girlfriend, would share with Marc and Simone the adventures of skiing and sailing and piloting De Havilland DH.89s. Once, during a festival weekend in Paris, they had soared skyward together in a hot air balloon. All those happy times had occurred before the war and belonged now to a far-flung and different world. But, whether they were adventuring together in France, Italy, Switzerland, or the Benelux countries, he would always notice the natural rapport between Marc and Simone. It was a symmetry that made of their relationship a rare and beautiful thing.

So he was to tell Henri months after this night when, as a concerned father, Henri had visited him in their barracks in the Free French Air Base outside London, seeking information about his son. At that time, he had given Henri far more information than that subtle gentleman had offered him. All that Henri had allowed himself to tell him was that Marc and

Simone were in trouble. It would be to their benefit, Henri said, if Denis told him what had spurred the Nazis to send some of their most proficient killers into England to hunt down the young couple. What Henri did not tell Denis and what Denis was to learn a long time afterwards was that Henri and Marianne had noticed the tremendous wedge that had grown between Marc and Simone. Because of this enmity between them, Henri and Marianne had guessed the truth. Simone was the cause of Marc's having avenged himself against an unarmed Nazi in Switzerland. Marc had refused to speak about the matter to Henri. Nor did Simone tell Marianne that part of the story involving Gerhard until much later. But, right after he and Simone joined Henri and Marianne in England, Marc sent word to him (a loyal friend and Jean-Claude's cousin, as well) to tell Henri everything that he knew about that evening.

On the night when they left Gerhard dying, Marc, Simone and he hurried away from the hotel without any untoward incident. Chance had worked in their favor. The desk clerk, alone on duty at that late hour, had been called to the east wing of the hotel. There, with a physician from the city, he was attending the needs of an elderly British nobleman. He neither heard nor saw Marc, Simone, and him leave the hotel. Nor did he see them enter the Aston-Martin that would carry them to a private airfield and to the De Havilland which, with Marc as the pilot, would bring the three of them to London.

For the few minutes that he was in Gerhard's room, Denis had noticed even the smallest details of the violence and the danger that had occurred there. The corpse-like body in the bloodstained bed eclipsed the pristine order of the larger space of the room. The ghastly images pressed themselves upon his senses so accurately, that he felt he would never forget the scene. Even later, when he was told that Gerhard had died, the horrific scene stayed with him. In that dark hour within the hotel bedroom, he had been witnessing the aftermath of brute force and savage hatred.

So, also, when he left the hotel with Marc and Simone and guided them and their luggage into the waiting Aston-Martin, was he witnessing the aftermath of Marc's revenge that continued to play itself out as though it were an evolving montage. Never before had he seen Marc looking grey-faced and guilty and haunted. Nor had he ever seen Simone grief-struck and depleted.

"Whatever had happened in that room had changed things for them," he was to tell Henri. "I knew at once that they were lost, and I wondered whether they were also destroyed."

Chapter Eight

Afterwards

Afterwards, Simone regarded her continuing bond with Marc more clearly than ever before as an unnatural and lingering obsession that fed not only their sexual need of each other, but also their unspoken desire for some safe personal haven in a chaotic and threatening world. In the first days after she and Marc returned to England, neither of them mentioned Gerhard. But Marc's murder of him was nonetheless a dark memory that festered inside her. It compelled her to perceive their relationship as a neurotic addiction and to look upon her husband with an ambivalence that eclipsed her tarnished love of him. The love that she occasionally felt for him in this war-torn autumn was a borrowed nostalgia that derived its loyalties and pleasures from the time that they had already lived out. To keep their love from dying, she found herself invoking idealized scenes of the past that, she was aware, she and Marc could never relive with the same ardor and spontaneity.

That her need of him anchored itself to bitterness and

hatred surprised her. Never before had she imagined herself drawing away from their love. Her feelings left her anguished and guilty. They pushed her once more to face the truth. By loving Gerhard, she had betrayed Marc. She had broken the pact that had made their love an extraordinary and honest thing. She was the catalyst not only in Gerhard's gruesome death, but also in Marc's self-defeating savagery. When Marc killed Gerhard, he also killed himself. He killed that Marc Roussillon who abided by honorable rules and who, without compromising his integrity, bravely played the hand that fate dealt him.

So, in moments of clarified awareness, Simone told herself.

In the first six months after their return to England, they avoided each other. Marc stayed in the RAF barracks in Lincolnshire, about a hundred miles away from his parents' home in Derbyshire. From his air base, he flew many bombing missions and in his free time, she imagined, brooded upon the ways that each of them had destroyed their relationship. She, not caring to devise even the semblance of reconciliation, stayed away from him and, for the most part, from his parents. All the days and nights of this bleak period, she drove herself through rigorous nursing assignments in the 28th Station Hospital in Sudbury. Sleepless even during the few hours she lay weary and depleted on a cot in the nurses' quarters, she too brooded about her shattered marriage.

Sometimes Marianne would work beside her, furtively watching her with cold eyes that sought to penetrate her most secret thoughts. Hardened and bitter, she did not permit herself to be intimidated by her mother-in-law. Only afterwards, after Marc gave in to his need of her and sent her a message that he wanted to spend a free weekend with her in Derbyshire, did she reveal the new hatred that was conspiring with her love for Marc. She refused to go to him. That refusal told Marianne that her son's marriage to her was in trouble. Something irrevocable had happened between them. That it involved another man, her mother-in-law—she sensed—became more convinced as the days and weeks hurried passed them.

Simone remembered the guilty confession that she had made to Marianne nearly a year earlier, on an evening after one of the parties that her in-laws occasionally hosted. Those parties dissolved or at least deflected the gloom that had overtaken everything and everyone in this terrible period. But they did not really cheer Marc or her. The festival colors of that evening seemed a will-o'-the wisp—a flare of hope and contentment that all too soon proved fabricated and impermanent. On that same evening, haunted by the guilt that she had carried with her from her first tryst with Gerhard in

Switzerland, she told Marianne the words that she meant to keep hidden. She confessed that, to save Jean-Claude Jordan from being executed by the Germans who had captured him after they'd shot down his Avro Lancaster, she had slept with a Nazi. She did not mention that she had fallen in love with this Nazi. But she did not have to speak the words that accused her of betraying the Allies as well as herself. Marianne knew. Though she had not once uttered Gerhard's name, her mother-in-law had guessed all.

Afterwards, after Denis Vidon told Henri what he had seen in the hotel bedroom on the night that Gerhard lay dying and after Marc finally told his father why he had killed Gerhard, Marianne and Henri worked together to bring her back to Marc. It was Marianne who initiated the plan that might draw her to Marc. When, however, her mother-in-law invited her to a holiday week at her home in Derbyshire, she did not mention Marc. Her approach was far more subtle. She mentioned her daughter, instead.

"Next week, Henri and I are giving a birthday party for Nicole," Marianne told her one afternoon in June when they happened to be sitting at the same table during lunch in the hospital refectory. "She's turning fourteen and has become quite an independent young woman. I know that you will want to help us celebrate her."

At first, not even the mention of Nicole prodded her acceptance. Though there was, because of Nicole's tough-minded nature and because of her mentoring influence upon the girl, a special affinity between Marc's sister and herself, she declined Marianne's invitation.

"I'll be on duty all that week," she said.

"You don't have to be," Marianne insisted. "You've earned so much leave time that nobody here is going to keep you from enjoying a brief holiday. Besides, Nicole expects you to be there. She thinks of you as her best friend."

The truth of Marianne's words made her pause. She had developed a close relationship with Nicole. With her, she had become not only a sister, but also a friend, a teacher, and a confidante. She had given her useful tips about horse-riding, skeet shooting, and swimming, always careful to enhance rather than subvert the lessons that her parents and her other teachers had already offered her. She had encouraged her plan to become a physician. She had worked with her to design the building of a gazebo on the Roussillons' Derbyshire property. She had taught her how to cook a fine soufflé. Nicole was an extraordinary girl. If she survived the war, she was going to make her life count for something special.

Now remembering all these things, she pushed aside, at

least temporarily, her plan to avoid any meetings with Marc and his parents in Derbyshire. She spoke the very words that she had not, even an hour earlier, planned to say.

"I'll be at Nicole's party," she told Marianne "I won't let her down."

Because of the many activities and the loyal friends who were going to be a part of the Roussillons' celebration, she decided to take a week's leave.

Upon arriving in Derbyshire, she was surprised by the pleasure she felt in being there. Friday afternoon and all of Saturday roused in her some of the life-loving capacities that she believed she had lost forever. During these first two days and the five that quickly followed, she was often in the company of the young couples—pilots and nurses, as well as artists and musicians and journalists—who had shared good times with Marc and her in happier seasons. She also joined Marc's sister for occasions that allowed them to renew their friendship while they were alone together. She and Nicole canoed on the nearby lake. They swam in the heated pool within the west wing of the main house. They rode cantering Tobianos and Sorraias across the wide span of the property. They cycled along the summer-colored Monsal trail in the Derbyshire Peak District.

They also spent an afternoon firing Remington skeet guns in a southwest meadow that stood, breeze-tossed and sequestered, opposite a forest of swaying larch trees. Whenever she was in her presence, she noted the uncanny resemblance between Nicole and the version of herself that, not so long ago, she had so naturally inhabited. Nicole was an emblem of self-discipline and steadfast determination, whether she was swimming, sailing, riding her favorite Tobiano, playing tennis and lacrosse, piloting a De Havilland DH.88 Comet, or firing a Webley & Scott 9mm semi-automatic handgun. She excelled in all the areas of experience through which she herself, as Simone Bergman, had earned a necessary confidence. Nicole was also a first-rate hunter, having killed her first stag on the Roussillons' *estancia* in Patagonia three years earlier. Dark-haired, brown-eyed, and long-limbed, she was extraordinarily beautiful. Her radiance might have shone even more brightly if it did not have to collaborate with her cutting-edge hardness. But she lived in a war-torn world and was playing with wily skill the hand that fate had dealt her.

"I'm ready to do battle with the Nazis," Nicole told her one morning after they had enjoyed a vigorous swim. "I am ready to work for the Resistance."

"How do your parents feel about that?"

"They have trained me to be a good fighter," she said.

"They have taught me not to be afraid of the things that I need to do. They have also taught me not to make my youth an excuse for staying out of the war."

Nicole's words pleased her. In those tough-minded words, she heard her own younger self speaking. Yet the words also saddened her, because Nicole was turning away from the carefree happiness that comes to a fourteen-year-old girl only once.

The loss of happiness is always a bitter thing, she told herself—not least when, looking back, you discover too late the casual manner in which you gave away your happiness.

During this unanticipated week which, she felt, was drawing her onto a different path from the one that she had sullenly been traversing, she often saw Marc. But rarely, in these public moments, did she speak to him on any but the most commonplace subjects— kayaking in Finland, for example, or parachuting from a B-17 Flying Fortress. Usually, she spoke to him obliquely—when they were in the company of their many friends and she was directing her words not at him especially, but at all the other guests who were in the room with them. It was in these moments that she noticed how care-worn and gaunt he looked. His brown eyes studied her quietly, and his sensuous lips that had so often worn a smile when he was in her presence held themselves tight in a grimace.

Not even when they were alone with his parents did she make an effort to appear as Marc's contented wife. Marianne and Henri were well aware of their troubled marriage. In the first days of this holiday week at their Derbyshire home, she refused to ease their misgivings or to devise a new accord between Marc and her. Yet she avoided angry scenes with him, always taking care to focus on the present moment unfolding around them and around his parents. She did not care to open her wounds for his bitter review and for her in-laws' too-careful inspection or to petition their understanding and compassion. The time when she might have saved Marc and Gerhard, and herself as well, had passed. Whatever happened to her life and Marc's hereafter did not seem to her to be especially important.

For five days she eluded tense confrontations with Marc and with his parents. But on the evening of the sixth day, when Marianne and Henri were hosting their grand birthday party for Nicole, Marc asked her to dance. An urge quickly rose in her to turn away from him without acknowledging his request. But their friends were dancing all around them or dining at nearby tables while watching them as they stood poised at the edge of the dancers' space. So, without offering him the words of assent that he wanted to hear, she allowed him to lead her onto the dance floor. She felt the warmth of his rugged left hand clasping the delicacy of her own hand and knew once again the press of his right hand upon her lower back. She noticed the intensity of his brown eyes, the new pallor that had overtaken his handsome features, and the gentleman's smile that, in spite of his sadness, he was working to maintain. A radiant young blonde was singing ballads about the true love that lasts, while a band of musicians accompanied her. Their blue notes kept floating across the crowded room and mingling with the exhilarated voices of the guests.

She danced with Marc in silence, consenting to their proximity with a nostalgia that surprised her. So moved was she by this unexpected moment with him that she refrained from speaking any words that might break the spell. She still felt deeply about him, and the truth of these feelings that she had been suppressing now awed and confused her. Still she accepted the spell. Over and over she gave herself to the whirl and sway of the dance with him.

Then, as the singer was ending her medley of songs about newly discovered love, Marc spoke the words that broke the spell and hurried them into the darker reality that was their own and that they had momentarily eluded.

"I want it to be the way it was with us," he said.

She recognized the tremor within the husky textures of

his voice. The masculine timbres could not diminish the emotional charge of his words. Lost inside his own wilderness, he still believed that they could retrieve their happier days. In spite of all the wrong that they had done, he had—she imagined—convinced himself that they could begin again and make their life together what it used to be.

She wondered whether he noticed the sadness in her voice as she found the words that answered him.

"If only we could begin again," she said. "But there is no way to undo the things that we've done."

The music ended now. The musicians had completed this set of ballads and were taking a break.

She was turning away from him now, freed of his clasp of her and of his searching eyes. But his voice, haunted still by his lingering sorrow, persuaded her to look upon him once more.

"I did it for us," he said. "Try to remember that."

In this moment, as she saw how much he was suffering, she wanted to open herself to him. She wished that their lives could be the way in happier times they had been for them. Even against her adamant will, she yearned for his embrace of her and for the words that could bring her out of the wilderness in which she had lost herself. But this feeling lasted only for an instant. The words that he had just now spoken were not the ones that might rescue her. They brought her no solace. They reminded her, instead, of her complicity in the killing of Gerhard.

Whether the friends around them who were leaving the dance floor noticed Marc's frown of dismay and her own unease as she hurried away from him, she could not say.

But Henri and Marianne noticed. They blamed her for Marc's abrupt return to Lincolnshire before Nicole's birthday party was over. They confronted her about the matter on the following day. On that Sunday afternoon, as soon as their guests had gone back to their barracks, to their air bases and nurses' quarters, and to their Derbyshire homes, they hurried to the elegant salon on the second floor of the east wing that adjoined the bedroom where she had been sleeping without Marc. At first, their anger held them to an uneasy silence. But the private place they had chosen for this meeting with her allowed them their stillness for only a minute or two. The warm rush of the winds and the rustling leaves of the trees quickly usurped the dignity of the stillness, while the afternoon's sunglow and the fragrance of lilacs and roses from the southerly gardens enhanced her impression of the pastel hues of the walls, the richly upholstered amenities of the room, and the burnished French doors that opened to a wide patio.

Marianne, sitting next to Henri on a needlepoint sofa, was the first to speak out.

"We've noticed that you and Marc are very unhappy," she said. "We'd like to help, if we can."

"It's too late," she said. "Marc and I have gone past being helped."

"You can't mean that," Henri said. "Not after all the good years that you and Marc have shared."

"Let go of your unhappiness," Marianne urged her. "Leave this problem with Gerhard Hauptmann behind you. Begin a new cycle with Marc."

"That is not possible, I tell you."

"Marc thinks that it is," Marianne said. "Henri and I think so, too. But, to save your marriage, you will have to work together."

"I don't know Marc anymore. He is not the person that I once knew so well and that I loved ever since I first met him. The Marc that exists now, I do not understand. I never imagined that he'd become a hardened murderer."

Henri spoke up now, defending his son in a brisk, matter-of-fact manner.

"Marc isn't so bad," he said. "It's the war that has done terrible things to him."

Hearing his words that meant to justify what Marc had

done to Gerhard, she threw out harsher words.

"I wouldn't blame the war too much if I were you," she said. "Marc's shooting Gerhard was worse than an impersonal retaliation against a war-time enemy. It was a vicious crime. It was an act committed by a cold-blooded killer. It was a crime not only against Gerhard's humanity, but also against Marc's. Gerhard was unarmed. He was no savage. In his heart, he wasn't even a Nazi. He played out the hand that fate had dealt him. If he were on our team, we'd have no trouble saying that he was honorable. Marc's made a mess of things. It doesn't make him look good."

She paused. The thought that, by saying all these things, she was betraying the man that she had always loved disturbed her. But she needed to face the grim truth about Marc if she were going to move on with her life. Her angry disappointment pushed her to say more.

"He's acted very badly," she said. "He's acted as though he is not fully human."

Marianne challenged her. Her voice was caustic and defensive.

"Marc did what needed to be done. He did what you should have done. He killed Gerhard."

In the face of her mother-in-law's remark, she lodged

another protest.

"Marc killed a good man," she said. "He killed a man better than himself."

"Marc killed a Nazi," Henri told her, his voice harsh and insistent.

"Gerhard wasn't a Nazi," she fired back at him. "He wasn't."

More tautly now, Marianne and Henri held themselves still. Then, as quickly as they had arrived, they rose to take their leave of her. Guarded while standing there at the door, they studied her for a long moment. Just before they shut the door behind them, they said more.

Henri was the first to speak.

"You are lost," he told her. "Maybe you are even more lost than Marc is."

With a softer voice, Marianne chose words that stayed with her for many weeks afterwards.

"I feel sorry for you," she said. "I wish that Henri and I could help you and Marc save yourselves. But we can't. Only you and Marc can do that."

The thought that, if they worked together, she and Marc might be able to save themselves from the dark wilderness that was overwhelming them pushed Simone forward now. Through all of the week that followed her return to her duties at the hospital, she recalled—in the brief rest periods that allowed her time away from her patients—the good things that made Marc a more-than-ordinary man. In spite of his terrible crime against Gerhard, she believed that some spark of humanity still worked as a fuse in his relations with most people. She remembered the affection and helpfulness that Marc expressed toward his friends. He was a loyal and fearless member of his bomber squadron. Extemporaneous and more genuine for being so, he had instructed his fellow pilots and many other friends not only about flying, but also—in their free time away from the war— about horse riding, sailing, and fishing even as he freely joined them in those activities. Marc had also shared with her memorable days of sailing, fishing, skiing, and flying. He had recognized her as a friend and lover to be valued. He had opened his heart to her, allowing her to see the uncertainty and the sadness that he kept hidden from almost everyone else.

More often now, she thought about Marc's reputation as an Allied pilot who had killed more Nazis and destroyed more of their aircraft than almost every other pilot. She thought, too, about his brave work for the underground Resistance. She kept reminding herself of his equally courageous work as an Allied spy. All these occasions demonstrated the humanity that Marc was still able to express in his relations with those whom he trusted and respected and perhaps loved. But, she told herself, they were not enough to exonerate him from his vicious crimes against Gerhard. Nor could they at first persuade her to forgive him for making her a catalyst in Gerhard's destruction.

Yet her guilt in having betrayed her husband began to override her reluctance to forgive him. His love for her had remained untarnished. In these solitary hours when her thoughts made him a constant presence, the tyranny that was a subtext of his obsession for her did not really matter. The intensity of his love seemed once again a magnificent experience. That her loneliness could bring her back to him did not surprise her. For so many years, he had been her lifeline. In spite of the anger and despair that he had roused in her, he was still her lifeline. Her dependence upon his love and her complicated responses to everything that made him who he was compelled her in these bleak days to admit her need of him. Loneliness taught her even more than that. It taught her, as if it were a necessary review of an earlier lesson, that she would never understand completely the intricacies of Marc's nature. Nor would she understand the disarranged nature that was her own.

Nearly two weeks later, Marc telephoned and asked her to spend five days with him in Derbyshire. They would be alone. Nicole was away at school, Henri was scheduled to fly in bombing missions over German cities, and Marianne was on duty at the hospital.

She accepted his invitation.

The morning after she agreed to be with him in Derbyshire, Marc sent her a message that said everything it needed to say in three words.

"Let's begin again."

During those five days, when early July stayed unusually cool, she and Marc hurried into many of the activities that in happier days had strengthened their bond and their love. They swam in the heated pool that made the west wing of the house a frequent visiting place. They rode Tobianos across the wide expanse of the Roussillons' property, and they cycled along the Derwent Peak District. They went skeet shooting at Henri's rod-and-gun club. They canoed across the breeze-tossed waters of the lake, and then they returned to picnic along the moss-covered bank behind the house. On that Saturday, they danced at a neighbor' s lavish party—in the midst of friends and with the pulsing fervor that clarified their vivid awareness of everything and everyone around them, not least of all themselves. And, after months of separation, they shared each other's bed.

Within these five days, and for the weeks that swiftly

followed, their lovemaking became an intense experiment, a way of testing one another and of finding their way back to the persons they used to be. Their pleasure, bound as it was to their melancholy, was spawned from their ambivalence and from their self-hatred. On one of these nights, for a half-hour after they had made love, they lay in silence together. Then, as her restless and anguished awareness came back to claim her, Marc turned to her. He was, she knew, as restless and anguished as she was. She wondered whether they would ever be able to rescue one another. Sex alone could not do it. The memory of Gerhard cast a long shadow across their marriage. It was a shroud, waiting to cover their union.

Marc's voice was matter-of-fact now. He was trying very hard not to show the sorrow that was leeching away his happiness with her. He was toughing it out, and because of that she felt the familiar spark of respect that had always strengthened the bond that she had made with him.

She understood that he wanted to know how it was with her. He wanted to find out whether they could get back the happiness that they had lost.

"It was good tonight," he said.

She told him what she really felt, even though what she felt on this night could not dispel the shadow hovering over them.

"Yes, it was good."

She sensed that he knew what she was thinking. His realistic perception compelled him to say more.

"But it wasn't what it used to be."

She hesitated before she answered, because she did not want to hurt him.

"No," she said. "It wasn't the same."

"Not yet."

That he was holding on so tenaciously to his belief in the two of them together impressed her all over again. She wanted to believe in them, too. But she could not find the words that might give him hope about their future. She merely echoed his words that told her things between them were not yet the way they used to be.

"Not yet," she said, her use of the same words sounding as heavy as his because of their shared sorrow.

His belief pushed him further. "Maybe next time it will be," he said.

"Maybe" was all she cared to answer before she turned away from him and pretended to fall asleep.

Eventually, she did drift into sleep. But, hours later, Marc's troubled moaning awakened her. He was, she felt certain, crying in his sleep. The light of the moon that was casting a ghostly spell upon their room clearly revealed to her his charismatic presence. In profile, he might have been the sleeping prince in one of the illustrated books that she read when she was a child. His rugged nakedness, only half covered by the silk sheets that fell across his chest and his legs, could well have belonged to a warrior prince. So she told herself, as she moved her warm body nearer to him. Gently, she touched his shoulders as a way to calm him. This was not the first time that she eased him out of an unhappy dream. Through all these years that they had been together, she had often calmed him, whether he was awake or asleep. Each one of those times had intensified her bond with him. Those troubled occasions always convinced her that Marc needed her as much as she needed him. Only after she lay closer to him tonight and after her familiar touch had calmed his uneasiness without waking him—only then did she glimpse a flash of the truth that, like a belated revelation, told her where she now stood with him. She still needed Marc. She had not yet learned how to live without him.

Nor had she learned how to live without Gerhard.

Before the irrevocable truth that Gerhard had been killed, she continued to grieve in secret. Over and over, in the long days and weeks and months following Marc's brutal attack of him, she wondered what she would feel if Gerhard had not died in that bedroom when Marc shot him. Though he would be counted among the living, he would be dead in all the ways he regarded as essential. The life that would cling to him could not retrieve his lost perfection. Gone would be the superb physicality that had been a fuse to his personhood and to the brilliant mind that had not known war or hatred or bitterness. Gone, too, would be the life-affirming experience that made him both artistic and sensual. Gone, as well, would be his hope and all of his dreams.

Yet knowing that he had died and had been spared such a ruined existence brought her no comfort. While he was alive, she could tell herself that one day she would go to him. She would tell him that she still loved him. That she still deeply cared for Marc was one of the perversities in her life that she did not yet fully comprehend. But the war had revealed Marc in ways that were new to her. The war had changed him. He had learned well how to be a savage. Without holding back the truth, she would tell Gerhard all these things. Now, she would say to him, he was the only man that she loved completely. She would offer her life to him. If he wanted to kill her, she would submit to his will, understanding that she had been the unwitting catalyst in his destruction. But if he allowed her to stay with him, she would do everything to make their life together happier and more fulfilling than he could ever imagine.

Her fantasy about meeting Gerhard in this way was, she now told herself, as unrealistic as Marc's expectation that, together, they would ever be happy again.

Try as she did, she could not let go of Gerhard. She felt that he was still alive. But she did not speak of him to anyone. The tough-minded surfaces of the image that she presented as herself indicated that she was already moving on to whatever future awaited her. She would not allow the past to encumber her. To those persons with whom she communicated daily, she appeared to be brisk and matter-of-fact. They did not see that she brooded secretly.

A philosopher of love, doting on ideal partnerships or even on the sublimities of tragic love, might have been intrigued by the accuracy of Simone's intuition. Simone had imagined that Gerhard was alive. He was. However, it was not love, but vengeance that would eventually drive him into Derbyshire.

Chapter Nine

Belated Discoveries

Only in retrospect could Gerhard Hauptmann imagine what Simone thought. Only after he discovered who she really was could he unravel the clues to the paths she had traveled as a spy and to the plans she had activated in the service of the Allies. In his eyes and in his fellow Nazis' assessment of his conduct as a hardened officer with a Prussian sensibility, his belated discovery of who she was weighed heavily against him. That he had been in her company for many weeks without recognizing the reality she concealed beneath a smoothly-crafted imagery was sufficient cause for his commanding officer's reprimand. As bitter as that reprimand hung upon him, as though it were a body of death he was condemned to carry forever after, it was his belated discovery of who Simone was that roused his fury and roused as well the fury of Hitler.

As uncompromising in his judgment against himself as he was against his enemies, he spent hours and days and weeks brooding over his acceptance and his love of Simone.

Sometimes, when he recalled with clear-eyed analysis the months in which she had been a part of his life, he told himself that his commanding officer and even Hitler himself would have accepted Simone for the woman she appeared to be. He did not know whether they would have fallen into love with her. He had done so. He had believed in her. She was upright and genteel. She was demure and honest. The beauty that attended her required no adornment. In his eyes, she appeared without artifice. He desired her in a way that he had not desired any other woman. There was in his feelings toward her a vaguely sentimental interpretation of all that he thought she represented.

Even when he discovered her betrayal of his love and his trust, he imagined scenarios that exonerated her from every charge his commanding officers were bringing against her. He told himself that her loyalty to her father had confused her. As obedient as she was respectful, she had no choice except to acquiesce to Knut Bergman's underground activities. Together, they must carry forward his plan to outwit and embarrass the Germans.

Only when he learned that Simone was married to Marc Roussillon did his memory of her turn bitter. But that occurred later, after he discovered her second betrayal on the night that they were together at the Beau Rivage in Switzerland. No longer could he think of her as untouched. But even then he did not league her with all the other women with whom he had casually made love. Simone had betrayed him, but she was not a whore. She was bright and brave and virtuous. Now, aware though he was of his emerging resistance to a sentimental appraisal of her, he found himself regretting that, to save himself, he would have to kill her. He would also have to kill her father.

Her first betrayal of him involved her father. She had joined her father in decoding German military correspondence.

The German High Command learned of their Resistance activities before he did. For more than a year, Simone and her father had been deciphering the Nazis' war messages. It was the professor and Simone who had first learned of the times when trains and aircraft would be carrying German troops into Norway, Poland, and North Africa. It was they, Bergman and his daughter, who became the catalysts in the Allies' successful explosion of the troop trains and their fierce bombing of the planes bringing the Nazis to the enemies that they wanted to overtake.

Hitler himself sent out the order that Bergman and his daughter were to be killed. But nowhere could the Nazis find them. Always a step ahead of his enemies, Professor Bergman had left Sweden with his daughter weeks earlier. It was many months before the Germans heard the news that he was working in England with a team of scientists on an atom bomb project. Bergman had outwitted the High Command, and so had Simone. They had betrayed the trust that he—as a young, hardened officer—had given them.

On the evening when Knut Bergman and Simone were hurrying away from Sweden, he was in Norway with his regiment. Two weeks earlier, after he had completed his assignment in Stockholm, he traveled to Berlin to deliver his favorable report about Professor Bergman. The remarks that he wrote into his report indicated that Bergman was sympathetic to Adolf Hitler's vision of a new world order. Furthermore, the professor had more than once suggested that, as soon as he had regained his health, he would join the atom bomb team in Berlin.

His report pleased Hitler as well as the primary members of the High Command. He was promoted to the rank of captain and sent to his new assignment in occupied Norway.

After discovering Knut Bergman's role as a code-breaker and his new alliance with the Allies' bomb team, the High Command laid much of the blame for Bergman's subversive activities upon him, the son of the invaluable Anton Hauptmann. He had been there, in Stockholm, while the professor and his daughter were deciphering the Germans' secret war messages. He had been there when Professor Bergman was initiating plans to join Allied scientists at Bletchley Park, not far from London. He had been there when Bergman's daughter, in various disguises, carried forward Resistance work that took her away from her father's home into France, Norway, Denmark, and even Germany. Yet he had failed to interpret correctly the professor's and her subversive activities.

The Nazis were even more enraged at him after they learned that Professor Bergman had fled from Sweden and had joined the team of scientists in England who were building an atomic bomb. Bergman would be heavily guarded and beyond the reach of even the most formidable German agents who were assigned to England.

But the professor's daughter was another matter. Because she was living in Derbyshire, she was now more vulnerable to an assassin's bullet. So was her husband, who spent time in Derbyshire whenever he was on leave from his assignments as a combat pilot. That he wanted to kill Marc Roussillon as much as he wanted to kill Simone and her father did not surprise his superior officers. He was not the first young man driven by sexual rage and jealousy to kill his rival. Yet the intensity of his hatred of Marc Roussillon impressed and intrigued them.

His militant qualities notwithstanding, he had failed in the mission that had brought him to Professor Bergman's home in Sweden. That failure demanded their stern punishment.

The High Command now decided to send him on a death mission—his own death as well as the deaths of Professor Bergman's daughter and her husband.

"You must accept this mission," his general, whose name was Bram Schlöndorff, informed him, "or you will be shot as a traitor."

He was the same general, noticeable because of his commanding gait as well as his red hair, aquiline nose, and combat-scarred face, who had arranged the exchange of prisoners that involved Major Helmut von Trotter and Jean-Claude Jourdan. At the moment, he was seated behind his desk within a Spartan office of the building that housed the German High Command. While Gerhard stood at attention, the general studied him with both hatred and disappointment.

"We expected great things from you," Schlöndorff said. "We did not expect this schoolboy infatuation with a Swedish spy."

Gerhard looked straight ahead, without presuming to make eye contact with one of the most formidable German commanders. When he spoke, his gravelly voice was low- key yet determined.

"I'll pay her back, sir. No matter what it takes, I'm going to kill her and her husband."

The general pressed his lips into an ambivalent smile. He was pleased.

"Yours will not be an easy mission," he said. "But you must do it effectively, even if it means that you will die. It is the only honorable way that you can make amends for your grievous mistakes."

"I promise to do my best, sir."

"Ah, you must not merely promise," Schlöndorff sternly asserted. "You must do your best."

Gerhard hurried to say more.

"I will, sir. My best has been good enough in the past. It will get the job done now."

"Maybe it will," the general conceded. "Until this disgraceful performance, you had a superb record. You have courage, and you have good instincts. Your wiliness might be able to get you inside England without being detected. You might even avoid being apprehended when you and your team of assassins sabotage essential rail lines, power plants, and bridges in many British cities. It is less likely that you will be able to kill Marc and Simone Roussillon without eventually being apprehended. They, too, will be heavily guarded."

"I understand the risks, sir."

"Of course, you do," the general said.

It was just before he signaled the two military guards who had accompanied him here to bring him back to the officers' quarters, where he was being held under house arrest.

"You are a man who, more often than not, lives on the realistic level. You well understand that all of life during wartime brings no more certainty than a gambler's throw of dice. To appease our Führer and the High Command and to reclaim your lost reputation, you have no choice but to accept the assignment. If you survive, you will enjoy new honors as an officer. Germany will welcome you back. If you die while succeeding in your mission, Germany will salute you nonetheless. Our country does not want its heroes to fall away in disgrace."

In this last remark, Gerhard detected no softening of the general's regard of him. Severe and hostile yet, Schlöndorff called a spade a spade. Not without calculation did he refer to his past heroism. It was the brutal standard against which the High Command as well as all of Germany would measure his conduct in the mission that was bringing him and his team into England. Germany was well aware of the courage he had demonstrated in every combat mission in which he had participated.

In late autumn of 1940, Gerhard had flown reconnaissance missions and submarine hunts against the British. Within an Arado Ar 196, a floatplane which had been catapult-launched from the Nazis' warship *Deutschland*, he had—as a radio operator manning twin 7.92 mm machine guns—successfully fired upon five Armstrong-Whitworth bombers belonging to the British Royal Air Force. He had in that same month also assisted in the capture of the British ship, HMS *Seal*. But a few weeks afterwards, while piloting a torpedo bomber, he suffered wounds to his chest, his right arm and his left leg in an air battle against a Bristol Beaufort, an English torpedo bomber. More than that, he lost three of his crew in the same battle.

When he recovered from his wounds, he learned that he was being temporarily grounded until he regained the complete mobility of his left leg. It was at this time that General Schlöndorff, who knew his father, recommended him for an assignment to Abwehr, the German intelligence-gathering agency. For several months, he was trained in sabotage and counter-intelligence. He learned how to plant false information, penetrate foreign intelligence services, exploit discontented minority groups in foreign countries, and sabotage large cities by laying mines along railroads, canal sluices, and water supply pipes.

Although in that earlier year he had requested an assignment in foreign territories such as France, Poland, and England, his father's influence had kept him in Norway and in Sweden. But now, in the spring of 1943, his commanding officer regarded his experience with the Bergmans in Sweden as unsatisfactory. After he recovered from the nearly fatal wounds that Marc had inflicted upon him in Lausanne, the High Command demanded that he give firm proof of his allegiance to Hitler and of his effectiveness as a military leader. His father, equally disappointed by his misjudgment of Professor Bergman and his daughter, strongly supported the High Command's plan for him.

It was not the first time that he understood that his father had no real love for him. He had not become a mirror image of his father, and for that reason his father disdained him. In one of his few meetings with him after the High Command discovered that Professor Bergman and Simone had tricked him, his father lashed out at him. This time, the same two guards had brought him to his father's office. It dominated a larger and more impressive space than Schlöndorff's office, because his father was a two-star general and the descendant of an eminent military line. A captain who served as his father's aide sat at the side of his father's desk recording every word that passed between them.

A sneer of contempt twisted his father's rugged features. Not even the silver hair, perfectly straight nose and glaring, brown eyes softened his appearance. He might have been a judge sentencing him to years of imprisonment or to a swift execution.

"You have tarnished our name," his father said. "You ignored the High Command's advice to keep your relations with the Bergmans impersonal. You allowed that renegade scientist and the promiscuous bitch who is his daughter to fool you. You've betrayed the trust that Germany placed in you."

His father paused, while still glaring at him. He was waiting for him to explain himself. Standing before him, rigid in his attention and precise in his choice of words, Gerhard spoke with clipped and even-tempered inflections.

"I'm not the only German they fooled, sir. Before I met the Bergmans, at least six other German officers were in their company for extended periods. The Bergmans convinced every one of them that they were sympathetic to our party. Some of those Germans were senior officers. They thought of the Bergmans as I did."

The facts displeased his father.

"Yes," he sternly answered him. "You thought as they did because you are a fool. Like them, you thought about the woman. You did not think like a Hauptmann."

Gerhard flinched. The memory of Marc Roussillon's shooting him again and again tightened his senses. His mind burned with rage, and his body ached with the phantom pain shooting out of it. He was a chipped replica of his once-hardy self. He was the enemy's victim who had not died. Fate, casual or indifferent in its dispensations, had granted him one privilege. He was devising his own death. If he made things work in his favor, his would be the death of a hero who, in the hour before dying, brought down all his enemies.

He found a bleak comfort in the fact that his father did not oppose the death mission that would send him into England. Standing at a soldierly attention, he offered words now that he hoped might placate his father's anger.

"I'm thinking like a Hauptmann now, sir. I'm willing to die as long as I can kill the Bergmans."

Still imperious and willful, his father accepted the words.

"That is good to hear. Perhaps, you have learned your lesson—as costly as that has been for Germany. The only way you can retrieve your lost honor is to kill the two of them—and not only them, but hundreds like them."

"I'll do my best."

"You have no other choice. That is the only way you can become my son again. That is the only way you can be a true German."

Now, with a peremptory wave of his hand, his father signaled the two guards who had brought him to this room.

"I'm through with him," he said. "Bring him back to his quarters."

He did not care to live if he could not avenge himself against Simone. His father was right. Together, she and Professor Bergman had tarnished the credibility he had earned through his skill as a pilot and as a captain attached to the Waffen SS. Nor could he live with his honor intact if he were to allow Marc Roussillon to go on enjoying the love of Simone. If the Fates allowed him to succeed, he would also kill Henri and Marianne Roussillon because they were Marc's parents and because they had killed many Nazis.

So it was that he directed his attention to the Roussillons. Upon finding that they had been warmly received in England, he looked to that country as the arena where, disguised as a Swede who was joining the RAF flying team, he would pursue his enemies and where his fate would test him.

Simone and her husband were rumored to be in Derbyshire. Because he wanted to kill them as soon as possible, he planned to begin his mission in the East Midlands. Only after that would he and his team of saboteurs wreak havoc in the major cities of England.

For months, he totally immersed himself in the role of the Swede who wanted to join the British war against the Nazis. With the leaders in his commando squadron guiding and challenging his every movement, he virtually became this person whom his commanding officer had named Erik Lundberg. With his fellow commandos, he devised Lundberg's complete biography, appropriating details from his own privileged background so that he might better assimilate the identity of a man who was his own age, but who had never existed. In these hard weeks, he sharpened his mastery of the Swedish language, and he carefully studied those areas in England that he and three other saboteurs were training to destroy. Years earlier, when he was an idealistic adolescent who had spent part of his summers visiting a school friend and his family in the Lake District, he had come to know England well. Even now, in spite of the hatred that was governing all his actions, he regretted that he was bringing harm to a country that had always given him the happiness that life in Germany with his tyrannical father had denied him. But so intense was his need to avenge himself against the woman who had loved him well and who had suddenly betrayed him that he quickly closed himself away from this belated nostalgia.

A Swede named Rolf Svensson was going to lead him and his team of saboteurs to the Roussillons. Svensson, a personable and wealthy sixty-year-old government attaché based in London, was a Nazi agent who served on the staff of Sweden's ambassador in England. He was a neighbor of the Roussillons. For many years, while he and his family spent some of their free time on their estate in Derbyshire, he often socialized with Henri and Marianne. He and his wife, as well as their two sons and their wives, shared many afternoons of horse riding on the Roussillon estate. They also enjoyed the lavish parties that Marianne and Henri hosted four or five times during the summer. As a Nazi, he hated both Henri and Marianne. But his tireless work on behalf of the Allies had won him their respect. Thus far, neither they nor any other Allied agent had discovered his affiliation with the Nazis.

Gerhard's commanding officer told him all that he needed to know about Svensson. What he needed to know most of all was that he and his team would be on their own. Svensson was not going to be involved in the killings of the Roussillons.

"On the day that you and your team kill the

Roussillons," his commander said, "Svensson will make certain that he is at his post in London. In that way, he'll separate himself from the killings. He'll be in the clear, and he'll keep his place on the ambassador's staff. But he is still going to be important to you. Because of him, you will gain access to the Roussillons."

"Don't worry about me or my men," he told his commander. "We'll get the job done."

The general had more to say.

"You are carrying useful baggage with you," he told him. "The personal vengeance you seek against Professor Bergman's daughter and against the Roussillons will spur you to do all the necessary things which the assignment demands. The killing of Knut Bergman's daughter and of her husband and his parents is not the most important part of your assignment. But it will serve nonetheless as a warning to those who work in secret against Germany. More essential than that act of reprisal, though, your mission as a saboteur will disarrange whole cities and render England vulnerable to a large-scale German invasion. You will begin by blowing up bridges, canals, power plants and munitions factories in Liverpool, Coventry, Birmingham and Manchester."

Gerhard had different priorities. The assignments in the

big cities might cost him his life. Then he could not avenge himself against the Roussillons. Even before he left Germany, he determined that, once they arrived in England, he and his team of saboteurs were going to hurry on to Derbyshire so that he could kill Simone and her husband.

Chapter Ten

Swift Judgments

For more than a week before they were to discover that Gerhard had not been killed, the Roussillons gave themselves wholeheartedly to new days of contentment. Too realistic to imagine that contentment would be a permanent visitor, they nevertheless embraced this respite from care and from imminent danger. Their tomorrows would bring them many cares and many dangers. In days to come, there might even be Nazis pursuing them here in England. But Gerhard Hauptmann would not, they were certain, be a part of their future.

The days that now unfolded around the Roussillons sparked their vitality. There were whole mornings of swimming in the heated pool that looked out upon the billowing woodlands and the rippling waters of the lake. There were afternoons of riding their favorite stallions along the winding trails that brought them inside the flourishing woods. There were equally favorable hours of canoeing across the wide span of the lake behind the Roussillons' house. There were light-hearted rides in a Hackney carriage; photography sessions on the beach, in the paddock, and in the greenhouse where Marianne's rare flowers and plants were thriving. There were vigorous games of tennis and of rugby and the quieter rhythms of croquet.

There was also a conversation with Marc that Henri would remember for the rest of his life.

He and Marc were walking together along the green banks of the lake. Dawn, with its blue-opal radiance, was rising over the sky-tinted waters of the lake. In wind-blown white cotton shirts and trousers, each with rolled-up cuffs, they walked barefoot and were seemingly carefree. They had risen early from their beds, eager to begin the day that awaited them. Even at this hour, they were wide awake and keenly aware of their surroundings. They were restless, too, before the unknown scenarios into which the morning and the afternoon might be drawing them.

As he walked with Marc along the smooth bank of the lake, he observed in the brightening distance the white stone cliffs rising out of the waters as if they were the remains of a world that had otherwise disappeared. Nearer than that, a flock of black-headed gulls was hurrying across sun-tinted clouds. Tall larch trees swayed in unison at the edge of the woods, where the fading shadows of night partially enveloped them.

Only by chance had he and Marc met, neither having mentioned on the previous evening that he would leave his bed to witness the July dawn making its appearance over the wind-stirred lake and over the ample house from which they had just emerged. As was their habit in this particular summer, they carried snub-nosed revolvers in leather holsters. Nearby, though out of their view, were two bodyguards watching their smallest move and scanning every detail of the otherwise deserted beach and the distant, mysterious woods and the unanticipated yawl that was hastening across the shifting colors of the quickening lake.

Henri had taken this opportunity of being here with Marc, while they were nearly solitary and morning-contemplative, to ask him what he planned to do with his life if he survived the war.

For a moment, Marc studied him quietly. His gaze was direct and the words that he chose now to explain himself were straightforward.

"I want to design and build modern houses and cities," he said. "If I can do anything of value, it will be that. In my small way, I'd like to make the world new. Fighting to win the war is one way to do it. But building new cities and new suburbs will one day be just as valuable."

Henri cheered him on. He was not going to throw him

off the course he had envisioned for himself. With this strong-minded son, there would be little chance of that. But he could encourage him and, in fact, endorse his son's aspiration.

"You are aiming high," he told him. "If there is anything that I can do to help, you know where I live. I'll always be on your team."

Marc allowed himself a smile. With a rough gesture that was meant as camaraderie, he patted his shoulder.

"I'll remember your promise," he said. "I may hold you to it."

Appearing more relaxed than he had ever been in his company, and more trusting, Marc shared with him now some of the thoughts that he had deemed too personal to tell anyone else. They were, Henri would tell himself later, part of his son's evolving awareness of himself in the larger world. For these next minutes, Marc would speak to him as a son confiding in his father. The minutes were to pass quickly, and the imagery of their stronger bond would flash like a will o' the wisp.

"Lately," Marc began, "I've been thinking that I've entered a new cycle of my life. The war has made me feel that this may be my last cycle."

"I've never heard you so solemn before," Henri said, trying to ease his son away from any dark thoughts that might be afflicting his will to go on. "You're a born fighter. You have a wonderful future to fight for."

"Even good fighters come to endings that they had not planned," Marc said. "I'll always fight hard. But that doesn't mean I'll always win. The world's a rough place and doesn't regard my dreams as especially significant. In the tangled scheme of things, the world doesn't even know me."

Still Henri tried to encourage him.

"We're all traveling in the same uncertain ship," he said. "But some of us do reach our intended destination."

"Very few, I think," Marc said. "For most people, the world's a crap shoot. It is wild luck or fickle chance that pushes most of us to a safe port."

They had paused now in their walk to peer across the dark wake of quickened waters and to catch sight of the chrome-green hills across the lake and the far-away trees that were leaning against the summer winds' raveling incursions. Nearer than that, a lonely yawl's white-flashing jib sheets were testing the wind's supple currents.

Henri spoke now. He wanted to bring to his son some measure of hope, some realistic words that would help him to find his bearings and find, too, the self that he believed he had lost.

"You'll find your way back after the war is over," he

assured him.

Marc eyed him skeptically.

"How do you get back the man you were before all the killing?" he asked. "How do you convince yourself that, in spite of being a temporary here-and-now killer, you can learn to be that man once again?"

"It can be done," Henri said. "I learned how to do it after my first war was over. You will do it, too."

"To kill enemies of war is a permissible thing," he said. "The laws of every country tell us so. But I have destroyed a good man not because he was my enemy in war, though he was, but because my wife fell in love with him."

This was the first time that Marc mentioned his troubled marriage to him. He, as his father, might have been pleased. He might have seen in this openness the possibility of his building a stronger bond with his son. But, in their conversation by the lake, blunt, tough-minded inflections had gradually overtaken Marc's borrowed ease. His son was not merely asking for reassurance that he would one day find his way back to the self he had lost. He was challenging him to prove that it could be done. He had not really wanted to ask. But his guilt and his wretchedness pushed him to it.

Henri could hear in his sullenness the voice of the

aggrieved youth he must have become after he lost the certainty that his parents loved him. This is the way he must have sounded whenever he opened his sorrows to his best friend, Jean-Claude.

But this morning he was more than that unhappy youth. There was in him a moral acuity that compelled him now to be his own judge and jury. He had judged himself guilty. Nor, Henri surmised, would his fatherly support alter that verdict or allay that guilt. Marc was keenly aware of the weakness in himself that sought out an opinion that would justify his crime. He would listen courteously, driven perhaps by his wish that some insightful advocate or some lucky chance would convince him that he had done no wrong. But kind words would change nothing for him. Whatever fate lay in store for him, he was going to have to meet on his own rugged terms and without lying to himself.

So, as his father, Henri mused. But his awareness that Marc had judged himself guilty did not dissuade him from speaking the clipped words that were meant to encourage his troubled son. As a man who knew the world as much as, if not more cannily than, Marc, he willed himself to resist a scrupulous assessment of Marc's treatment of Gerhard Hauptmann. Other men had committed similar offenses and had gradually come to accept their more fallible self-images.

His temporizing words, drawn from the skillful casuistry of his world-weariness, would not answer Marc's need for stark and uncompromising truth. But later his son might recall that in this moment the father who had been lost to him for so many years wanted to comfort him. That Marc was seeking his advice, while using him as a sounding board or as a momentary refuge from his brooding memories, was a hopeful sign. One day, he might come to him without the bitterness and without reverting to the guarded distancing of himself from a father who wanted to help him. With this idea before him, Henri hurried to defend him.

"Gerhard Hauptmann was your enemy because of the war," he protested. "If there had been no war, Simone would never have met him."

"But she did meet him, and I destroyed him," Marc said. "And because I did, I'll never find my way back."

So haunted was his son's face as he spoke these words, that Henri was hard-pressed to find the thought that might comfort him.

"Give yourself time," he said, after enclosing himself within a moment's stillness. "Give yourself a chance. Wait and see what happens."

Having said so, he resumed walking toward that corner

of the lake where in the palpable distance the hard whiteness of the wind-scoured cliffs seemed to rise endlessly. He was intrigued by the subtle way in which the cliffs resisted a too-easy definition of themselves. A viewer noticing them in an hour like this one, when traceries of night fog and new-born morning radiance partly concealed them, might imagine that they were strong pillars, holding up an uncertain sky.

Marc easily kept pace with him, while he enclosed himself within the privacies of his own silence.

The ambivalent solace that visited her family in the temporary lift of these days before Gerhard's arrival touched also a conversation that Marianne shared with Simone on a warm morning in July. Henri was to learn of it a few days later, when she recalled the scene for his own pensive analysis.

With her team of able gardeners and with Simone's assistance, she had immersed herself in the careful transfer of camellias from the beneficent atmosphere of the conservatory. There, the camellias had thrived within a controlled climate and a glass-and-metal, roomy habitation. Now, with Simone's help and with the proficiency of her crew, she brought the camellias to a southerly corner of the garden nearest the main house. The blooms shone brightly, and all of them swayed gracefully, inspired perhaps by the soft rhythms of summer breezes. Many of them stood as high as fifteen feet and, with their cream-white, pale pink and rose colors, would create a plush backcloth to small shrubs and azaleas.

After they had overseen the correct placement of the camellias in the southwest garden and after the gardeners had gone on to other landscaping assignments on the Roussillon property, she and Simone found themselves seated inside a gazebo that looked upon the beauty of the flowers that they had helped to transplant. Mrs. Dowling, her primary housekeeper, had brought each of them a mint julep and her extemporary praise of the dazzling look of the flowers.

Left alone now to admire the work of their morning, Marianne conversed more openly with Simone than was her habit when they were in each other's company.

Influenced by the flare of colors around her and impressed by the languorous quiet of late morning, Simone eased into their conversation. At first, she seemed relaxed and as happy as her troubled spirit could ever allow her to be.

"I could become used to this kind of living," she said, "but only as a brief retreat from the cares of the real world. I'd always want the real world as my prevailing resource. Gardens, even when well made, tend to be artificial constructs. They can be havens of a sort. But they can't tell me where I stand in the full-scale reality of things. Having some knowledge of random chance and of danger, I've learned to distrust the safe and the hermetic."

Against her habit of suppressing her emotions, Simone allowed a frown to subdue the tenuous energies of her solace. Noticing the bitter edges that enfolded themselves within the young woman's inflections, Marianne gently prodded her toward a different way to see. She wanted Simone to stay out of the war. She wanted Marc and her to have a baby. Maybe that was the only way they could save their marriage. She pushed herself to say more. Though her tough-minded sense of things might ordinarily have told Simone that she should go on fighting the Nazis, she hurried to say the words that might bring her daughter-in-law to a different path.

"Being safe can be just as real as being endangered," she said.

A stillness taking hold of her, Simone calculated the authenticity of this remark. Then, having made a matter-of-fact assessment of its implications for the life that she had built from her day-to-day experience, she answered her with words that were as terse as they were honest.

"I don't really believe that," she said. "I can't even imagine that such a world exists. But maybe one day, if I survive the war, I will see things differently."

"Don't think of going back into the war. You've taken enough risks. You have done more than your share for the war. Take a different path. Stay here in England. Start a family."

Simone listened to her counsel with a courtesy that nearly concealed her surprise as well as her disdain.

"My having children is a pretty thought," she said. "But I'm not certain that Marc or I want children or that we would ever be good for them. Too much has happened to make us altogether different from the persons we used to be. Besides, I want to finish the job that I've begun. I'm going back into the war—this time as a pilot."

It was now that Simone told her about her new assignment in the war. She would be staying in England, where she would be a part of the Air Transport Auxiliary. It was a civilian organization that ferried new or repaired aircraft from factories and assembly plants to trans-Atlantic delivery points, to active service squadrons, and to airfields. Both men and women ferried these planes and, by doing so, freed the much-needed combat pilots for aerial fighting. Simone would be flying the Royal Air Force's front-line aircraft: Spitfires, Hawker Hurricanes, Mosquitoes, Mustangs, Avro-Lancasters, Handley Page Halifaxes, and Fortresses. Already proficient as a pilot of light, single-engine airplanes, she was going to be trained in stages to fly the more powerful and complicated planes. She would be flying in a non-combat role, but in combat conditions nonetheless.

That Marc would continue to fly with the Free French Air Force which was partnered with the RAF seemed less important to Simone than her re-entering the war.

"Why are you doing this?" she asked her. "You'll be a special target of the Nazis."

"Am I any safer here?"

"Yes, I think you are," she said. "Gerhard and his Nazi gang are behind you. You needn't concern yourself about them anymore."

"Maybe so," Simone answered her, though reluctantly. "But France and England will need me. They need all of us. You and Henri are right in going back, too. Helping Europe is the thing we have to do now."

Marianne did not dispute her words. In spite of her momentary wish that Simone might choose to become a mother and possibly salvage her marriage, she found herself approving Simone's realistic viewpoint. Marc, Henri, and she were not going to stop fighting for their country until the war was over or until they were killed in action. Simone, she was pleased to see, was still made of the same stern material.

So Marianne explained to Henri a few days after her

conversation with Simone in the southwest garden. There, Simone had received the garden as a merely temporary haven. Its solace for her seemed a trick or a disguise. It was both a spurious rescue and an insufficient refuge from the violence that was destroying the real world.

"She is right, of course," Marianne said, while pondering the trouble in the far-away world that they would be able to keep at bay for only a while longer. "This is not a year for believing in the safety of gardens."

She and Henri were walking on the path that led to the flourishing woodlands behind their house. As was their habit, they watched the crimson glow of sunset upon the tall greenness of larch trees that stood wind-blown and eerie at the edge of the dark woods. In the far distance, a yawl, a catboat, and a cutter glistened with stippled energies across the hastening waters of the lake, leaving in their wake the heave and surge of the lake. Still the white cliffs rose into the nebulous regions of dusk. Still a bodyguard, furtive and reliable, trailed behind them. Still Henri carried a snub-nosed revolver, hidden tonight within the deep right pocket of his windbreaker.

He had listened attentively to all the news that she had to tell him about Simone. Now he offered his point of view, which brought forth an assertion as well as an indirect question.

"She is very unhappy," he said. "I wonder whether she is returning to the war this quickly so that she can get away from her marriage to Marc."

Marianne mused upon his remark for a moment or two. Then, because she was ready to assess his words and to add clarifying words of her own, she answered him with a compelling possibility that in her brisk delivery sounded matter-of-fact.

"That may well be so," she said. "But Simone may also be hurrying back to the war to fulfill a secret death wish."

Though she was struggling against a sorrow not unlike despair, Henri noticed how Simone willed herself to resist all visible show of sadness. In these days when happiness seemed a carefully modulated plan, Simone gave herself almost completely to the happier occasions of their Derbyshire experience. He saw how she suppressed her sorrow and reached out to help the Hoffmann family, whom the Nazis had pursued in France. The Hoffmanns, who lived a few miles from their property here in Derbyshire, were often their weekend guests. Simone recognized the three of them as kindred spirits. They had lost their parents and their relatives in the massacres perpetrated by the Germans. She had lost relatives, too. And she had lost Gerhard.

The Hoffmanns were French Jews whom Henri and Marianne had rescued from the Nazis a year earlier. Since then, Franz, a renowned neurosurgeon, had become an indispensable part of the medical rescue unit at the 28th Station Hospital. His tall, lean physique and even-tempered manner gave him the look of a steady forty-year-old man capable of withstanding formidable emergencies and unexpected enemies. Rachel, his wife, served at the hospital as his nurse. At thirty-two, she was still a raven-haired beauty, and she had a heart of steel. Their daughter Talia, who was eleven years old, might— Henri imagined—one day become as lovely as her mother. She had dark curly hair and an alabaster complexion. Right now, though, as quick-witted as she was, she often appeared reticent and even anxious. The dangers and uncertainties that surrounded her parents and herself had stolen some of her confidence.

"I can't be brave," Talia cried out one day when her mother had remarked to Simone and to Henri that the war required everyone to be brave.

"Of course, you can," her mother said. "You already are brave. You are being brave every time that you do the things that need to be done, even when there is danger around you."

Impatient and brooding, Talia resisted her mother's words. Her voice was barely audible and gave the impression that she was speaking to herself.

"I'm tired of being unhappy," she said.

Usually, in moments when her anxiety stole away her peace, her father's presence was enough to calm her. But on that afternoon he was not with them. Instead, Franz and Marc—always on the lookout for enemies—were riding swift Tobianos while reconnoitering the wide span of the property.

It was Simone who now offered comforting words to the girl. In his scanning glance of his daughter-in-law, he recognized the haunted look of her blue eyes and in her voice the bitterness that she was learning to endure.

"All of us are unhappy at least some of the time," she said. "You just have to make the best of things. You have to learn how to live with unhappiness."

Now Henri found the words that might help Talia and, at the same time, might keep Simone on the path that was right for her.

"Never give in to it," he said, as he directed his remark to the girl. "Never allow your unhappiness to rule you."

His matter-of-fact words and gentle patting of her shoulder eased her tension.

"I'll try," she said. "I'll try not to give in."

For her part, Simone remained very still. Whatever influence his words had upon her, she was unwilling to show him.

For this entire week, Franz Hoffmann and his family were his and Marianne's house guests. He was pleased to witness once more their positive influence upon Simone. Carefree or seeming so on many days, she joined Nicole, Rachel and Talia in a meadow that offered its vibrant colors a quarter of a mile or so from the main house, though it belonged to the Roussillon property none the less. There, in the midst of scarlet, blue-gray, and gold ornamental grasses, Simone and the three others spent time at their easels painting three roan-colored palominos that were grazing in the distant paddock. With them, she was always blithe and even merry. They thought of her as a helpful friend. So Rachel Hoffmann was to tell Marianne, and in that way he eventually heard of it.

On other days, Henri accompanied Simone, Nicole, and the Hoffmanns to his rod and gun club for an afternoon of skeet shooting. With him, Simone continued to assist both Rachel and Talia in their use of the Beretta and Remington skeet guns, and—as an experienced sharpshooter—she subtly competed with the accomplished Nicole while firing a Browning XS Skeet model. During other favorable mornings or afternoons, she spent time with the two girls and with Mrs. Hoffmann recording by means of Leica cameras a clarifying imagery of those persons with whom she was sharing this summer season: he and Marianne looking sun-tinted and buoyant as they entered their yawl and as the restless waters of the lake slapped against the long and sleek jetty which they had only then traversed; Franz and Rachel pausing by the lake at dawn, a crimson glow attending their pensive faces; Marc, rugged and intense, mounted on his favorite French Trotter and cantering along the smooth stretch of the sun-gold beach and at the edge of the excited waters of the sea that appeared to be hastening after him; and Nicole and Talia, pensive and even melancholic as they peered into the blue-rimmed well in Marianne's rose garden.

There were days and days when Simone swam and sailed and when she made glamorous appearances at three of Marianne's and his lavish summer parties and at an equally festive evening that celebrated the Hoffmanns' wedding anniversary. Sometimes on these occasions Henri noticed in her responses to Marc either the underpinnings of a taut enmity or the suggestion of a suppressed and weary bitterness.

"If only we could help them," he told Marianne when, alone in the privacies of their bedroom, they spoke of the tensions between their son and his wife. "If only it were possible for them to hurry away from the past and to become new again."

He tried to think of ways that he might help Marc and Simone. His saving them, if he could, would be an intricate thing, like rescuing persons who have set themselves on fire.

Early afternoon of the next day gave all of them their final happiness for that summer. With the cautious aptitudes of a sentry, Henri had more than once reviewed what everyone would be doing that day and where they would be located. Nicole, Rachel, and Talia were using that hour to work on the paintings they had begun a week earlier. Rachel, a talented artist who had exhibited her canvases in Paris, Brussels, and London, had accompanied the two girls to the fragrant meadow of scarlet, blue-gray, and gold ornamental grasses that stood a quarter of a mile away from the main house. There, she worked on her own painting and from time to time, if she was invited to do so, advised the girls about the progress of their canvases. She and the two girls were dressed in large straw hats that protected them from the glare of the sun and in pastel artist smocks that gave them a picturesque appearance.

So, a half hour earlier, Henri reflected as he watched Rachel and the two girls driving toward the meadow in Marianne's Mercedes. A security guard was going to meet them there to ensure their safety. Today he was the only guard whose presence Henri required. Gerhard's death had given them back at least a portion of their ease. Neither he and Marianne nor any of his European guests felt the need of a security guard on this perfect summer day. Nevertheless, to make their sense of security even more secure, he had assigned a guard to follow Rachel and the girls to the northwest meadow. Marianne, Franz, and he himself were carrying Enfield revolvers within the inside pockets of their jackets.

At this same time, he surmised, Marc and Simone were walking through Marianne's luxuriant garden in the southeast wing of their property. Gradually, after they had savored the beauty of flowering trees and exotic plants and ornamental shrubs, they would make their way toward the lake.

For many years later, Henri remembered this afternoon as a dazzle of colors. He, as well as Marianne and Franz, began that hour by riding their Arab bays across the emerald-green land. Because the afternoon was offering them the crispness of July's cooler presence, they were wearing mint-green shirts and tan quilted jackets, brown jodhpurs and summer jodhpur boots, and cobalt-green protective hats and gloves. Around them always was the shimmer of colors and forms. There was the stippled imprint upon their senses of the paddock and stables and barn hurrying past them, vertiginous and soaring. Past them too was the gleaming whiteness of the ample main house, half-timbered and authentically gabled and at once a spun velocity inside their seeing. Keeping pace with his wife and with Dr. Hoffmann, he glimpsed in cantering passage the sculpted geometries of architecturally-cut verdant slopes and fieldstone retaining walls. He glanced at ornately paved and planted surfaces and at the many-tiered, bluestone terraces. In scanning review, he also noticed double rows of aureum maples that wore coral-red branches and shoots. The leaves of these trees were lobed and brightly green and rimmed with golden yellow.

Intense and excited, the recurring montage of radiant flower fields and shimmering grasses rose before his brisk cantering. So also did the tall symmetries of red-leafed and bright orange hedges hurry by him as their Arab bays lightly skimmed the sloping greenery of the hills. Proficient riders, he and the two others sat tall in the saddle without leaning backward or forward. They took their weight down through their legs and heels to allow each horse to balance itself by using its head and neck.

On their reliable stallions, while holding their bodies well forward and over their knees so that their horses' backs were not carrying their weight and could move freely, they ascended green, northerly hills and hastened across heather-covered moors. Once more they rose to the trot. Lightly, they balanced their feet in the stirrups, and they wrapped their lower legs around the horses' bodies. Relaxed and independent of their hands and rising with the horse's movement in the ease of their proficiency, they rode past winterberry holly, sedum, and sweetspire and past oak leaf and hydrangea and permisetum grasses.

It was here that he noticed two pretty, olive-skinned girls. The diligent and sisterly daughters of the primary grounds-keeper, they were gathering hay in a field. With mellifluous timbres, they were singing a folksong in Spanish. He noticed also, in an orchard nearby, the girls' sturdy father and their four muscular brothers poised on high stepladders while picking large, burgundy plums from beneath dense canopies of trees. At this time, as supple riders, he and his companions squeezed their legs inward against their horses' sides and decreased the forward movement of their hands to negotiate a smooth and proper halt. Now they arrived at the edge of the untamed woodland and before the cultivated gentility of an efflorescent grove.

Once they dismounted, they permitted their horses to graze in a green field enclosed by a split-cedar fence. Lighthearted and refreshed, they strolled into that portion of the property garmenting itself with a rare sumptuousness. All about them, tall, graceful laburnums with pendulous sprays of cascading yellow satisfied their ease. In fragrant union with the windfall crispness of a cool afternoon, equally tall and decorative hawthorns offered flowers pink and white and red. Tamarisks enhanced their visit with fluffy, rose-tinted plumes and fine, feathery leaves.

Afterwards, he would remember that it was then. It was in this specific moment, when they stood quiet and contented before the day's flourishing beauty, that he and the two others knew their last unqualified happiness.

He wondered months later whether his happiness had made him feel uneasy, as if he had not fully earned its rewards. Why else would he, rather than his guests, have been the one to intrude upon the silence that was not only intensifying their bond, but also persuading happiness to stay? At that later time, he would tell himself that no happiness that he experienced could have been adequate or seemly when he knew that Marc and Simone were so troubled.

It was the thought of their unhappiness that compelled him to push away the silence so that he could speak openly of their problem to Marianne and to Franz Hoffmann. Now, as they attended his words carefully, he reviewed his perceptions of Marc's and Simone's disguised estrangement from each other.

"Gerhard Hauptmann is still at the root of their problems," he said, as a conclusion to all the other words he had spoken. "Not even his death has changed things for them."

For a moment Franz turned away from him and from Marianne. He was, Henri imagined, considering his remark while enclosed within the privacies of his own space. As he stood at the split-cedar fence, he glanced upon the Arab bays grazing in the field. Then, with a more decisive movement, he turned back to him and to Marianne. But it was to him that he directed his words.

"Things will never change for Simone," he said. "Marc and Gerhard are her obsessions. She will never be rid of either one of them."

Franz's direct glance toward him and his matter-of-fact expression told him that he had more to say.

"You must not forget that, even dead, Gerhard will always be a part not only of Simone's life, but also of Marc's."

Now he offered both Franz and Marianne his own thoughts about the matter, imparted as they were within the intricacies of urgent questions.

"But how can they go on?" he asked, his husky inflections and his hint of a frown defining his pity and his apprehension. "How, when their memory of Gerhard will not leave them, can Marc and Simone ever be happy again or even stay together?"

With a muted brusqueness and a cool-headed manner that dismisses both alarm and sentimentality, Marianne quickly answered him.

"They will go on, and they may very well stay together," she said. "But first they will have to learn to live with Gerhard Hauptmann's ghost."

Chapter Eleven
Avenging Specter

A quarter of an hour later, as though his ghost could appear incarnate and grim-faced, Gerhard was suddenly there. With three other Nazi commandos, he was making his way to the stables where he and his henchmen intended to mount swift Lusitanos and to go in pursuit of Marc and Simone, as well as Henri and Marianne. Four days earlier, he and his cohorts had made their way into England as the guests of Rolf Svensson. All had gone well. Every official who examined their passports and their other identification papers accepted them as the persons that they said they were—well-trained patriots and experienced pilots from Sweden who had served in the Home Guard there and who were now seeking to join England's Royal Air Force. The British liked the rugged look of them and their willingness to do their part to win the war.

Gerhard played this game with the confidence and determination that, he felt, made him instantly plausible. As the Swede he was supposed to be, he appeared older than his twenty-four years. But his imposing height, the wide range of his knowledge, and his supreme self-command nearly deflected an onlooker's notice of his faded blond handsomeness, the traces of weariness within his straightforward regard of them, and the occasional flash of a grimace that suggested the bearer had made a stern and private pact with bitterness.

The first of his three companions, and the most sadistic, was Bernd Dietz. Two inches shorter than his own six foot, four inches, Bernd had curly brown hair, blue eyes, an aquiline nose, and full, sensual lips. His wholesome features and his good humor won him many British friends who never imagined that Bernd had tortured and killed many Jews, as well as innumerable French Resistance agents. Upon hearing that the Roussillons shared both French and Jewish blood, he was—he told him—looking forward to spilling as much of theirs as he possibly could.

The second of his associates was Volker Henze. He was an efficient killer. From his viewpoint, there was no need for delay or questions or torture. He killed quickly, because his aim with a revolver, a rifle, a grenade or a stiletto was always accurate.

The third man on his team was Klaus Rimbach. He stood at exactly six foot. Though he carefully understated his virility, he was the epitome of strength and masculinity. He had light blue eyes, rugged features, tow-colored hair, and a hard yet lean body. Klaus took pleasure in killing women, possibly because his mother had abandoned him when he was two years old and because his father kept marrying women whom Klaus regarded as well-paid courtesans

That Gerhard was leading these three fellow assassins into the danger did not diminish the complexity of the missions. As far as he was concerned, the killers with whom the German High Command paired him were liabilities. They were not sufficiently detached from the episodes of violence they were sent to perpetrate upon the hated Roussillons and their equally hated British allies. Bernd, Volker, and Klaus had a craving for violence. They were powder kegs that could explode at the wrong time. They were hair triggers firing their powers indiscriminately. They were land mines that inadvertently destroyed their teammates.

From the start of his association with them, Gerhard was hard on them. Thus far, he had anticipated their misjudgments and impeded their rash actions. By the time they made their way into Derbyshire, he had established himself as their formidable commander. They knew that if they crossed his will, he would shoot them. They understood who he was. He was a killer, and for that they both feared and respected him.

On the Saturday when the Roussillons and Dr. Hoffmann were riding along the trail that would bring them into the woods behind the main house, Rolf Svensson and his wife had not joined them. He had been called to London unexpectedly, and Mrs. Svensson had accompanied him. But their sons and their wives had remained in Derbyshire, where they continued to receive their parents' guests with polished grace and with genuine cordiality.

Before he and his wife left for London, Svensson spoke to Gerhard in the privacy of his study. In this meeting, he discarded his personable manner. Blunt and imperious now, he told him how he and his team should proceed after they arrived on the Roussillons' property.

"Leave nobody alive who could connect you or me to the killing of the Roussillons," he said. "Kill everyone who crosses your path."

On the same Saturday that Henri, Marianne, and Franz had begun riding their horses around the expanse of the Roussillon estate and then on to the flourishing woods, the young Svenssons were giving a festive luncheon for twenty-five guests. In the midst of a wide expanse of lush greenery and a bountiful array of banquet tables with sun-gold canopies, foreign ambassadors and business moguls, poets and scientists, and artists and philosophers mingled with precise assurance and sometimes with the hint of panache or of debonair flair. On the southwest terrace of the main house that overlooked the burnished greenery, musicians orchestrated the lighthearted voices and self-reflective conversations of the guests with the equally fluent intonations of piano and violin, oboe and piccolo, trumpet and clarinet and tuba. Some guests danced to the melodies of Gershwin, Porter, and Franz Lehar. Other guests swam in the heated pool in the west wing of the house that overlooked the blue-green waters of the bay. A few played croquet or went boating, piloting adeptly the yawls and yachts that were among the amenities which the Svenssons offered their guests.

Gerhard and his three associates were among those guests who—by choosing to pilot Rolf Svensson's newest yacht—took their leave of the extravagant party, even while they remained anchored to it by participating in one of its pastimes. They were wearing white cotton shirts and slacks, comfortable navy boat shoes, and yachtsman's hats that were made of white brushed cotton with anchor embroidery and navy trim. Wind-tanned and athletic, they possessed a casual affinity with their craft that gave each of them a clean-cut and wholesome persona.

Yet among their gear, concealed within the deep pockets

of their weatherproof khaki jackets, were Beretta pistols, Enfield revolvers, and Mauser and Walther Model 8 handguns. Their intention was to use them with sharpshooter accuracy, as they made their way over the excited waters to the private dock that was part of the Roussillon estate.

Gerhard docked the boat without incident. As he was doing so, an aged fisherman hobbled along the jetty to meet the heave of his mooring line. His name was Leif Wallen, and he was as adept in all things maritime as he was tight-lipped and grizzled. It was his job to maintain, with the assistance of two equally fine mechanics, the precise workings of the Roussillons' yacht and their three yawls, as well as the smooth running of the boathouse. On this afternoon, Leif was alone. Not even the security guard who had for many weeks kept sentry duty at the boathouse was on duty. He, in fact, was attending the safety of Rachel and the two girls who were busy at their easels in the shimmering meadow that stood a quarter of a mile from the main house.

Leif saw in his face and in the faces of his friends only a wholesome appreciation of the summer day. Young, agile, and proficient, he and the others impressed the fisherman because of their easy affinity for their craft and because of their respectful exchanges with him in Swedish concerning the Svensson yacht and their happy (though fictional) boyhood in Sweden. Leif had heard that they were visiting Mr. Svensson and his family and was therefore not surprised that he and his associates had suddenly appeared at the Roussillon dock. That they were guests of the Svenssons gave a plausible context to their being there, on the sun-flecked dock where an incautious wind occasionally bestirred the solace of the afternoon.

After he and his cohorts had allowed old Leif a nostalgic reminiscence of his homeland, Gerhard asked where he and his friends might find Mr. Roussillon. The three of them were bringing greetings from their fathers, and all of them were eager to see young Mrs. Roussillon and her husband. They had known her as the extraordinary daughter of Professor Knut Bergman.

The fisherman (Gerhard was to guess later) was not aware that, at the last minute, Simone and Marc had decided to go for a walk through the southeast gardens and then onto the beach, rather than to join the horse-riding party.

"They've gone riding," Leif told him and the three others, with raspy though friendly inflections. "But you can join them. Juan Tomas will help you saddle up, and you'll soon catch up to Mr. Roussillon and his party."

So they did saddle up.

Juan, the rugged groomsman who may have been forty, provided him and his teammates not only four of Henri

Roussillon's swiftest Lusitanos, but also Crosby close- contact jumping saddles. Their forward-cut flaps allowed the rider to carry his legs close to the saddle, while making his position more secure. Juan also supplied them with fine breeches and boots, quilted jackets, and hard hats—each with a protective chin harness.

"Today," Juan said, "you fellows will ride fast."

To his friendly remark, they said nothing.

As soon as he and the three others were well equipped for a smooth and fast ride, Gerhard watched as Klaus and Volker fired their Beretta pistols into Juan's mouth and forehead. Blood spewed from the back of his head and sprayed out of his eyes and ears, while his body lurched and buckled before it fell backward. Then, when he and the three others returned momentarily to the boathouse, Volker fired his Enfield revolver into Leif's heart. Again, he watched the killing. He saw surprise overtaking the fisherman's cragged features as he fell upon the dock. He also noticed that, even in death, the old man's faded blue eyes kept staring at all of them.

Only after that did he and his fellow Nazis go in search of Marc and Simone, as well as Marc's parents.

Confident that they were about to achieve their mission, they cantered toward the trail that would bring them into the woods where the Roussillons were riding. But, as they hurried into the northeast portion of the property, he saw in the proximate southerly distance a tall graceful woman and two pretty girls busy at their easels while they recorded their impressions of the summer day and its burnished imagery. He as well as Bernd and Volker accepted the sight of them as a scanning flare upon their senses. Without a pause, they hurried forward to kill the enemies whom they regarded as most essential.

But in that fleeting instant he noticed that, with an impulse that was both sadistic and murderous, Klaus left the group and rode along the path that would bring him to the woman and her young charges within the ample meadow of sweet-scented grasses. He knew what Klaus meant to do. He would kill all of them, but not before he raped the girl who appeared to be fourteen or so and whose beauty to his eyes appeared an exotic blend of French and Jewish.

No sooner did Klaus reach the undulating path that hurried to the meadow, than Rachel saw him take from the inside pocket of his jacket a Beretta semi-automatic pistol. Hearing the hoof-beats of the horse, she and the two girls had looked away from their canvases more startled at first than frightened. From the palpable distance, about four hundred feet away, an unknown man was riding toward them, and he was pointing a gun in their direction.

It was in this moment that the security guard who was assigned to protect both her and the girls rushed forward from his guardian place about two hundred feet from them to intercept the passage of this intruder. He was raising his Enfield revolver to take aim, when Klaus fired his Beretta and instantly killed him. Rachel saw the bullet enter his forehead and the blood explode out of the back of his head. The security guard's body fell upon his knees, swayed momentarily toward the right, and then fell face down.

At the sound of this first shot, the horse whinnied and neighed and rose upon its hind legs. Now she noticed the assassin leaning forward to the right side of the horse's neck and keeping the reins slack. Then, with whip and spurs, he drove the horse forward.

In this same instant, Talia screamed, dropping her paint brush and raising her arms and hands as though they might shield her from the tall, strange man who kept riding toward them on her favorite Lusitano stallion. Her daughter ran to her, accepting her as the steadfast adult there who would protect her. The prettiness of her tan oval face seemed disarranged because of the fear in her brown eyes and because her mouth had twisted its delicacy into another scream, conveying now both her protest and her fear.

"Don't do it! Don't do it!" she yelled.

Rachel gave her daughter a comforting pat with her hand and, nearly at the same time, instructed Nicole to take hold of her and run as fast as they could into and through the tall, shimmering grasses that might conceal them. Her intuition told her that she was going to die. But, if that were so, she would die trying to protect the girls.

She stood by her easel and waited for the stranger to ride up to her. Only at the last moment was she aware that Nicole had stayed with her, positioned as she was a few feet behind her. But she was only vaguely aware that this strong-minded girl was struggling to lift a Colt pistol from the inside pocket of her smock. It was caught there, within the drawstring of her garment.

Now, as he reached them, the stranger fired upon Rachel, deliberately wounding rather than killing her. The bullet penetrated her shoulder, and its impact pushed her back so hard that she lost her balance and fell to the ground. She winced in pain and for a few seconds reeled in and out of consciousness.

Though the imagery before her was blurred, she could see that this strange killer was about to dismount. She saw that he had begun to pull both of his feet out of the stirrups when

Nicole hurried forward and, with her Colt Pocket Hammer pistol, shot him again and again. The bullets tore through his left ear, his right arm, and his heart. At this barrage of bullets, the horse neighed and reared once again and galloped away. His right leg caught in the stirrup, the killer was dragged across the path for a hundred or more feet, his body battered and blood-smeared before it fell away from the Lusitano.

Something like a shock wave took hold of Talia as well as herself. Nicole had killed a man, and she had done so out of necessity and with right reason on her side. Yet her savage and tigress expression unsettled them. Suddenly she had become a person altogether different from the one that she had been. Without guilt, she was no longer innocent. Nor were they, because they had witnessed what appeared to their eyes as a scene of madness.

Rachel grasped this thought for merely an instant, while the imagery before her kept reeling in and out of her perceiving. Talia began sobbing once again, but this time she was making an effort not to cry. She kept her mouth tightly closed and clasped her hands into fists, as though that gesture might anchor her to an acceptable behavior.

Nicole was holding her senses taut. She hurried toward recognizable tasks as the proper method for negotiating with their fates. Always ready to do the things that needed to be done, she was placing under Rachel's throbbing head two pillows which she had retrieved from the Mercedes that had brought them to the meadow. Just as carefully, she wrapped a blanket about the wounded woman's chilled body.

Rachel heard her own voice now offering her daughter a familiar motherly calm and the encouraging words that she willed herself to summon, in spite of the pain that she was experiencing.

"It's all over," she told her. "The worst has been done. If there are any others like him, I don't think they will be coming this way."

Talia, sobbing only intermittently now, blurted out the thought which was now impelling her fear.

"Will they hurt Father?" she asked.

Her daughter's face was flushed not only because of that fear, but also because of her anger and sorrow.

"Of course, they won't," Rachel answered her. "The Roussillons and your father will protect us."

She imparted these words with such conviction that Talia gradually grew calm. If any doubts or fears were hovering near to overtake her once again, she pushed them back with a steadiness that was as resilient as her own.

"Everything is going to be all right," she told her.

Talia even managed a smile. It was clear that she was willing to believe in her optimism.

Only Nicole demurred. Though she admired her, Nicole could not believe Rachel when she told her daughter that everything was going to be all right. Unlike Talia, who was sitting by her blanketed body, Nicole stayed at a distance. Wise beyond her fourteen years and conscious of the ambivalent powers of a war-torn world, she did not believe in storybook endings. But she did believe in doing the things that needed to be done.

It was Nicole who made the sensible suggestion that Talia must go for help, so that her mother could receive medical attention.

"Don't go to the main house," she advised. "If there are any more men who have come to harm us, they may be waiting there. Go to the foreman's house behind the north meadow. His wife is certain to be there, and she can alert the police and the hospital."

Talia surprised them. She readily agreed to carry out this directive.

Weaving in and out of consciousness, Rachel was vaguely aware that her daughter had quickly left them with the hope that she would accomplish her mission and bring back the necessary people.

She was aware as well that Nicole was standing by her, the Colt Pocket Hammer held tight within her grip. She looked steadily about her, a fierce and adamant expression indicating that she was prepared to confront whatever enemy might try to enter the territory the two of them were now inhabiting. She might have been a tough-minded military guard or a political sentry. Even in her pain, Rachel detected as a subtle tracery upon Nicole's face a vague shadow of the fear that she had nearly mastered. She recognized in the straight-backed posture and the incisive awareness of danger the girl's realistic sense of things. For Nicole, the only surety in this moment (and a tenuous one at that) was the Colt short-recoil, semi-automatic pistol that looked like an almost natural fit for her firm hand.

As the Nazis galloped toward the northwest field, Gerhard was the first to see that Marc and Simone were not with the three persons who had dismounted from their horses and were lingering by a grove. Not far from them, their Tobianos and Criollos were grazing in a field, where pretty girls were busy picking hay and singing a Spanish ballad.

To Gerhard's scanning glance, the three riders looked complacent and vulnerable. He guessed that they were the senior Roussillons and their American host. Within the secure privacies of this setting, they would be carrying neither snub-nosed revolvers nor semi-automatic pistols. Bernd and Volker did not need him to assist in their killing. They could take the three of them by surprise and shoot them quickly. Believing so, Gerhard left the rider's trail which they had been traversing and hurried back toward the south portion of the property. Simone and Marc, he told himself, had stayed at the main house or they were on the beach, swimming or walking.

Bernd and Volker did not object to Gerhard's leaving.

Already, when they were seven hundred yards from Henri, Marianne, and Franz, the two Nazis took from the inside of their jackets their Beretta revolvers.

Their Lusitanos were galloping now, each of them at full stretch with body and neck lengthening and each leg fully extended as they powered across the winding trail. Behind their horse's neck, Volker and Bernd tucked their upper torsos precisely and fused the outline of their forms. They lifted themselves out of their saddles, so that they could drop their weight down into their heels and push it further back, allowing their upper bodies to tuck in behind the necks of their horses. As they went galloping toward their targets, the Nazis were riding with shorter stirrups to make it easier to lift their weight out of the saddle. They kept their lower legs on the girth and kept their arms extended forward, as their horses stretched their necks within each stride.

While the two Germans galloped along the undulating trail, trees and brush, sturdy plants and ample fields—stippled and iridescent and instantaneous—flashed by them.

Then they saw their targets—three well-groomed riders who were pausing by a field that was encircled by a cedar-wood fence. The two men and the woman were standing about three hundred yards ahead of them.

Now each of the Nazi riders pushed his lower leg forward while still squeezing both legs against his horse's sides. Each man braced himself against the stirrup and shortened up his reins, all the while putting the hand that held one of the reins tight into the horse's neck. He used his other hand to keep a strong hold on the second rein, as the horse started to listen and to slow down.

They were almost upon their targets, when the two men and the woman saw them and saw their revolvers pointed at them. Without a pause, they rushed deep into the grove of flowering jacaranda, hawthorn, laburnum, and golden rain trees, concealing themselves within their bountiful sprays of flowers, within the foliage of barberry, pieris, smoke bush, and juniper, and within the sun-flecked haze that appeared to well up from the shadow of the grove and from the flowers and foliage.

The Nazis were forced to dismount or become easy targets of the persons they had come here to kill.

Agile and stealthy, they hurried into the grove. Always taking cover behind foliage shrubs or the flowering blossoms and thick trunks of trees, they made their way through the sun-tinted haze and toward their unseen enemies. They could hear the breeze-stirred whisper of leaves and the mellow chirping of birds. A squirrel scooted up a tree, and a young deer with graceful energy hesitated before them and then sprang away from their witness.

When he reached the top of a grassy knoll, Bernd saw Marianne aiming her Enfield at him. There, in the palpable distance, she was crouching behind the profusion of flowers that belonged to a laburnum tree. The surprise of her having carried a revolver while she was out riding took him off his guard. Even with his Beretta cocked, he paused for a split second or two before firing.

He missed. But her bullet tore into his left arm. He would have fired at her again, if chance had favored him. But, with a speed that overtook him, Henri rushed forward from his place behind the trunk of a hawthorn, firing his revolver twice and each time hitting him. The first bullet tore through Bernd's chest and the second ripped a hole through his forehead.

Instantly, Bernd fell dead. Not only his face, but his entire body collapsed into itself, tumbling over and over the grassy knoll and landing at the foot of a beautiful tupelo tree.

Henri hurried to the tree where Marianne was still crouching. He saw that she was unharmed and that she had lost none of her fighting spirit. They exchanged no words. Instead, they used the stillness between them as another strategy for concealing themselves. Only the excited chirping of birds in the trees and the flutter of their wings and of breeze-roused leaves rode upon the air.

As he took a crouching position next to his wife, he surveyed the terrain around him with a penetrating and militant gaze.

For a minute or two, they concealed themselves more adequately there within the fragrant cover of flowers and of foliage. Marianne also peered about her, cautious and accurate. Then, satisfied that no enemy was in their immediate range and maintaining always a crouching position, she and Henri hurried forward to confront the second of the men who had come there to kill all of them.

They had taken only a few steps when they saw Franz. No farther than a hundred feet in the distance, he was already firing his Enfield revolver at the murderous Volker Henze. The first bullet ripped through the German's left eye, and the second smashed through his brain. Thrown back, the body dropped away. It landed on its back, the distorted face wrenched and the one remaining eye wide open and startled.

In silence and with soldierly effectiveness, Henri and Marianne then joined Franz in reconnoitering the territory around them. Only when the three of them were satisfied that no other assassin had entered the area did they run toward the field where they had left their horses. Before he mounted his Tobiano and while Marianne and Franz were mounting their Criollos, Henri allowed himself words as terse as they were pragmatic.

"Our battle isn't over," he said.

"No, it isn't," Franz answered him.

That Nicole, Rachel and Talia, as well as Marc and Simone, might be in danger or might already have been harmed hurried them forward. Minutes later, Franz and Marianne were galloping toward the south meadow where they had seen Rachel and the two girls painting at their easels. Marianne looked tense and distraught. Fury and anger were transforming her face into a mask of murderous hate. Franz looked somber and fatalistic.

Henri rode with them, though his thoughts summoned an image of the meadow where Rachel and the two girls would be painting and of the banks of the lake where, he expected,

Marc and Simone would be walking. Doubt and apprehension and wild courage were propelling his every move. He imagined that Marianne and Franz felt as he did. They were in danger of losing the persons whom they loved most of all.

He thought first about Nicole and, right after that, about Rachel and Talia. Nicole, Rachel and Talia, he knew, were far more vulnerable than Marc and Simone. Yet Marc and Simone were also in danger. On this tranquil-seeming summer afternoon, they were not anticipating an attack by Nazi assassins. They believed that Gerhard was dead and that they had eluded any immediate danger from him or from his fellow Nazis. He wondered whether Marc and Simone had armed themselves with Colt pistols or Beretta revolvers before they began their walk through the gardens in the east and west portions of his property and then on to the path by the lake.

What happened by the lake before he hurried there to help Marc and Simone, he would learn later.

Right now, his bitter awareness that Nazis had overtaken his home quickened his fear for them. But the thought that he might yet be able to help them worked like a fuse to ignite whatever energies he would need to save them.

By the time he arrived at the lake with Simone, Marc had achieved a measure of calm. Though he was not walking hand-in-hand with her, he had revived some fragments of the natural rapport with her that they used to enjoy whenever they were in each other's company. Sauntering through Marianne's exquisite gardens, he had allowed the vivid colors of the flowers and the foliage shrubs, the precise contours of the topiaries, and the symmetry of ornamental and fragrant trees to soothe his senses. Though he shared very few words with Simone, there was between them an unspoken pact that they would try not to bring any further sorrow to one another. If their staying together meant that they would never be happy, then they would have to part. Only time would reveal the path that was right for each of them.

"You will never be away from me, even if we separate," he had told her a few days earlier. "You are in my blood, and to let go of you completely would be, for me, a kind of dying."

His words had brought with their sullen implications the understated emphases of silence that lingered about her for a moment or two. Then, because she wanted to tell him how things stood with her, she responded with words that were as direct and as honest as his own.

"We have a strange life together, you and I," she said. "Sometimes I think that I can't live with you or without you."

He had smiled then, his intense gaze upon her both

melancholic and sensual.

"Yes," he said. "We have a very strange life."

He imagined that, as they made their way along the tawny sands of the beach, a passerby might regard them as a romantic and attractive couple. The thought, with its bittersweet fervencies, pleased him. They wore white shirts and windbreakers, as well as white slacks and sandals that brought to their tanned faces the subtle emphases of youthful well-being and an ingrained *joie-de-vivre*. Their shirts and windbreakers and slacks billowed in the breeze, and their lithe, confident movements offered to any observer additional emblems of whatever charisma they might possess.

As he sauntered with her along the winding path of the lake, he saw sailboats hurrying across the waters in the distance, their shimmering velocities so many gem-like tactics upon the blue-green sea. A brisk July wind was rousing the waters, while spume-fed waves rose and dipped with acrobatic proficiencies. He saw a flock of black-backed gulls navigating their way through sun-flecked clouds. Their cacophonous flight was an italic riff upon his senses. He and Simone saw, as well, the stark white cliffs gleaming in the sun and ascending skyward, arbitrary and predominant.

Then, quite suddenly, as if he were a ghostly apparition or a belligerent image from their troubled dreams or a star-crossed reality they had not anticipated, he saw Gerhard Hauptmann. He and Simone had turned from their scanning view of the sea to clarify the sound of running feet not far behind them. Gerhard was standing a hundred feet away, and he was pointing a Walther P-38 handgun at him.

With hair-trigger swiftness, Marc was reaching for his Colt pistol, which he was carrying within the inside pocket of his windbreaker, when Gerhard shot him and then shot him again. The first bullet penetrated his left shoulder, and the second grazed the left side of his temple.

He fell backward, his hand held still near the inside pocket of his jacket. He groaned in pain as he struggled to pull the pistol out of his pocket. His hard brown eyes stared with brooding fury upon this Nazi who had shot him, this inescapable nemesis, this war-battered man, this Gerhard Hauptmann who was going to fire his Walther for a third time and kill him.

Gerhard ran forward and stopped only when he stood a few paces from Marc. He saw the handsomeness of the man whom Simone had married. This was the man who had shot him in Switzerland. This man had killed all his dreams of future happiness. This was the same man whom Simone really loved.

This brooding face and perfect, athletic specimen was Marc Roussillon. It would give him pleasure to kill this man whose love for his woman was unlike ordinary love. It was an obsession, a sickness enclosed within its wayward and hermetic intricacies.

But in this same instant he also saw Simone. She was more beautiful than he had remembered. Her blond flowing hair, her lightly tanned sculpted features, and her statuesque form might once have roused his passionate nature, even as the ethereal sight of her had offered a promise to ease his need for her. But, trapped inside this death mission, he could look upon her only with anguish and self-hatred. On this afternoon, after he killed Marc, he planned to kill himself.

For many months now, as a vague imprint of his childhood religious lessons, he had wondered whether there was an After-life. Because he had become an avenging specter even before he left this life of his which had turned hollow and punishing, he had spent many sleepless nights wondering whether he would be condemned to roam the world, eternally anguished and alone. He did not think that he or Simone would ever meet again, even if life were given back to him at some far-flung, nebulous time. To be her lover, he would need to be someone else. He would need to be innocent of his Nazi crimes. He would need to believe in his future.

These brooding thoughts were an instant's flare upon his senses. They could not change the facts of the Now that he inhabited.

He kept his pistol aimed at Marc. He intended to fire the bullet that would kill him. But then he saw that Simone was aiming an Enfield revolver at him. Once, when he first knew that he loved her, she had made him feel whole. She had set him free from a war-driven world that had stolen his future from him. She had inspired him to take hold again of that future. She taught him to believe in the plans that he had been making for a happy life before the war came.

Now, perhaps, she could free him once more.

He was cocking his handgun and stood ready to fire upon Marc.

Simone stepped closer to him. There was so much love in her voice and so much anguish and fear.

"Don't make me kill you," she said. "Run away from here while you still have time."

"I have no time left," he answered her. "It's all used up."

"Run away," she implored. "Live and accomplish the great things you told me about."

For the flicker of a moment, his eyes flashed with the love he still felt for her. But just as quickly an expression as stern as it was hardened brought a grimace to his face. Her words meant nothing to him.

"Do it," he said, as if he were giving her a direct and militant order. "Shoot me, or I'll kill him."

She hesitated.

Then, because he appeared to press his finger against the trigger of his Walther handgun, Simone fired her pistol. It ripped through his heart, and he fell dead.

No sooner had she shot Gerhard, than Simone threw down her pistol and hurried to him. When, close up, she saw that he was dead, she fell to her knees beside him and began weeping uncontrollably. Gently, she lifted his head and placed it against her breast. His blue eyes were half open, as though they were squinting and, from far away, were trying to decipher who she was. Yet they saw nothing. Her cries grew into a wailing, as she caressed his ruined, handsome face and kissed his lips, which were still warm to the touch and life-like.

Lying wounded, Marc looked on with muted and bitter sorrow.